Tituba

THE INTENTIONAL WITCH OF SALEM

Dave Tamanini

This is a work of fiction. All of the characters, organizations and events portrayed in this novel are either the products of the author's imagination or are used fictitiously.

ISBN: 978-1-7348308-0-4 (trade paperback)
ISBN: 978-1-7348308-1-1 (ebook)
First edition: 2020

Please visit: http://www.DaveTamaniniAuthor.com
to sign up for my newsletter and to contact me.

After you finish reading, if you'd be willing to leave a customer rating or review for me, I'd appreciate it very much. I hope you enjoy *Tituba.* Thank you

Dedication

To all the women who helped me be a better man. I know who you are.

Chapter One

No one could possibly understand what the day meant for him. Samuel Parris paced the floor of their narrow Boston townhouse, tucking and re-tucking his loose-fitting white shirt into his breeches. "And look at this collar, Elizabeth. Why can't that African starch a simple shirt after all these years?"

Elizabeth Parris sat on the edge of their bed brushing her husband's waistcoat. "Tituba ironed it twice. I see nothing amiss."

"This appointment with Cotton Mather is a blessing for us and I must be presentable." His outward appearance was something to hide behind, as if it kept others from seeing the pounding inside his chest.

Cotton Mather was the grandson and son of the Puritan church leaders John Cotton and Increase Mather. Although congregational ministers were equal in rank, the Mathers were considered by many to be first among equals.

"If Mr. Mather cannot tip the scales for me to secure that vacant pulpit in Salem Village, we shall soon be paupers."

Three years at Harvard studying the classics had not prepared him to manage worldly matters in Barbados nor here in Boston.

Elizabeth helped him into his doublet and jacket. He eyed her as she smoothed out the fabric; she was always the calmest person, but blast it, there was no sign she understood what wracked him.

Nor could he say it; this is maybe his last chance to find a life that pleased God and brought down His blessings.

She dusted his shoulder one more time. "Do not fear God's will today."

"Do you think I fear it?" he snapped.

Of course, he feared God's will. Samuel chided himself for his sharp tone. She meant well. He tugged at his collar again. "Mather must have noticed me during the weekly Scripture discussions at the meetinghouse. I've helped as much as any of his deacons, too. You don't think he might suspect my knowledge of our convention of faith because my father adhered to the Church of England; don't look at me that way, I know how they are."

He glanced at his slave Tituba entering the room without a sound, eyes cast down at her folded hands. "Where are my boots?"

"Akanni is cleaning them, Master."

"They best be well brushed, and a better job than this collar." The twelve-year-old needed closer supervision. "Hurry him."

He rechecked the jacket buttons until Tituba left them.

"I do not fear God's will, Elizabeth." He said it as much to assure himself rather than as a rebuke. He was worn out after months of demonstrating his faith during forays to far-off farming communities looking for a pastor.

The trips began with hopeful good cheer but ended with sober reflection and maddening uncertainty. Last week the tiny hamlet of Stow offered only a pittance for pay and constant threat of Indian attack. At the least, he needed a decent wage to provide for his family. Accepting less would sidestep his responsibility before God and his community.

"I know it will go well, Samuel. Our family is already proof He loves us. Our daughter Betty is healthy, and my niece Abigail is settling in nicely."

That part was true. The care and protection of children was the highest requirement of good citizenship and the proof was there for all to see. But today, he needed more; a glimmer, that's all, a glimmer of proof that he was in good standing with the Almighty. He was offering to serve Him with what he regarded as his best skills, virtues, actually. Clear thinking and discipline were his strong points. As a minister, he could discern sin from virtue, truth from falseness. And if the Creator was merciful today, Mr. Mather would see he possessed the knowledge and skills to teach the chosen people to live by the absolute and undeniable truth revealed in Scripture.

He needed a ministry for the solid footing it promised. No more for him, the life of commerce with its whimsical market and unreliable men who shirked paying their honest debts.

Elizabeth had turned to other work, hanging the jacket he usually wore on the door hook and brushing it clean. She was doing the same on his woolen breeches as he watched. Her calm demeanor was one of several reasons he had wooed her after opening his business in

Boston ten years ago. They signed the civil marriage contract within months. He didn't know of her poor health, but fair enough, she knew nothing of his liquidity problems.

He'd given everyone many reasons why he'd sold the plantation he inherited in Barbados. The poor weather, the economy, and the smallpox decimation of his slave workforce had all excused his inability to run the place at a profit. The larger plantation owners had pounced to buy him out at a depressed price. Still, that sale of the plantation and the seventy remaining slaves gave him enough capital to masquerade as an island gentleman even though his export and land agency in Barbados was failing. And as badly as that ended, his recent business venture in Boston did no better.

Elizabeth Eldridge. Born and raised in Boston, she seemed the perfect match for him. Her father had proved his fierce rejection of the Church of England and its papist influences, and her own devotion to God was never in doubt by anyone. The Puritan patina she provided made life in the city of open sewers and forever damp and tight quarters bearable if not profitable. And it was more important now as he answered his new calling as a clergyman.

John Indian, his other adult slave, arrived at the bedroom door carrying Parris' spotless and buffed boots. It was clear he had done them rather than his son, Akanni. After pulling them on, he stood to allow Elizabeth to survey him one last time. She took his hands. "At first, I was not eager to leave when you became interested in Salem Village's congregation. But now, having prayed over it, I feel certain God will grant your desire and I welcome it."

Elizabeth kissed him hard. "Now leave. You have no time to spare. And you are as handsome as always, Reverend Parris."

He returned her encouragement with a dubious look. She would be optimistic. Failure was never just around the corner for her.

"Project confidence, and Mr. Mather will respond as you wish." Elizabeth led him to the stairs and watched him descend before returning to her sewing.

Parris descended the steps while suppressing an impulse to call the entire visit off as a waste of time. But at the front door he thought his wife might watch for him through the upstairs bedroom window, and so, Parris sucked in a deep breath and set off at a firm pace, stepping carefully over numerous piles of horse manure in the street.

The streets were uncrowded because Boston was still recovering from yet another unpredictable pox outbreak. Sinfulness had brought it again, certainly. And while the disease raged, people cowered indoors and searched their souls. But when the angel of death retreated from his mission and worthy souls recovered their health, people ventured out timidly, but only to conduct overdue business or necessary personal matters. Samuel Parris' business was personal—and urgent.

His uncle John Oxenbridge suggested he seek personal counsel from Mather. As much as Parris disliked asking for favors, even from family, his uncle had offered to open a door. It was time to forget scruples. He had to provide for his family and make a new start. And he needed God to smile on him again.

Yes, Elizabeth was right. He must sound like a confident preacher might. Make clear how, with divine grace, he would care for the souls of his congregants. He pulled on the cursed shirt collar again as he turned a corner.

When Parris reached the street running into North Square, the appearances of the homes and shops made his own street seem like a workmen's lane. He stopped at Mather's three-story brick residence marked by multiple gables and a high-pitched roof. The leaded diamond-shaped glass panes in the casement windows sparkled. Once he might have afforded this kind of neighborhood. He looked east and west and, seeing no one, straightened his jacket before mounting the stone steps to the varnished double doors. Someday he might move into a place like this. God willing.

Parris hammered the brass knocker an extra time or two. He refrained from gawking through the glass panel next to the door frame, not wanting to appear like an awed supplicant. When the door did not open, his blood rushed. Was the appointment today?

He knocked harder. And waited. And then he peered through the side glass into a large dark-paneled hallway. No movement. Parris felt like kicking himself in frustration but got a grip on his emotions. Well he did, and just in time, too as the door opened a few inches.

A small woman dressed in the simple blue attire of servants and slaves squinted. "Yes?"

"Reverend Samuel Parris, for Mr. Mather." The pretender already. He felt sweat beads on his upper lip and swiped at them. Be bold.

"This way, sir. Mr. Mather is in his study." She led him across the parlor and bade him to wait while she walked to a heavy oak door and knocked once before opening it. "Your appointment is here. A Mr. Samuel Parris."

"Thank you, Jenny. How now, Mr. Parris?" From the next room, the voice of a master. "Excuse me while I finish the last few paragraphs here. Please sit. And Jenny, tell Mrs. Mather we shall have a guest for dinner."

Parris took a seat at the window bench of Cotton Mather's parlor, eschewing the white ash Brewster chairs near the fire. The large central hearth was putting out too much heat for his comfort. During the walk to North Square, despite the chill of early spring, he had been sweating from anticipation.

Parris reviewed once again what he needed most from this meeting: he needed a benefactor.

The daily burden of his dwindling inheritance money clogged his mind with a constant refrain: you were an inept planter. At this moment, he carried it further. Had you worked harder, you might have kept God's favor instead of begging for Mather's favor today. He closed his eyes to pray for calmness.

At the sound of rapid footsteps on the hardwood floor Parris straightened. The short plump man entering the room rubbed at brown-black ink stains on his hand and fingers. Parris thought he detected a look of surprise on Mather's face, as though he'd forgotten the reason for the meeting, but upon making eye contact, his tone was warm. "Mr. Parris, is it? Welcome." He extended a soft hand and Parris stood to take it. "My day has been so full. I confess to wishing I could be two places at once."

Parris looked down from his six-foot height. Longish hair framed Cotton Mather's pink face, extending back over his collar.

"The wait was nothing at all, sir. I've been admiring your library."

Cotton beamed as though the library was a favored child. "Herr Gutenberg did God's work. His holy word is now in every home." Mather admired his leather-bound collection. "And as for my humble collection…" He swept his arm in a wide arc toward the walls. "There we have the holy books in the sacred languages, Hebrew, Greek and Latin. And in this corner the works of our greats, Keeble, Burton and Glanvill."

He moved closer to the shelves, touching the book spines. "Sermons by the most inspired divines from England like Mr. Baxter, and my grandfather John Cotton and my father." He stared at them a moment. "One hopes his own poor sermons and commentaries will be read as widely as theirs."

Parris wondered at the seeming false humility of this man of stature. Everyone read Cotton Mather.

"You don't read the heresy out of the Royal Society, do you, Mr. Parris?"

"I do not. Searching outside Scripture for God's plan is the Devil's work, isn't it?"

"Quite."

Parris savored his response. It came off his tongue rather well. Emboldened, he considered showing his knowledge of Scripture. But before he could say a word, and, to his relief, Mrs. Mather called them to the midday meal.

The small dining area near the kitchen surprised him. It was windowless and walled with wide floor-to-ceiling hardwood panels. A half dozen sconces lit the room with a warm glow from bayberry candles.

The tantalizing aromas from the table almost made Parris faint. He had not eaten since yesterday and he was ravenous. At table they dug into dishes of marrow bones, poached cod, and a loin of veal. It was the best he had eaten in a long while. Better than the efforts of his slave Tituba. Although, he considered as he dug into the pink slice of meat laid before him, he didn't provide Elizabeth with the means to buy anything better.

After a serving of dried fruit sweetened with cane juice, Mather led Parris back to the parlor, and took his place in a large leather wing chair near the hearth. Parris pulled one of the Brewster chairs across from him and waited for Mather to speak.

"So, what may I help you with today?"

The sumptuous meal filling him, Parris launched into his reason for coming. "One always wants to follow the family business, I suppose. But unlike my father, I found no way to reconcile the mercantile life with the reason God placed me on earth. I have the mettle to mediate between God and his chosen people here in our colony if given a chance."

"Then God bless you."

"Thank you, Mr. Mather." Push on, he told himself. "Recently I gave several demonstration sermons to the

Salem farmers. Thomas Putnam Jr. and the village committee have expressed some interest in me, but they have not yet invited me to negotiate a contract. Would you happen to know any people there?"

"His grandfather, old Thomas Putnam, was an honorable man." Mather seemed to recede into his thoughts. Was he perhaps hesitating?

Parris forced himself to speak. "Mr. Mather, may we speak candidly? What advice can you give me about securing this position?"

Mather pulled an ear as though searching for gentle words to answer a fool. "These are difficult days even for men holding a master's degree in Divinity, Mr. Parris. The competition here in Boston has forced them to accept part-time and interim positions."

"Yes. After I responded to the Lord's call, I saw how acute the competition was for the scarce paid openings." He picked at a fingernail, holding his breath. Patience, he told himself.

Mather burped. "That veal was tasty, but my indigestion is raising its flame." He gulped for air and swallowed. "As I was saying, these times are challenging. The economy flips this way and that for many reasons. For instance, there is the growing uncertainty whether the Crown will recognize our Puritan freedoms in the new charter being planned in London."

Parris knew it was not just freedom to practice the faith that needed protection. The real battle was for the Puritan church to keep the power to govern, and why not? This, he told himself, is what he needed, nearness to this center of influence and security.

Parris paid closer attention as Mather continued. "Old land boundaries under the revoked charter are under question now, and the uncertainty slows cultivation and development. Those farmers in Salem Village are resisting their obligation to contribute to the larger Salem Town militia. They argue their homes are vulnerable to Indian attacks when they are drilling miles away in Salem. And well they should. Given the nasty skirmishes with the Abenaki tribe and their French allies."

Parris added, "With good leadership in the meetinghouse, they will find God's providence to support them."

"Remind me again, Mr. Parris, how many in your household?"

He stiffened, wondering if the man was about to dissuade him from pursuing an outlying pulpit on account of the dangers to his family.

"A wife and child make three of us, plus a young niece, and I have three slaves from my father's estate."

"Few country pastors can afford slaves."

"I inherited them. My African woman, Tituba, never causes trouble, and she follows every instruction without objection. She cares for our children and the household when my wife is not in the best of health. Her husband, John Indian, is capable with livestock and I shall lend him out to earn money. They have a son. I hope to lease him out like his father, as soon as he is able."

Mather had been nodding his head in a pastor's way, saying yes, and yes, until Parris finished speaking. "I wonder if you have the tenacity, the spirit of sacrifice, for your vocation, Mr. Parris."

"What do you mean, sir?"

"Men of God must prepare for the imminent, our imminent reckoning. The coming of days are nigh. The Devil and his dark hosts are backed up and preparing for the final fight. Will you be able to join us as harbingers of biblical prophecy?"

Parris suppressed a smile. On this subject he could converse for hours. "You will not find one more committed to this calling than me."

Mather nodded, at least at the brevity of his answer. "As for those dear brothers in Christ of Salem Village.... They have a poor record of abiding by agreements with their ministers. They forced out the last three. Be adamant for your needs."

Parris searched the man's face. Was he offering encouragement?

Mather coughed dryly and called out for drinks. "They want a covenanted congregation and an ordained pastor. It is their weak spot. Between us, their desire for a covenanted church is part of their plan to break from the control of Salem Town."

Parris gripped the arms of the chair to keep himself steady. Go on. Show Mather what you know, he thought. "I know they have two or three powerful clans. The Putnams supported the last minister."

"Yes, Deodat Lawson was their choice, until they decided against him."

Mather scratched his shaved chin as the servant brought their drinks. "Mr. Parris—Samuel—your uncle says you are a discreet man, so I will speak plain. I want to help you. But the Putnams are a tough lot. They have lived in the civil courts battling neighbors in Salem and Topsfield. They think using the law helps them get their way." Mather laughed, almost to himself. "They do not differ from many of our people, but they are wrong. Solutions to all conflicts come from Scripture, through us the ministers as their mediators and not the magistrates and judges of cold civil law. Are you ready for the challenges?"

"I did at one time have some negotiating skills," Parris said. "Perhaps I shall navigate their rivalries and resolve disputes as an interested pastor."

Mather leaned toward Parris. "But beware in your relationships with them. They will use you to support their conflicts."

Bile rose into Parris' throat and he wanted to think it was from the heavy meal. "I will dedicate my entire being to God's work, favoring no one." He wiped his hands on his thighs. It was time to press for the ultimate favor. "I wonder if you might do something more for me, Reverend Mather."

"What is it?"

"If you could put in a word… somewhere, I shall be everlastingly in your debt."

Mather clapped his hands, startling Parris. "Quite. But we must use care. As you know, our congregations are fiercely independent." Mather's smile looked almost conspiratorial, and it unsettled Parris. Was there something he missed?

"I shall make further inquiry on your behalf to pastor Higginson in Salem Town, in occulto. The village must not sense outside interest in their internal affairs."

With what he needed so seemingly near, Parris could not help second guessing himself. Mather appeared so quick to help him, an under-educated supplicant. Had he taken on a personal indebtedness to this man unnecessarily?

He managed half a smile, hoping it showed proper gratitude. When Mather raised his cup to empty it, Parris heaved a breath and repeated in his head: all is well—all is well. He might have just secured the best ally in the colony.

"Give us two weeks then, and ready yourself for a call from the villagers. Demand every guarantee for your personal needs, Mr. Parris." Mather stood. "Because once in office, you must feed your congregation the bitter and the sweet of Scripture's messages. There can be no conflict of interest between saving souls to honor God and your family's requirements."

"Thank you, sir. I know I shall succeed." Parris could not think of an apt scriptural reference because he was already considering Thomas Putnam and the committee in Salem Village. With a sense of newfound confidence, he would show them what an experienced negotiator could get.

Mather put a finger to his nose as if remembering one more thing. At his bookshelves, he reached above his head to pull down a dusty volume. "Take this Perkins octavo…" He wiped the leather cover and read the title aloud, "Discourse of the Damned Art of Witchcraft. Remember, we have great power from the Lord, but Revelations seventeen: fourteen tells us, 'There are Devils even among the holy saints.'"

"Thank you. And our simultaneous duty from Exodus twenty-two: eighteen. 'Thou shalt not suffer a witch to live.'"

"There it is." Mather nodded approval. He stood back a moment staring at Parris. "Yes, and I want you to have this, too." He turned back to the shelves and standing on his toes pulled more books. "Trapp's Commentaries are invaluable. As the Romans said, 'ab ovo usque ad mala,' a meal from the eggs to the apple dessert. I relied on Trapp when I began preaching."

He took Parris by the sleeve and led him toward the doorway. Parris abruptly shortened his stride to avoid clipping his host's heels on account of Mather's smaller steps.

Mather turned to send him off. "Pray remember me to your family, Mr. Parris."

"I shall. God be with you, Mr. Mather."

Parris made his way down the street to a corner just beyond sight from Mather's with the books in his arms. He let loose a yelp that echoed in the empty street. Kissing the great Mather's hand had been well worth it. This new association was a sign of better days ahead.

He hurried homeward, a fresh bounce in his step. Yes, in his bones he was certain of this good turn. He would get the pulpit in Salem farms and then he would remind his congregants, with the fire of truth, that failing to honor Christ is to side with the Devil. Parris liked the ring of that last phrase. He would use it in a sermon one day—after he negotiated a suitable contract with those rough farmers.

Chapter Two

Tituba and Mistress Parris sat near the small hearth, repairing worn clothing when Master fairly skipped into the room. Tituba watched him drop a stack of books on a table and toss his coat on the wall peg. He had been out of sorts earlier, griping over his shirt collar. She prepared for more now.

"I have good news!"

Mistress lowered her needle and smiled at her husband.

"Mr. Mather will help me secure the pulpit in Salem farms."

"That is glorious news!"

The wide grin on the master's face, a rarity, looked almost comical.

"He said he likes my approach to serving God and wants to help me." He clapped his hands. "I shall have an answer in two weeks! I feel it, Elizabeth. God is smiling on me once again and Mr. Mather will come through."

Tituba looked to her work as he chortled. True to her name's meaning in the old Yoruba language, Tituba was first an appeaser. For more than thirty years, since slavers kidnapped them from her village, Tituba lived by the promise her Mama forced from her to always appease. She said it was the only way to survive the red-faced Englishmen. Today, like every other day, Tituba stifled her judgment on the fickle nature of the master. She knew his mood could turn yet again to gloom followed by a hint of lightness, followed by more gloom or outbursts of anger. Mistress labored to keep him level and for that Tituba was grateful, even though Mistress was not always successful.

Tituba's two highest concerns were to appease the master and to nurture her young son. The slavers had killed her Mama in Africa, and she would make certain Akanni learned how to survive so he would not be lost to her, too.

"Tituba, come. We shall celebrate," Master said.

At least for now, his spirits were up. Whatever had occasioned that, she and her family might benefit from his present good humor.

Master dug into the purse on his belt and pulled out six pence. "Tonight, we shall feast and give thanks. Out with you, Tituba. Fresh bread, and a leg of lamb. And a bottle of Spanish wine."

Tituba was eager to comply. She pulled on her well patched wool cloak and braced for the chill on the street. Even in springtime, the Massachusetts weather forced everyone to bundle up, and most still wore hooded winter cloaks. She dressed like all the others and took comfort in that. Few would notice her complexion as she headed to the market shops. Except for her hands peeking from her long sleeves, nothing betrayed that she was not white. She tired of the local English children and more than a few adults pointing at her in public. There were hardly any Africans here, compared to the thousands in the Indies of her youth.

She bought wine at a shop three blocks from home, and the bread next door. When she headed toward the butcher shop, Tituba turned a corner and halted as though jerked by a rope. Crossing in front of her, armed white men were leading two black African men and a child. They had bound and yoked the black men by their necks. One of the captured men was holding hands with the black child, a girl. She appeared to be ten or twelve years of age; her untended hair caked with dirt overwhelmed her skeletal face.

The slaver gang's sudden appearance on the street so shocked Tituba, she stumbled on her long skirt, banging hard against a moss-covered wooden wall at an alleyway. Had she looked as forlorn as the child after arriving in Barbados on the slave ship? Cold sliced through Tituba that these white men might grab and take her with them and she pressed herself against the wall.

No, of course they wouldn't.

Tituba straightened herself to proceed, but she could not shake the image of that filthy child. The little girl's huge eyes left Tituba's heart feeling like an iron band enwrapped it even after the wretched troupe turned a corner. She stepped a short way into the alley gasping to subdue a wave of nausea. She leaned against an empty fish barrel for support.

They kidnapped Tituba thirty years ago, but the terror slammed her like it was yesterday. Two men had breached the village fences. Their ritual facial scars marked them to be from another tribe. One man was much bigger than the other, and the smaller one grabbed Tituba, covering her face with a hand as hard as rawhide. They barged into the mudbrick hut where Mama was preparing fresh catfish for mid-day meal and soon, they were weeks away from home and heading toward the Englishmen at the coast.

They'd almost escaped during the journey, when Mama unleashed her mystical powers and almost freed them. Mama always promised to teach Tituba how to attain her powers but she never did. Before they killed her, Mama had said she would somehow return to help Tituba discover them inside herself, no matter where fate and the slavers took her. But she never did.

Tituba wandered out of the alley, unaware of how she got to the next shop. She opened the door and entered.

"What can I get for you?" the butcher said.

Tituba stared in bewilderment at the fat smiling man.

"Yes?" he asked again.

She must look like a sleep walker. "A leg of lamb, sir."

"I sold the last one not two minutes ago. I have nothing left except that turkey." A lone gray and brown-feathered fowl hung by the legs on a whitewashed wall.

Tituba's heart thumped. Master would be cross, but at this hour she knew he was expecting her. Some meat was better than none.

After paying, Tituba headed homeward. What would she say to avoid punishment? I thought you wanted a turkey, Master. Appeasement. For so long she had practiced the art of appeasement while never discovering her supposed powers.

She managed well enough without them, did she not? She had John Indian, and their son, Akanni. They were all the comfort she needed. Yet, as she wended through the crooked lanes, Tituba thought once more of Mama, wondering why she had never visited as she promised. It would be so nice to see her again, anyway.

Chapter Three

Samuel Parris sat at a bench near the large hearth in Ingersoll's Ordinary and Tavern in Salem farms. At the front of the hearth they had arrayed pine-knot candles, and the smoke from the Indian torches curled up and out through the fieldstone chimney. The pitchy droppings from the pine knots had built up, and they flared now and then. Still, the room was dark and smokey, like Parris' thoughts as he waited for the outcome of his demands.

The Salem Village committee and he had been negotiating for hours, and he had still not gained the pulpit in the Puritan farming community.

Parris felt comfortable speaking of money and salaries in the country tavern, with its low ceiling and exposed beams. It was easier there, away from God's house. And, unlike the unheated meetinghouse, the hearth diminished the perpetual chill he felt in this forbidding country.

Thomas Putnam was conferring with his committeemen over Parris' last demand. Two farmers sitting in the corner were drinking from a new keg of strong water, and one of them laughed loudly. The sound went unnoticed by Parris in the midst of a pang over his past. If he'd somehow worked harder on the Barbados plantation, he would still be a gentleman rather than a parson begging for a decent salary.

Putnam cleared his throat. "Mr. Parris, we have already agreed the meetinghouse needs repair. Have we not? And haven't we also agreed to deliver logs to the sawyer to cut the boards for the work?"

"But I must have the covered doorway, the two small window shutters and that part of the wood siding all completed within a fortnight."

Parris knew they had haggled over the construction and maintenance of the meetinghouse for many years. The building stood only twenty-seven feet long by thirty-six feet wide and twenty-eight feet high. Five buildings that size would fit inside Second Church in Boston. Still, it took the villagers five on-again, off-again years to complete the building. Afterward, argumentative members disputed the need for continued upkeep since basic materials required additional donations, supplies or money from the parishioners.

If they were going to make the repairs, he must force them to agree now while he had leverage. Parris kept a confident smile for appearances' sake while Deacon Ingersoll poured refills of fermented pear cider. He had learned a valuable lesson from those vultures in Barbados. They had leverage on him then, demanding he reduce the asking price of his plantation because of the hurricane damage to the main house and fields.

"Very well, Mr. Parris. You have our word on it—in a fortnight." Thomas Putnam took a long pull on his drink. "But mind you, we must remain firm, then, on your annual salary. Sixty pounds, one-third in coin and the rest in provisions. That is all we have."

"As long as you will reconsider my pay when we next have good harvests, I am satisfied." He cleared his throat. "Do I have the committee's guarantee of sufficient dry firewood for the parsonage? My blood is still thin from life in Barbados, and I will need at least fifty cords per year."

Seeing the consternation across the table, Parris was quick to add, "If I am to be your minister, I must have certain essentials to free me for the care of all souls in the congregation. That part of my salary in coin will barely be sufficient for me to buy grain and foodstuffs." They still looked doubtful, so he said, "And if I have no wood for heat, I cannot study Scripture to prepare my sermons, nor then bring more souls into our church."

They must recognize this common necessity, he thought. Everyone needed heat. He raised his voice a notch. "I need a firm guarantee from each of you for sufficient cut and delivered firewood."

The clear dismay from across the table felt like a slap in the face. But he had laid out his stake and unable to back down, he waited.

And maddeningly, Putnam drew out the moment. He scratched the back of his broad freckled paw before saying, "Trust us, we will make certain one way or the other you get all the wood you need."

Parris sipped the dregs from his cup. He knew pleas for trust were fleeting when memories faded. If they had offered enough money, he would feel more secure in case Putnam's assurance proved false. "I shall rely on your good faith promise. But...there may be one other way, perhaps to give me more money."

The faces of the men across the table twisted into suspicion, looking at him skeptically, so Parris hurried to explain. "I have always lent out my Indian man and soon his son, perhaps, for income. How can you accommodate me in this?"

Ingersoll was setting a candle on the table against the sun's fading illumination through the small window of the tavern, and Putnam caught his arm. "If Deacon Ingersoll here can find work for your Indian man, we as a committee will make our best efforts to find something for the younger one. Can you do it, Deacon Ingersoll?"

"Aye, at the minimum I always need help during planting and harvesting seasons and, more often lately, here in the Ordinary."

An abrupt bang from the tavern door opening and slamming shut drew everyone's attention. A rush of chilly air carried a buckskin-clad man into the room. He peered around. "Mr. Thomas Putnam Jr.?"

"Aye, over here."

"I have a letter from Reverend Higginson in Salem Town."

Putnam read it and smiled. "Thank you, lad. Go see Mr. Ingersoll for a drink on me."

He handed the letter to the other committeemen, and while they read it, Putnam said, "Good news, brother Parris. Salem Town has reversed course. They will not object to your ordination here in a newly covenanted congregation. Our own Salem Village church!"

The others at the table congratulated each other on the good news. The letter meant they no longer need travel to Salem Town, particularly in foul weather, for the Sabbath communion.

Parris barely believed his ears. Could he be so blessed? A covenanted gospel congregation of his own? Thank you, Father. I shall serve You first, before all other needs.

He steadied himself and kept his lips tight to hide his feelings. It wouldn't be proper to clap his hands. A covenanted church! Even Deodat Lawson and George Burroughs, his predecessors in the village and both four-year Harvard graduates, had been denied the privilege of ordination. He needed to end this negotiation before the committee changed its mind on anything they'd already agreed upon. What to say?

At a loss for words, he merely offered his hand to Thomas Putnam, and they shook. The other men grunted approval, as Parris and Putnam said, "Done and done."

After slapping their hands on the oak table, the committeemen stood and bade fare-thee-wells to one another and the new parson.

As they left, Putnam motioned Parris to sit again with him.

"I shall expect your support in village matters, Samuel. If we continue to work together, I will do all I can to ensure you have regular pay for your family needs."

If?

Putnam reached into the leather purse hanging from his belt and tossed coins to pay for their beverages. "Reverend Lawson has said he will be pleased to assist you during your ministry. And so shall I."

"Thank you and God bless you, brother Putnam. Er, will you hold a moment more?" Parris saw the Salem

Town messenger rising from his drink and making to leave. "Hallo, lad, can you take a message to Boston posthaste?"

Chapter Four

Tituba stretched her back and stepped away from the empty iron kettle. Since early morning she had ladled melted tallow from it for candle dipping. The autumn duty of scalding and skimming meat fat to make two dozen scores of candles for the parsonage and the meetinghouse was all but finished. Without the candles, she would have to toil in semi-darkness every day of the year. She sucked on a blistered burn from earlier. It was a small price to pay, making candles, especially for her, a child of sunshine and warm breezes.

In the distance, a quarter mile off, she saw the master homeward bound after another day of pastoral visits. Two years here, and he never stopped searching for new people to baptize. He was back and they hadn't cleared the last of the hanging candles from the main room.

Inside the parsonage, Mistress, Tituba and Akanni had finished dipping the last batch. They worked among sets of lug poles positioned in the room. Each set of poles supported cross laid dipping sticks, and each one of those had half a dozen new candles suspended from it. Tituba entered and said, "Master is almost home." The three of them hurried to remove the last of the hanging candles. As soon as the master entered the house, he spotted Akanni. "You, go tend my horse."

"Yes, Master."

When Akanni hurried through the kitchen and out, Tituba nodded ever so slightly. It was rare he did not throw a furtive glare after receiving orders. Akanni must carry that last whipping fresh in his mind, she thought. The older he got, the worse were the punishments. She had felt the willow branches laid on Akanni on her own legs, and worse, anguish at keeping silent instead of asking mercy for her son.

Tituba backed away into the kitchen, as was expected while the children and Mistress greeted their master. She heard Betty rush to him and hug his waist as she always did. "Father, we have been copying the Lord's Prayer, and now Abigail can read the words."

Mistress said, "To keep them busy when not helping us dip."

"Well done, children."

"Father, may we play a guessing game with you?"

"No."

"Riddles?"

"No games. Frivolity is an invitation to wastefulness."

Tituba looked in from the kitchen as Master drew the girls near the hearth fire, where he warmed his hands. "Have you obeyed the mistress of the house today?"

"Yes, Father," Betty said.

"And what did you do to help her make candles?"

As they answered him, he called out, "Tituba, bring me a large cup of our pear cider."

Fermented pear cider. Two days ago, she had told Mistress the barrel was empty, and they were low on apple cider. What to do? She could not explain the problem to him. He often said explanations were mere excuses for shirking duties. Nor would she be more the fool to implicate the mistress and invite the switch across her own back for speaking out of turn. Tituba brought a cup of apple cider instead and readied for come what may. He drew a mouthful, only to spit it out. "I said pear cider."

She waited, expecting another threatening outburst, but he surprised her by digging into his belt purse and tossing her a coin.

"Send your son to the tavern for a bucket of *pear* cider. Tell him to run."

"Yes, Master." Tituba returned to the kitchen, thankful for her master's strong thirst. After so many years of service she puzzled over his continued bad temperament. Had he not gotten his church? He had seemed pleased for a while, until lately when he reverted to his old habits.

His sermons, which he made her attend, were becoming more emphatic as he reminded his sinners how Judas betrayed Christ. Could he have felt himself betrayed also? Some of his people were no longer listening with bent heads and silence, but instead coughing excessively and grimacing while he chastened them.

She heard Master's grumbles from the main room as he stacked unused lug poles out of his way.

"Father, are you angry at us?" Betty asked.

"No! No, child. Where has your mother gotten?"

The clacking spinning wheel in the bedroom drew his attention. Mistress knew how to read her husband and when to withdraw.

"Abigail, go help Aunt Elizabeth."

The child stared at her uncle, slow to respond. Was it any wonder the child was slow? Only five years ago, a warring tribe had slaughtered Abigail's parents during an attack in York. How many times had she helped the mistress console the child when she called for her mama? She had missed the butchery while visiting in Boston, but how could she move on amidst the never-ending tales about savages burning captives alive? One moment the poor child was gay and the next as cold as a stone.

Parris was on her in three quick steps, pulling Abigail's arm. "Did you not hear me?"

The child's knees gave out beneath his grip. She looked up at her uncle as if pleading for a kind word.

"Elizabeth, give Abigail something productive to do upstairs. Unless she learns her duties, she will never find a proper husband." He looked down at the girl. "And we shall have no choice but to keep you to care for us in our old age."

Tituba grimaced at his sharp tone. Unless the girl got some tenderness from her uncle, she might carry her burden the rest of her days. From the kitchen Tituba saw Abigail stop halfway up the steps, out of sight of the master, watching him pull his wooden armchair, the only one in the house, nearer the fire. He held out his arm for Betty to come nearer. "Very well, now tell me what other task you performed this day."

Betty climbed on her father's lap and snuggled close to him. "This morning I helped cut apples to string for drying."

On the stairs, the look of longing on Abigail was clear. And Tituba wondered if Betty on her father's lap could see her cousin standing there. "Wait, Father, I'll show you."

Betty hurried into the kitchen and hefted a large clay bowl. Tituba had no chance to slow her down before she rushed to show him. Betty tripped on the uneven plank floor. Awkwardly, she pitched, falling against the stacked lug poles. Dozens of apple pieces bouncing helter skelter. By some odd luck the bowl did not break while skidding along the floor.

Betty's immediate loud bawling seemed excessive, and it filled the room even after her father scooped her up with both hands, cooing to her and rubbing her bruised knees.

Tituba smiled at Betty's manipulation of him. It was rare for Master to stumble into tenderness.

When Master summoned Tituba to come and clean up, she was there before he finished calling her. She had swept up half of the mess when Akanni returned with the bucket of pear cider.

"Your cider has arrived, Master," she said.

"Bring it up to me in the study."

Betty followed her father up the stairs, as Abigail was descending. Tituba glanced at her and whispered to Akanni, "Wait here until I come down. I have a task for you."

As Tituba picked her way across the main floor with pear cider, she addressed Abigail. "Clean up the rest of the pieces until I return."

When Tituba descended the stairway after delivering the cider, she stopped and stared. Akanni had gathered and restacked the lug poles without being told to do so. He was eating a piece of apple and laughing softly while dodging pieces Abigail playfully threw at him. Her eyes sparkled as they played.

This form of gaiety was not allowed. Akanni had not seen her, and he scraped a mashed piece of apple from his boot and tossed it back at Abigail, snickering until he saw his mother. Tituba did not return his smile.

Abigail might be slow, as some said, but she was past twelve. She was developing the same urges as any young woman. They might forgive her for being playful with any lad, but never with Akanni.

Tituba would remain alert for any troublesome signs of forbidden friendship by Akanni and quash it before anyone noticed.

After dinner Tituba cleaned up and scoured pots in the lean-to. She caught sight of the master as he added two armfuls of wood to the main fire. The pale warmth of October days had given way to freezing nights. She watched the family from the kitchen and awaited Master's call to join them in front of the hearth for prayers. He led them in several psalms and then he spoke to Abigail, "You must remember, as with your kin, that the Lord gave, and the Lord took away. Blessed be the name of the Lord."

Mistress, as if guessing where her husband was heading, took Abigail's small hand in her own.

"Remember when the Lord commanded Moses to avenge the children of Israel for the evil by the Midianites?" Tituba saw Abigail's eyes widen. She had heard parts of this story before, and the children knew it well.

"And Moses said the people must arm themselves and go against the Midianites. Just as we brethren of Christ shall soon go to avenge our dead brothers and sisters against the black heathen Indians, those infernal worshippers of Satan."

When Abigail let a whimper escape, Tituba hoped Master would assure the child that justice was coming from their god. But he seemed not to concern himself with the tears welling in the girl's eyes.

"And the Lord commanded they slay all the males and females and take the children captives—"

Abigail burst out a screech. Her terror unlocked, she screamed louder and longer with each breath.

Tituba stifled her alarm, waiting to receive an order, watching impotently, as pandemonium followed.

"No-o-o!" Abigail wailed. "They will find me and take me away! And they will kill Betty and everyone!"

She yanked her hand from the mistress and, in the effort of breaking free, sent her herself reeling backward. She stumbled, then spun to face the hearth. Tripping on the firedog irons, she grabbed them with both hands. Tituba winced as the hot metal searing her skin sounded like bacon dropped into a pan. Crying anew, this time in severe pain, Abigail pitched the wrong way, deeper into the hearth. Only her heavy clothing shielded her from the blaze, and she backed against the rear of the hearth, trapped behind a wall of grasping yellow flames.

In a panic the mistress shouted, "Samuel, get her! Get her out of there!"

"Come on, Abigail," he coaxed, braving the heat as he extended a hand toward her.

Abigail refused him, shaking her head, clinging to the only spot the fire could not reach. Her scorched clothes were already smoking from the heat, and flames began to climb from the hem of her dress.

"Abigail, come out! I command you to come out of there!"

By this time Mistress had pulled Betty to herself and backed away.

"Abigail, come out!"

As he shouted at her, Tituba couldn't help but wonder if the child was more terrified of him than the fire.

"Abigail . . ."

Furious, Master dove into the hearth, shielding himself from the heat and her pummeling hands until he controlled her. With his forceful pull they toppled backward out of the fire, setting several of the logs askew in a massive shower of sparks.

Mistress turned Betty's face away from Master and Abigail as they gasped for fresh air on the floor, smoke tendrils rising from their singed hair and burnt clothing.

"Look for burns!" Mistress cried.

Abigail was sobbing as Master roughly checked her smudged face and neck. Fat blisters already had formed beneath the blackened skin of her palms.

Tituba ran into the lean-to and back with a bucket of water, slopping it as she hurried. Master took it and doused the last burning spots on Abigail's dress. He whirled on Tituba, snarling. "Her hands are burnt. Fetch grease!"

Tituba headed back to the kitchen, angry at him. Did he think she did not know how to treat a burn? She scooped a gob of lard into a small bowl and, grabbing clean rags, rushed the grease and bandages to Mistress' outstretched hand.

Tituba watched them, ready to do as needed. Abigail lay whimpering on the plank floor beneath her aunt's gentle touch as she applied the ointment. Tituba backed away from the master, not wanting him to transfer his foul temper to her. Couldn't he see that his callous Bible story had terrorized the child and caused the accident?

Betty had found a corner of the room farthest from the fire, where she hugged her small arms around herself, her lips moving as if praying to save her frail cousin.

Tituba turned to catch Akanni staring at Abigail from the kitchen, crying soundlessly. There would be no more of that. "Come on," she said, herding him in her arms and out the back door. "Go check," she snapped at him, "the animals in the barn. Go on. Make yourself useful."

Chapter Five

Reverend Samuel Parris pursued his duties in Salem Village during the first year with the fervor of God's most grateful apprentice. Ordination day had signaled great days ahead. Reverend Nicholas Noyes of Salem Town embodied the church, and Reverend Hale ordained Parris with the laying on of hands, all of it promising a life blessed by God. At last.

For months at a time, he'd not battled thoughts of Barbados or Boston and the humiliations he'd left behind. His flock had embraced him so warmly in the beginning. His exhortations to saintliness, that everything was possible through the blood of the Lamb who died for all men, had stimulated appreciative discussions and several adult baptisms.

But now, nearly two years into this new work, God's work, he smelled faint whiffs of that old familiar stink. Every morning he hid from it in the refuge of prayer, burying himself in it deeper for relief from self-doubt and, increasingly, anger at his disrespectful flock.

He was an ordained messenger from Christ. And more often than he had expected, disrespect was spreading. People sat on the benches like knots in a log when he pointed out the sparse attendance at meetings. Didn't they understand he was giving all his energy to bring them into Christ's arms? Here they were, acting as though he was a common laborer to be bullied and denied fair pay for his work.

Yes, perhaps it had been unseemly to renegotiate his contract so soon, cajoling the committee to convey the deed to the parsonage to him. But with the new baby, Susanna, he had to make up for the back pay they already owed him. He'd given up trying to shame them even before they inexplicably voted to cut off his stipend for firewood. They'd given their word!

Parris assured himself he'd been right to demand the parsonage land as added security. Scoundrels and cheaters, they were. And heartless with winter soon upon them. Cutting and hauling logs was not for Harvard men, or men of the cloth. He would need to scavenge for firewood one way or another by the end of winter.

Today, while he rode homeward atop his chestnut beast after a pastoral visit to John Proctor's farm, Parris' mood matched the leafless maples bereft of autumn warmth.

Goodwife Proctor had a brood of children scurrying about the house; she seemed to half listen to him. Her servant girl, Mary Warren, seemed to be having as much fun playing along rather than helping her mistress. "Mary, shall I tell my husband of your inattention to work? Settle them down."

Parris waited as Mary ducked her head and hurried the children from the room.

After they were alone, Goody Proctor said, "Beg your pardon, Mr. Parris. We must supervise that one close. John has laid on the rod for her laziness. It seems the only way to keep her attentive."

John Proctor had a large farm and recently opened a tavern under license. Parris knew the Proctors enjoyed God's bounteous providence, selling their overstock of nuts and grain, dried fruits and smoked meats. And he could not miss the fifty cords of cut firewood behind their farmhouse.

"My neighbors told me to expect your visit, Mr. Parris." She motioned him to sit on a bench. "I have been searching my soul, longing to be closer to Christ and able to testify to my conversion. There is nothing I want more than to become a full member of our village church."

It was the reason he'd come. "I would be happy to baptize you and your husband."

"I am sorry to say John is away this day, but he is less likely to seek it."

Parris suspected Goodman Proctor and his wife, like everyone else, knew of his income disputes with the rate committee. It galled him they might suspect his motives during visits like this though he told himself it was first for God's glory he was there. Still, bringing in newly baptized landowners like Proctor had personal benefits, because they would be required to pay into the rate assessment and his salary.

He had little inclination to linger, knowing the master of the house was not there, but he stayed long enough to examine the two children over the age of five, checking how well they could read scriptures.

"Keep them reading, Goody. What was the Reformation but the liberation of the mind by reading the sacred word of God?" He'd said it on so many visits to examine children, he suspected the people joked about it among themselves. And where was it getting him?

"Thank you for visiting, Mr. Parris. Mary, bring that small box of salt cod for the Reverend." She passed it to him. "Please take it for Goody Parris to make a nice stew."

"Thank you and God bless this house," he said, thinking they could have thrown him a half cord of wood, too.

Parris reined up to dig for a piece of dried fruit from his bag. He chewed on it for a moment before another thought on his pay occurred. It was time to press his lackluster patron Thomas Putnam for a solution.

He found Thomas sitting on a stone half-wall at a corner of his fields, dressed in homespun and leather work clothes. He at first wondered if Putnam noticed him, as the man remained intent on his task of scraping gobs of mud from his boots.

"Evening, Revert. What can I do for you?" He wiped his work knife clean and looked up. Putnam evinced that dry smile he flashed from time to time. To Parris, it gave the impression Putnam was calculating what value he might derive after granting a favor.

"You can offer me a cup of beer, so we can talk parish business for a while."

Inside the Putnams', they sat close to the hearth in the main room. It seemed every blessed season of the year needed the warmth of fire.

"I see little prospect of quickly resolving my deficient pay. What can we do about it?"

Putnam looked at him. That smile was back, but he said nothing.

"The rate committee does not appreciate my efforts at bringing new members into covenant. I have baptized men, women and children. Yet rather than an increase I must beg for what they owe me."

"You want appreciation now, do you?" Putnam drained his cup. "You know, I am no longer leading the rate committee. Joseph Porter is in control, and he is not as inclined to take care of you the way I did."

"But Thomas—"

"You have not forgotten my help from before, have you, Samuel?"

"No, but—"

"We broke the restriction in the village deed and granted the parsonage land to you even though there was no prior consent in the village."

Parris didn't want to hear those details, then or now. He preferred to stay ignorant of them, and Putnam's reference to the unusual transfer of title made him feel soiled.

He was uncertain now why he decided to see Putnam.

"Oh, by-the-by, parson. Have you heard any rough talk in the parish about my legal problems with those thieves up Topsfield way?"

The parties had been in court over boundary lines and timber harvests from lands claimed by both the Topsfielders and the Putnams. The mention reminded Parris of last winter when Putnam had sent two cords of firewood to the parsonage after he ran low. He never inquired over its origin. Was it tainted by disputed ownership?

"I have heard nothing other than a grumble here and there," Parris said.

"I ask you as a friend, Samuel. If you hear such talk remind the gossipers, it is sinful to tell lies."

"I shall."

"And I shall find a cord or two somewhere for you, before it gets cold and people get stingy."

"From which neighbors?"

"Worry not where it comes from, Revert."

Goody Putnam joined them. "Mr. Parris, will you eat with us?"

"Of course, he will!"

"I shall." Parris said, trying to nod appreciatively, though he had little appetite a moment ago.

Goody Putnam laid out roasted venison, carrots and piles of boiled cabbage, along with fat loaves of bread with butter and beer for all. She set wooden trenchers with a knife for the adults. Parris took a large napkin made from old linen from a thick stack on the table; eating meals with hands and fingers as they did, required their use at every meal.

Thomas Putnam took the solitary chair reserved for the man of the house. Parris joined Goody Putnam on a rough barn plank bench while the rest of the family stood around the well-used oak table board.

"Mind the splinters," the mistress cautioned.

"Goody Putnam, your abundant table is more than any visitor could expect. A splinter is a small price to bear to partake of such fare."

"Tempt me not with the sin of pride." Her tone sounded agitated to Parris, and he chuckled to distract them from thinking he had noticed. His wife had told him of Ann Putnam Sr.'s frequent flights of melancholy, but he scoffed at it. She seemed normal enough in the meetinghouse, never missing a Sunday or Lecture night.

Thomas added, "Aye, she might forget her other faults and throw your compliment in my face the next time I correct her mistakes."

Parris wondered what dance he was seeing.

"Is illness a fault to you now, Mr. Putnam?" she shot back and stared at him as though he'd told a secret about her.

Thomas ignored his wife until she rushed from the room, spilling unexpected tears.

Parris was unsure what to make of this turn of affairs. "Thomas, may I be helpful?

"No, t'is my business, thank you."

They finished a subdued meal without Goody Putnam and afterward, Thomas produced the family Bible. Parris read several passages from Psalms. Upon finishing he laid the book on the table and turned to the oldest child, Ann Jr. Her head and shoulders rose a mere six inches above the table level.

It had shocked Parris when he first learned her age after arriving in Salem Village. Though shaped like any other child, she was smaller than his Betty, who was the same age. And now that he looked closer at her, she was extremely thin.

The child smiled in a way that reminded Parris of her father.

"Do you say your prayers before sleep each night?"

"Oh, yes, Mr. Parris." Her eyes darted toward her father.

Goody Putnam returned to the table, rolling her eyes at her daughter's answer. She had recovered her emotions somewhat, though her face was flushed.

Parris looked back at little Ann. "Do you obey your father?"

Ann nodded vigorously.

Parris placed his hand on the Bible. "And the Lord will punish those who do not obey Him. Just as these words of God tell us obedience to his laws is our duty, so his punishment will follow, not only those who disobey Him, but those who also disobey their earthly father.

"Do you understand this, child?"

The child shook her head, but at her mother's instructive hiss stared at the floor.

"I fear she understands only what she wants, Reverend," Goody said.

"Remember, young Ann, the Devil is always trying to tempt us from Christ's loving arms."

Parris patted her on the head. This was the shepherd's work he longed to do without worrying over a secure income. "When you come to the parsonage next, will you show Betty and her cousin Abigail how you card wool and make thread from linen? I am sure they can learn other things from you as well."

Chapter Six

Outside the parsonage vicious November winds slashed at the wooden siding, scratching icy nails along the rough grain. It searched for gaps to suck away warmth before exhaling its frosty breath into the house. Tituba kept the fires burning throughout the night, but the unstoppable wind roared down the chimneys and froze the sap sizzling from the logs.

During these never-ending cold seasons, Tituba slept in the new lean-to kitchen on her mat, almost inside the hearth. Usually the wood she laid for the fires gave enough heat to keep them alive until morning, but tonight she could not stand one more cold moment. She had piled extra wood on the fire and silently apologized to Master for being weak.

In the dim light from the glowing coals half buried in white ashes, Tituba watched the flames catch until the fire crackled. She rubbed a sand crystal from her eye. She had been dreaming about Mama when a powerful burst of air down the chimney awakened her.

The dream was about the day she was taken. It had started much like every morning of her pleasant childhood. Eleven years old and yearning to become a woman just like Mama. Someday she would teach Tituba how to be a seer and possessor of mystical powers. As Tituba tended yams baking in the cook fire outside her mudbrick hut, the village seemed asleep. All the men, women and older children were working the communal fields for the next planting.

The kidnappers seemed to appear from thin air just as Tituba looked up from the fire.

Inside the hut, when Mama resisted them, the big man subdued her with such punches and kicks Tituba thought Mama would die right then.

Tituba filled with adrenaline, but the man's grip on her was too strong. Soon, they were beyond the village fences and in the forest. The big man carried Mama on his shoulder, her head was bouncing as he ran. The other man having tied Tituba's hands with leather straps pulled her along, sometimes dragging her when she tripped. Mama's swollen face was a mass of blood, unrecognizable if Tituba hadn't seen them beating her unconscious.

Another mighty gust shook the walls of the parsonage. Tituba wished it was only the storm that caused her stomach to hurt.

She raised her head to search the small room for John Indian, Skitôp as she called him. As blast followed blast, puffing white ashes onto her, she rolled to where he was sleeping up against the wall, away from the drafts. He had arrived in the middle of the night. At least once a week, he snuck home to her. Each time they made love urgently but silently, the way house slaves must. Master forbade him to leave work at Ingersoll's tavern without permission, so he made his way back and forth in darkness. She told herself to sleep lightly. She would awaken him before dawn so he could return to work at Ingersoll's undetected.

The colonists had captured Skitôp and his father during King Philip's War. They rounded up the Pequots of his tribe not killed in battle or escaping to sanctuary and sold them into bondage in the West Indies. He was a mere youth then, but he preserved his tribal identity as if he were still among his kinsmen.

It was still so cold, even after she added her woolen blanket over his. Spooning gave more warmth both to body and soul. Skitôp mumbled in his native Indian language and then in English, "We can run for freedom with my brothers, the Nehântick tribe. Many Pequot people still live there, and their huts are warmer."

Tituba nuzzled closer to him. "You long for freedom we cannot describe. We have been captives since Barbados. What do we know of it?"

"My heart understands freedom."

This sort of talk disquieted her. Not ten days ever passed without Skitôp railing against their bondage. Since they arrived here on the frontier, closer to the tribes, he spoke of it more often, and she hoped tonight would not be a repeat. She could not deny his yearning, but how would he protect her on the run? Or Akanni? And what would they do when the English came to get them from the Nehântick? "There is no way for you to protect me, as you promised so many years ago."

"I fail to protect you each time the master beats you and our son." His voice rose, and she tried to shush him with her hand to no avail. "Each time I see a mark on you, I want to make him suffer and beg for mercy. I refrain, knowing they will tear us apart or worse if I act alone." He rolled to face her. "This is why we must run together. Soon, before fate takes away the chance."

Tituba rolled him back and kissed him, not out of love, but to silence him, and keep him from pressing her. She knew what she was doing, what Mama wanted her to do, and it had kept them all together.

While Skitôp always spoke his mind to her, he still hid his thoughts from Akanni, as she had asked. But he, always a rebel against her prodding to service, was asking questions. Recently Akanni blurted out his anger about the indentured Irish and English set free after seven years of labor. He realized it was not his fate because he was black.

Tituba had not laughed at Skitôp's retort. "Better than being Indian. They shoot Indians."

She knew very soon the father's thoughts would become the son's. Why could they not endure their lives in servitude as she did?

Skitôp seemed to relax again, as his wave of anger passed. Tituba knew he would never leave without her, true to his vow. But as for Akanni? How long did she have? Tituba wished there were a similar way to hold on to her son. But it would take a greater power than she possessed.

Akanni was growing too fast, right under her nose, giving her scant time to tame his inherited impulses, command him to obey without explanation, and to always keep the master happy. And as Akanni pulled away from her, as every son must from his mother, it seemed she would never teach him lasting secrets of survival.

She hugged Skitôp tightly to ward off another chill, this one coming from within her, rather than the frigid room.

When Skitôp started to snore, Tituba was still searching for elusive sleep. Ready to give up, she tried to imagine the sunshine of her lush village in Africa. But thirty years of captivity had fractured and veiled her memories. She could recall nothing with certitude except two things: Mama's command to appease, and she would come back one day.

Tituba massaged her belly. She'd been feeling odd pressure from within lately and breathing was harder when it happened. She thought frontier slave labors or the cares of a mother caused the condition, but rare good nights of sleep made little difference.

She thought again of Akanni. How could she protect him? Though Tituba never had found the powers Mama possessed, she survived without them by appeasing. Once, she hoped and expected Mama would return to teach her how to find and use the powers. Then she might've given Akanni some shield against the future.

Once more that pressure arose in her stomach. Perhaps it was the storm in the waning night. Tituba waited for the pain to ease and soon she grew drowsy.

In that half-sleeping state, she whispered, "*Mama, nibo ni o wa?*" The old language came back to her. Mama, where are you?

The next Tituba knew, the rooster called from the barn, signaling time to begin her daily drudgery: bring up the kitchen hearth fire, heat water, milk the cow, gather eggs, and cook the morning breakfast.

In his sleep Skitôp gripped the knife in his belt. She finger-combed his long black hair, caressing him. *Do not forget your promise to never leave me, husband.*

Skitôp opened his eyes, and she thought he had read her fearful thought. But he smiled, and she knew he remembered his promise without being asked.

"Come closer, woman." He looked as though he had set aside what they talked about during the night. "We shall talk no more about leaving the English until you are ready."

She leaned to kiss him.

"Do we have time?" He smiled and looked toward the door way from the main room.

She slapped him on the chest and pulled away. "For you a little time is enough, but we must wait until next you come."

They giggled together as Tituba arose and laid flaky elm logs on top of the burning fire.

From early hours like this until long after sunset she must complete one task and begin another. She did not differ from women in every household, except, she thought, other women did their work by choice, and slaves did not. She caught herself. Such thinking was forbidden, and out of habit she felt guilty.

Skitôp moved more wood closer to the hearth to help her as she gathered a hunk of day-old bread with some cheese and a small cup of beer. "Here, eat," she whispered. The contract with Ingersoll required him to feed Skitôp, and Master might chastise her for using their sparse supplies unnecessarily. But her man needed nourishment. Too soon, he was gone.

Dragging feet on the second floor told Tituba that Master was awake. She used the bellows to speed the fire for hot water. After his first prayers and a wash and shave, he wanted his breakfast before retiring to his study. Once she provided for him, she must awaken and feed the rest of the family. After eating, they would join Master for prayers while Tituba planned the day's chores for the girls and waited for further direction from Mistress.

As she ladled hot water into a washbasin for Master, Tituba reflected on a fun memory of childhood gamboling with playmates in the cool air beneath the central village tree.

Yes, the great tree! She felt herself ease into that happy time, enjoying the daydream until her mind flickered abruptly. Tituba sensed Akanni at Raiment's farm, three miles away. He had been banished from the parsonage for another infraction, and sent to work for a foul-tempered farmer whose son had a broken leg.

She visualized him through a frame of hazy indigo and black. The farmer was snapping a horse whip at Akanni as he backed away, holding out his arms and shaking his head as if denying what was being said. Tituba clutched her apron, twisting it. Akanni was so thin compared with the burly farmer, even though he ate for two. When Akanni bumped into a chopping block, he reached behind and found a hatchet stuck there.

"No!" Tituba shouted, "No!"

She blinked and instead of Akanni and the farmer, she saw the kitchen's whitewashed wall and the cooking tines and frying pans hung there.

What had just happened? Tituba felt the painful pressure recur and grow. It was squeezing her unbearably. Did she just have a vision from afar? As Tituba shuddered her skin turned to goose flesh. She sorted through what happened, recalling the Raiment farmyard exactly, down to the way their barn door hung slightly crooked to the right. But search provided no clue of what had happened between the farmer and her son.

A kettle boiled, and Tituba jumped to attend it while worry distracted her. Her hands shook as she tried to maneuver the kettle off the fire with an iron poker. Before she could stand straight again, a hard lurch in her stomach and a mouthful of saliva brought on a wave of dizziness that tipped her off balance and into a squat next to the cutting table. The overwhelming sense her Akanni was in danger, no matter how the argument played out, if there truly had been one, pierced her with urgency. Laboring to inhale a breath, she regained her feet and tried to swallow her anxiety. How could she know if she truly saw anything?

No, it was not possible. This was nothing more than a mother's farfetched fearfulness. But Akanni—

"Tituba!" Master's voice made her jump. "My water. Now!"

She had forgotten it. She struggled to overcome the trembling that gripped her. "Yes, Master." The shaking would not stop. Nor would the distracting thoughts.

How could she have been so near Akanni? It seemed she could have touched him! Vivid dreams such as this had come to her deep in the night, but never during the light of day, catching her so unaware.

Tituba had over-filled Master's clay shaving basin with hot water, spilling a good portion as she carried it to him. What ought she do? He would never give permission for her to leave and verify the truth of a daydream.

Her only escape from the distress of not knowing what happened was work. Make the cheese-bread and bake three loaves, boiling the peas for porridge and steam two large pompion, cooking them down into a sauce while plucking the fat goose Deacon Ingersoll had sent instead of pay for Skitôp's labor. Churning butter from the gallons of fresh milk allowed her to escape into monotony, at least for an hour or two.

Though exhausted from the inner debate, she could not stop it. She had seen something. She'd seen nothing. Tituba squeezed the sides of her head to stop the thoughts, and tried one more time to find Akanni in the distance. She kept at it even as she despised herself for her lack of self-control.

"Tituba, come help me with the baby."

"Yes, Mistress."

Chapter Seven

Alone that night, Tituba could not let go of the daydream. Her mind kept returning to the scene at the Raiment farm. She had to know how it ended. But each time her thoughts went to it Tituba suffered the worse for having tried and seen naught.

The parson's house was silent early since Sabbath was observed at sundown on Saturday.

With nothing else to do, Tituba needed to dowse the candle of her racing thoughts and search for a little sleep. But it seemed impossible.

On her mat in the kitchen, she closed her eyes for the hundredth time and searched instead for the solace of her Mama's face. Nothing.

She huffed, chastising herself. Why look to Mama? How might a memory of her ease Tituba? She clenched her jaws, determined to dismiss the uncontrollable thoughts as nothing more than an overactive imagination. Dreams and daydreams, indeed.

The next morning, unrefreshed, Tituba grumbled to herself in the waning darkness and loaded more wood into the hearth. The sharp popping and crackling from the fire comforted her and she lay down again to steal a moment of respite before facing the day. She reclined on her mat and filled her lungs with a deep breath, closing her eyes and exhaling slowly, searching for clarity.

And that was when Mama seemed to appear. It was as though Tituba could see through the roof of the lean-to, and beyond into the clouds as Mama approached her.

My daughter, hear me.

Tituba tensed, not daring to open her eyes. She kept breathing evenly, deeply, and she relaxed. If this was a hallucination, she would see it through.

Yes, unclutter your thoughts, daughter. I am here. And if you maintain this state, we shall be together.

Despite years of cursing her mother for abandoning her, Tituba was charged with a warmth she had long forgotten. Instinctively, she opened herself to Mama. She smelled the arid jungle floor of Africa and other long-forgotten scents of the forest. She dampened an urge to smile, fearful it would end the spell.

There was no need for speech as they communicated wordlessly. *Mama, have you come because of my calling? To teach me your powers?*

No, child, I have come because you are ready.

For what am I ready?

To know what is inside your heart. I cannot come to teach what you must learn. Look inside. Think purposefully.

Tell me, Mama, and show me the powers.

Patience, child, but for now, I say—

The deep voice of Master hammered Tituba's spell to pieces like a broken glass. Once more aware of her surroundings, Tituba blinked upward at him from her mat.

"Are you going deaf? Or shall I heat water for *you*?"

She blinked again to clear her head, not sure what he had said. And then she remembered it was Sunday morning! And, once *again* she was late with hot water for him to wash and shave. When preaching about the filth of mankind, the master had to be a model of cleanliness.

"…or shall I heat water for *you*?"

Tituba rolled to her knees.

"One more time slacking like this and you will cry for mercy from my belt." He stomped from the kitchen.

When Tituba stood up, a wave of nausea struck. She gagged to vomit but her stomach was empty. She struggled to reorient herself, gripping the cutting table to find her balance, but failing, fell back on her haunches. Sweat drenched her collar.

Waiting for the dizziness to pass, Tituba stared into the hearth, at the tiny yellow and red flares from under a mound of ash. Then, feeling better, she sucked in a hard breath and forced herself to stand. Moving by habit she ladled hot water for Master. How long had it been since he hovered over her, a mere moment? Five minutes? She hurried as best she could to deliver the water.

She hadn't slept over the last two days. Akanni and Mama, Mama and Akanni. They would not release her.

Tituba fed the family and saw them off to the meetinghouse. Alone, she checked the germinating malt barrel, mixing and smelling it for readiness. She cleaned and re-cleaned morning pots, trenchers, and bowls; the eating knives and wooden spoons, until she could barely remain standing. And after a bare moment of rest, she dried her hands on the soaked apron she wore, feverish for more diversion.

Hours later, when renewed anxiety demanded answers again, Tituba ground her teeth. She turned in a full circle, surveying the lean-to cooking area. What else needs be done? The meal was cooking and the family would be home for midday meal soon.

She wished Skitôp was with her, but he was at Ingersoll's, helping to prepare for hungry parishioners after morning services. He brought the best gossip to her, faster even than the congregation women visiting the Master or Mistress, and she wanted foolish talk to sidetrack her.

She jumped from her reverie when the door popped open and Akanni rushed in, closing it with a bang. Tituba looked for telltale signs of fighting or, forbid the thought, blood. As Akanni inspected the food cooking over the fire, she inspected him. He was dirty from outdoor work, but she saw nothing unusual.

"I am hungry," he said.

"You give no better greeting to your mother than to demand food?" She was ready to burst into tears, as relief welled. But just as quickly, uncertainty returned. She pulled a clean shirt for him. "Take off that filthy waist coat and shirt."

"What?"

She needed to see his back for signs of a whipping. "Do it now!"

Her manner must have shocked him because he peeled off his clothing. There were no scars.

Tituba hugged her child for longer than he wanted and laughed giddily as he squirmed for her to let go. He was unhurt. "I am sorry for my harsh tone. I missed you." She handed him the clean shirt with a smile.

Even though she felt better, she could not avoid rethinking; the absence of signs he'd been whipped proved nothing.

"Help me," she breathed and then covered her mouth.

Akanni stopped chewing a mouthful of bread and peered at her.

"Er, the family will be home soon. Raise the fire in the main room and lay out the board for their midday meal. Then carry the empty commode and buckets to the sleeping rooms. I'll gather food for you to eat, and you may tell me how your work for Goodman Raiment has gone."

Akanni moaned. "When will my indenture to you end, Mama?" But he set to the tasks she gave him, still eyeing her in a questioning way. When he returned, Tituba handed him a steaming bowl of meat and pompion sauce.

"Now, tell me why you are here. Is it for a day of rest?"

"Yes."

He did not look at her when answering, and she told herself he was too hungry to talk.

When Tituba heard running feet approach the lean-to, she knew it was Betty and Abigail. As usual they were the first home.

Not wanting to see if Abigail and Akanni shared a glance, she diverted him. "Here is cornbread. Take your food and sit over there." She pointed Akanni to a stool in the corner. "We shall talk in a moment."

The girls rushed in, their cheeks red from the cold, eyes glistening at the short freedom from supervision after church. Neither seemed to notice Akanni.

"Tituba, why were you not at your seat in the gallery of the meetinghouse?"

"I did not feel well, child."

"What illnesses have you?"

"Mind you not."

The girls were always hungry for a treat. But Mistress demanded they get permission from her to eat between meals.

Despite the rule she knew very well, Abigail asked, "What can we have before Uncle Samuel arrives?" She eyed the cornbread in a pan and a bowl of butter next to it, as another child arrived at the door.

Ann Putnam entered the kitchen in her bashful manner, which Tituba often thought affected. The child always unsettled her for reasons Tituba could not determine. Instead of the healthy complexion of most village children, Ann was very thin and had a sallow face. Her white blond hair was pulled back as all girls kept it, but near the hairline was a small but ugly pink scar. Perhaps over exuberant administrations of corporal punishment kept her… secretive.

The girl was pouting. "What troubles you, Ann?"

Her lower lip protruded. "They did not wait for me." She began to grow teary until she noticed the cornbread and sniffed the cooking food.

Mistress' arrival at the front door drew squealing appeals from Abigail and Betty for something to eat, and the two cousins whooshed back into the kitchen.

Knowing the likely answer from the mistress, Tituba had set out small squares of corn bread for the three.

"But Mother says no butter until we eat dinner—with Ann as our guest." The three scrambled for the stairs.

While Mistress hung her cloak on the wall peg, cooing to the baby, the girls scrambled all the way up the ladder to the third-floor loft. "When those growling stomachs are silenced, settle and regain a respectful temperament for a Sunday. Read the Lord's Prayer and copy it. We will have our meal upon Father's return."

"Yes, Mother." "Yes, Auntie." "Yes, Mrs. Parris," they replied at the same time.

Tituba realized Akanni had made himself scarce. She had to know what had happened out on the farm. Sometimes that child....

She felt a wave of regret for failing to be strict with him. She seemed to always give in. Skitôp said she coddled him.

Thumps from the loft alerted Tituba the girls were going to need supervision. When Elizabeth entered the kitchen, Tituba stepped back from the cooking fire so she could inspect the progress of the meal. "Will everything be ready for my husband?"

"Yes, Mistress."

"I hear too much noise going on up there. Climb up to check the girls. I shall watch the food."

Tituba nodded and ascended the stairs toward the second floor. When Ann let out a long and extra-loud burp in the loft, Tituba also heard it and the children giggling at Ann's audacity. Tituba knew they had wolfed down the food and licked their fingers clean, and would have wagered no hornbooks or papers were in their hands yet.

After reaching the base of the loft ladder, she moved silently upward, stopping halfway, just able to see the children sitting on the loft floor with their backs to her.

Ann picked up Betty's child-sized book of prayers and leafed through the worn pages. "Tell me, why are we damned?"

Both girls looked to Betty for an answer.

"We ought not to talk of the spirit world," she said carefully. "Without Father to help us, the Creator might think we blaspheme."

Abigail was in no mood for solemn talk, however. She reached inside Ann's apron and pulled out a poppet doll. She hugged it like a mother, then smiled. "Aunt Elizabeth says playing with poppets is sinful."

"She does not have to know," Ann said. Tituba saw she was grinning. "My father says even if we try to be good children, God may still not allow us into heaven. He picked all the elected at the beginning of creation."

Abigail lay on her back, looking upward as if staring at a knot in the ceiling. "How can God even remember which of us He picked to be saved?"

She craned her neck toward her cousin Betty. The pastor's daughter sat straighter on the braided rug next to her cot. "My father says we must do what God expects, and believe we are saved through the Savior's blood, and never sin."

Ann knit her brow. "My mother says I do bad things all the time, and she lets me play with my poppet." She fluttered the prayer book pages back and forth without reading. "She says we must be vigilant for the Devil and his familiars. They are ever ready to lead us into sin."

"What are Satan's familiars, Betty?" Abigail asked. "And what should we do if we find one?"

"Father says witches are familiars. The Devil sends them to hurt us if we reject him and his temptations. Have you not heard father preach it? He says his friend Mr. Mather found a witch familiar in Boston."

Ann tucked the poppet back into her apron pocket. "My uncle Edward says animals that come in the night are familiars. A wild dog or a frog or yellow birds are forms taken by witches. If we see them, we'll tell." She began a soft growl. "Why don't we practice? I shall play a wild dog familiar." She snarled a little and bared her teeth.

Abigail grabbed Betty and scrabbled behind her. She was shaking and squeezing her eyes shut.

"Stop it, Annie," Betty cried out uneasily, but Ann was enjoying the game. She rushed toward the girls on all fours, growling louder and snapping her teeth.

Ann nipped at Abigail and then leapt onto Betty, pushing her face into Betty's neck as if trying to tear open her throat.

Shrill screams of fear burst from both girls, but Ann replied by howling. Among them, they raised an unholy chorus in the parsonage.

Responding to this outburst, Tituba hauled herself the rest of the way up the ladder and into the loft. She pulled Ann roughly away by her arm. "What foolishness is this?" she hissed.

Betty and Abigail remained clasping each other, huddled against the roof gable, gasping mixed fear and relief. Ann turned sullen for an instant, but then stared up at Tituba, panting like an animal.

At a sharp call from below, Tituba let loose of Ann's arm. "Tituba, what is going on up there? They were to keep quiet in prayer! Bring them down. The Master has just arrived."

Tituba held back as the girls descended, clattering the whole way down. First Akanni, then Mama in her mind day and night. She had felt goose flesh run up her arms as she watched little Ann's imitation of an attacking dog.

That thin girl seemed to enjoy frightening the girls as she performed her act.

Sinful dolls, witches and wild dogs! Bah, Tituba thought. What things they believe in.

Chapter Eight

During an unexpected December thaw, Betty was visiting the Putnam farm. Goody Putnam, flustered, was re-tying the laces on Betty's winter cloak and hood. Her hands were shaking. She had lost track of time and should have sent the girl home much earlier. Darkness was certain to drop its cape, and enormous clouds were piling in from the east. The scent presaging a fresh snowfall permeated the air, even inside the house.

She chastised herself. One more thing she was inadequate about. Blood pounding in her head reminded Goody Putnam how she felt when her husband complained about some act or omission of hers.

"Annie, best if you walk halfway with Betty to get her home. And come straight back." She opened the door for them. "Stay along the road, not on it, or you will sink into the mud. At Wolf Meadow, you turn around and allow Betty to proceed home."

She touched Betty's shoulder. "You ought to find your way straight home then."

"Goody, I am afraid to go alone in the dark."

Goody Putnam wiped a pale hand across Betty's cheek. "Very well. Ann, go to the parsonage with her, but do not dally or your father will fetch the rod upon your return."

The girls grabbed hands and ran through the doorway, scampering around the raised box garden holding the remains of a few carrots, parsnips and turnips. Two shriveled cabbages had gone to rot, one more sign of Goody Putnam's failed husbandry.

"Lord, protect them from harm," she said, biting her lip and closing the door.

* * *

Two miles away inside the parsonage, Elizabeth Parris had trouble feeding the infant. She was fussing, and with Betty not yet home, she gave up trying.

"Abigail, take Suzannah upstairs and watch her."

She circled the room every few minutes, checking the door each time. As Tituba watched, her impatience swelled into anxiety.

"She was to come home well before sundown!" she cried.

Tituba knew the Master's wrath would fall both on Betty and Mistress if the child was not back before he returned from a parish meeting.

Tituba brought the mistress a warmed cup of cider. She understood a mother's fears, for she had them, too. She had heard the village women repeat worries to each other over their precious children. One lost to illness, another to an accident. How many mothers had lost three or four children less than a year of age? The blacksmith's first wife had gone mad over her losses.

"Tituba, send Akanni to fetch Betty." The mistress was picking at her fingers.

Tituba went out to the barn, where Akanni was working. Fat snowflakes had started to fall. She handed him his winter cloak. "Mistress wants you to find Betty. She has not returned from Goodman Putnam's and should have been here hours ago."

"Why must I go?"

The mistress' unsettled mind was affecting Tituba. Akanni out in the dark searching for a missing girl made her stomach twist.

"You must hurry. Already the snow is worse and soon even this cloak will not keep you warm."

Akanni left at a run, shooting looks left and right as he disappeared into a white curtain. Tituba strained to catch a last sound of him, but there was only the silence of falling snow.

* * *

An hour had elapsed without a sign of Betty or Akanni before Parris entered the parsonage, followed by Goodman Putnam. Master was saying, "As you see, I have just arrived myself."

Tituba knew by Thomas Putnam's sodden breeches, muddy past his knees, that he had come on foot. Mistress said, "Thomas, at seeing you, I hoped you had brought our daughter."

Putnam's face showed that he was troubled as well. "I know not where she is, Goody. I am here for my Ann, who was walking Betty home." His eyes darted around the room as if searching for his daughter.

"But our Betty was in your care, Goodman."

"She was, they were…"

Putnam trailed off as Mistress rushed to her husband. "Samuel, something evil is at hand. If our child has come to mischief...."

Master said, "We shall find them both." He looked at the ceiling, his lips moving as if in prayer. Tituba wondered if he was seeking patience with the mistress or guidance on how to proceed with the search. He opened the door to a hard mixture of sleet and snow.

"Tituba, call Akanni. He's to make three torches and come with us. Elizabeth, fetch my dry boots upstairs."

Tituba remained in place, eyes fixed on the plank floor. Should *she* explain that Akanni already was searching somewhere out there for the girls?

Master turned on her and his tone betrayed the same rising fear she felt. "Mind me! Find your son. We need the torches."

Tituba shook her head and kneaded her hands. The mistress finally spoke up, her voice quavered. "I had Tituba send Akanni to search…"

Tituba swallowed an urge to cry out.

Mistress said, "But more than an hour has passed since he left, husband. I am afraid—"

"God's flesh!" The profanity shot from him. He turned to Putnam as if searching for a solution, and finding none, whirled around and slapped Tituba so hard she banged her head on the wood floor where she fell. She saw flickers of light from the impact, but she gained her knees. She had gotten worse from him.

"Where is my daughter, then?"

She knew he expected no answer from her and she kept out of his reach, furtively glancing up at him. Had he no concern for Akanni? Even for a moment? Was she so low that her son's welfare could not tear at her equally?

Tituba stood shakily.

"If your shiftless son has not done his duty…. You should hope no harm has come to my child."

Tituba's face was stinging, but she dared not touch it. She cursed her silence, wanting to demand the master find *all* the children. Then backing up a step, she told herself, of course he would.

She watched him pull on a dry heavy cloak.

Just then the door swung open and the two girls tumbled inside. The wind blew the foul weather in with them. Both had the blissful look of childish adventure until they saw the faces of the men, then Tituba.

"Father, what…?"

Tituba struggled to keep her feet, searching beyond the girls into the darkness outside. Perhaps Akanni was circling the house, preparing to enter from the back door. Yes, he must be. But she dared not move yet, knowing she would fall at the first step.

"Shut the door and attend your fathers," Tituba whimpered.

Ann's eyes flicked at her father. There was no mistaking his anger, but she let slip a nervous giggle, as if she knew what awaited her and didn't care.

The girls' boots and cloaks were muddy through and through. When the mistress tried removing Betty's sodden garments, Master shouted, "You have frightened your mother and me beyond words. You will have a beating for this. And if you become ill, you shall have another beating."

He pointed toward the stairway. "Put on dry clothes and return. I will know more of this misadventure." And then, as if an afterthought he said, "And where is that black bastard?"

Tituba's heart thudded. Akanni had not returned.

"At the beaver dam, Father."

"At... the beaver dam?" Master's eyes widened, and he turned on Tituba. "Is he to blame then for this tardiness? What else might he have been doing with our girls?"

Tituba was unsure to whom he was speaking, or whether she should speak and risk another cuffing. All she could muster was a thought; my son is no more a bastard than you, Master. Tituba fingered the welt on the side of her face where he slapped her. No more a bastard than you.

Thomas Putnam grabbed little Ann with a rough hand and led her to the door. She gasped as if expecting immediate harsh punishment, but she followed without another sound.

"Brother Thomas," Master called to him, "take my chestnut mare from the barn. Use my pillion saddle."

After Putnam departed, Master slammed the door and threw the bolt. Betty was cowering back inside her mother's arms. "What of this beaver dam, then? And do not sin by lying, else your punishment will be the greater."

Betty answered with a sneeze and a red nose. When she spoke, her voice was a whisper. "We were coming straight back. But there was splashing from the beaver pond. A-A-Ann said we should watch the beavers, and we threw sticks to help them build a house. We-e were not there long, Father, before Akanni came upon us."

Master pointed his long finger at Tituba. "If you taught your lazy son better, he would understand to obey orders rather than lead children in play."

Betty said nothing and Tituba tried to catch her eye to signal she must say more, say where Akanni was.

Master glanced at his wife and shouted at the top of his voice. "Abigail!"

"I am here, Uncle." She had been standing at the head of the stairs, quiet as a bird. She took two steps down and stopped.

"Help your auntie to bed."

Elizabeth was looking very poor as she held onto Betty. "I can go by myself. Abigail, help Betty change clothes and bring the soiled ones for Tituba to dry out and brush clean."

Left alone with her furious Master, Tituba shuddered. He took his seat, glaring into the yellow flames dancing in the hearth. After a while he spoke. His voice was cool. "You and your son will both pay for this laxity." He reached for a poker and at first Tituba thought he would strike her, but he settled the fire and ascended the stairs. She watched every slow step.

From the second floor the master called back, "Bring hot porridge to us. We shall eat in our rooms."

Two hours later, Tituba was sitting in the dark kitchen. Only the dwindling fire lit the room when Akanni arrived. The air went out of her at the sight of him, wet to the skin and like a captured animal, frightened and fierce at the same time. He threw something at the fire, but it sailed off the mark and hit Tituba. A child's mitten.

"Half the night to find that."

Tituba, not knowing what he meant, pulled off his cloak. It was sopping wet. She wrapped him in her own dry hooded coat. "Give me your boots." He needed help prying them loose. Together they yanked them off, then his sodden stockings "Your breeches and shirt, too."

She pumped the bellows to raise the fire, sliding a small pot along the lug pole closer to the fire to warm cider for him.

"You took all that time to find a mitten?" She flashed back to the day Abigail had flirted by tossing apples at him. Could Betty or Ann have done the same?

"Yes! Betty's mitten." Akanni glared at her.

"What more have you to say?"

"Nothing."

"Do you understand what this looks like?"

Akanni was shivering so hard, Tituba could barely understand him as he blurted, "I found Betty and Ann idling alongside Beaver Brook. Ann said she was afraid to go to her farm at the late hour. I implored Ann to go her own way so we could come home. She would not leave until the wind whipped up, blinding us, and Betty said she could return with us."

"And then?"

"I lost the way once, but as we came upon Thorndike Hill, Betty cried she could not find her mitten. She said I must find it or she would get a beating. She said if I did not go for it, I would get a beating for disobeying."

"And so, you obeyed." Tituba tried to wrap the dry cloak tighter around him.

After a swift jerk to avoid her touch, he leaned into her warmth, but as he spoke to her, the words cracked like a whip. "You and your ways. I searched for the mitten because you said we must never argue with them. But, Mama, I thought I might die in the cold… for a mitten."

He shuddered, and she brought him the hot cider, which he gulped, grimacing at the heat of the liquid he needed inside. Tituba rocked him until he fell asleep in her arms. She struggled to move him onto his mat, nearly tripping over his long legs.

She kept the fire blazing that night.

An hour before dawn, Tituba heard Betty sneezing and coughing.

When Master descended the stairs in the early morning dark, he surprised her in the lean-to. Tituba's first thought was he came to punish Akanni.

Akanni rose on an elbow as the Master approached him on the mat.

The Master seemed under control as he spoke. "Do not tell me a fabrication. Stand up." He towered over Akanni. "As you like to tarry in the rain," he looked at Akanni's muddy wool coat on the wall peg, still soggy wet, "you will need no dry garment against the weather while feeding the chickens and the livestock. Then muck out the barn. Hard work will warm you."

Master stomped off, and Tituba hurried to find food for Akanni.

"I thought you might tell Master what happened."

"The girls will call me a liar to avoid being punished. Besides, he will believe nothing I say against his children."

While he ate, Tituba dug a dry shirt from Skitôp's canvas bag and cut a hole in her blanket for him to use as a wrap. "Here, wear this, and…" She tightened it around his waist with a cord to trap body heat.

Betty's coughing reminded her that sickness often spread inside homes and sometimes became deadly. She hung Akanni's heavy wool cloak near the fire to dry, wishing she could do more to keep him from falling ill.

After serving the family at breakfast, Tituba called Akanni to the kitchen to eat while she laid out foods for the midday meal. He hunched over a pine wood trencher of food, shivering though he sat so close to the hearth that steam rose from him, scenting the air with animal vapors. She checked his blanket wrap, running her fingers down it and squeezing out moisture. "Wear your cloak outside, it is more dry than wet now."

Master came in and found Akanni dozing over his uneaten food. He kicked at one of his muddy boots startling him. "Someone will deliver a wagon of firewood today. Finish cutting and splitting what we have and then do the same to the new logs."

One look at her son told Tituba he was on the verge of talking back, and she dropped a skillet to divert him as Master left the room.

From the afternoon and into evening, Tituba listened to Akanni cut and split firewood, stacking it along the outer wall of the parsonage. At one point he must have paused for rest. A moment later the Master shouted, "Get back to work!"

Akanni answered half under his breath, using Pequot curses learned from his father, but loud enough for her to hear. She froze at his insolence, but nothing came of it.

The crack of the ax and rumble of split logs against the house, though slower and slower, continued into the night.

The pressure Tituba had felt before returned in full force. Only this time she knew its source. Didn't she have a right to be sorely vexed? Master blamed her son for the late return of the girls even though it was Akanni who went out in the storm, and found them. And his irresponsible child thanked Akanni by sending him back to find her lost mitten.

Swallowing her feelings about the injustice increased her suffering rather than easing it. Her son was freezing again outside over a sin he never committed.

Master blamed Akanni. But she had let him.

Yet, with such self-awareness she could not break from her lifetime of appeasement. Perhaps she was not brave enough to confront him… even for her son. This torture would end soon, wouldn't it?

Chapter Nine

Hour after hour Akanni worked into the cold night. And each time he paused, Tituba came awake, worrying about the consequences. After midnight, she brought him hot food to maintain his strength and fresh torches to light his work.

As she handed Akanni a bowl of cornbread soaked in honey and hot milk, he glared at her.

"Why the hard look, my son?"

"You, Mama. You are the cause."

She knew what he meant but said nothing. A failure at protecting her son from their Master's reaction, yes. But a cause of what happened, no. How could she be?

It was not a time to argue out there in the cold, in the middle of the night. And she was afraid the Master might overhear them, but Akanni had not finished.

"Why do you remain a groveling slave? You talk about obedience to Master. Where has it gotten *me*? Father knows our only way to freedom is to run."

Tituba shrank down into her shawl, waiting for him to finish the food. Had Skitôp disclosed his own yearning?

When it was clear Akanni had more to say, she moved close to him, hoping he kept his voice low. "Do you think I have not heard Father whisper it in the night?

"I don't want to hear this."

"I want to run away with Father, but he will not leave without you. What are you so afraid of, Mama? Suffering? Haven't you suffered enough here?"

Tituba shuffled back inside the lean-to. After closing the door, she fell to her knees and slumped back against it, stifling sobs with her apron. He was ready to go, and she was unprepared to let him. Her only son knew so little of a crushed spirit. Why could he not bear up to this temporary punishment? He did not know the full barbarity of bondage, the slavers and their disregard for life.

He could never understand what she had gone through before he was born. The crossing, the rape, a new world in which she had to do everything she was told.

Her first master had been fond of telling plantation guests from England the story of the island. "Barbados was like an emerald stone that leaped out of the sea as our first ship tacked against the wind. It was uninhabited when we took it from the Spanish. Those papists had killed or shipped the island natives to their silver mines. Not a single one was left on the island until we came and learned to grow tobacco and cane with the Africans."

She was one of those Africans. By the time Tituba's ship had entered Bridgetown harbor, half of those on board with her had died from sickness or suicide en route across the Atlantic Ocean. The stench of body waste and vomit and death filled her nose for endless days on end.

After the first weeks of the voyage, Tituba had scant energy to do more than stare at those around her, hopeless and uncaring.

When the ship docked in Bridgetown, she hardly noticed the thump against the pier. After debarking, they scrubbed the slaves with goat water. After that, they rinsed away the smell of animal piss with buckets of harbor water. As they dried in the sun, Tituba felt the scrub brush burns on the tips of her breasts, and touching them, noticed for the first time her body had changed. Mama had said the change would make her a woman, but Tituba felt no joy in it, feeling too much a forgotten piece of debris to care for anyone's approval. Rough sheets of burlap became fresh new clothes.

"Are we to be eaten?" a woman asked. Fat at the beginning of the journey she was boney now. Tituba remembered what a fellow captive had told her months ago.

"No, we are more valuable than sheep."

A man already chained in a line with others said, "But they will work us to death in their fields."

As white men mounted slaves on blocks and sold them, Tituba hooded her eyes while she watched the bidding.

The ship captain's voice came from off to the side, drawing Tituba's attention. It sounded as if he was arguing, but then he laughed and Tituba saw him shaking hands in a hasty manner with a man in brilliant white clothes. She later would learn he was the planter, Mr. Thomas Parris.

The captain waved for a surly sailor he called Bill and ordered him to take charge of Tituba. A chained African man still next to Tituba whispered, "You shall become a gift for his wife in England."

The captain was not on board when Bill delivered Tituba into the empty captain's cabin. Soon he relieved the single watch, and she heard footsteps hurry across the deck and down the gangplank. They were alone.

The next Tituba remembered, she was curled on the floorboards of a carriage and the man in brilliant white was driving it.

Tituba tried to move, but her body responded as though she were an ancient woman incapable of getting out of bed. Laying her head back, she searched her memory. Why was she in a moving carriage? Why were her numb lips split? And that metal taste.

Once she would have sobbed, but she did not even feel an urge to cry. Her left arm was bent wrong, and she knew someone had broken it. And there was a deep ache growing below her navel. Upon reaching down there, she touched a thick cloth wad extending between her legs.

The ship's boy was next to her in the jostling carriage. She only noticed him when he adjusted the blanket covering her. He was not an African, and would not understand her language had she been able to speak. He climbed forward into the driver's seat along with the man in the white clothes. Tituba wanted to believe the man must have saved her from some calamity, and if it was so, she felt grateful for his protection. She pushed a fleeting thought about Mama away, along with a spike of anger before falling asleep.

Whether the rest of the journey to the plantation took an hour or three, Tituba knew little since she was conscious for brief periods only. In one lucid moment she heard Mr. Parris speaking to the youth, though she could not understand the words.

"What's your name?"

"John, sir."

"How old are you?"

"About fifteen."

"West Indian?"

"No, *Skitôp*. I am Pequot."

"You take care of the little one back there until she heals, John Indian."

Weeks would pass before Tituba could stay awake longer than the time to consume broth. Her new master's African cook, Izzie, was her nurse, and she arranged a mat for her beneath an open window. As Tituba's body healed, she hid her recovery by remaining still, head turned to the wall. One moment gladness filled her for having survived the sea voyage and the next moment deepest despair as she searched for Mama's presence everywhere, hoping she might come and soothe her.

John Indian always seemed to be nearby, his black eyes searching for some sign of recovery. In her mind she knew him by his Indian word, *Skitôp*, and she took small pleasure from hearing the cook shoo him away when he was underfoot. She felt anxious if he was away too long. But he returned at night to sleep near her, head to head under the window.

One evening she asked him if he had seen who hurt her.

"I saw when he died. And wished I could have done it."

What he said next thrilled and terrified Tituba. "If anyone, master or slave, hurts you like this, I will kill them. I will guard you forever."

Slowly, Tituba's melancholy lifted. The plantation kitchen, she came to learn, was Izzie's domain. She kept it filled with food. Fruits and fowl hung on one wall. Nearby a gutted pig was laid out on a huge block of wood. Large metal pots lined another wall.

The kitchen hearth was as large as half of the hut she had grown up in. It contained no less than two small fires at all times, one in the near part heating water, another smoking meat beneath the chimney.

Tituba's lost appetite stirred when she detected the wonderful smell of fresh bread, made the way the English preferred. When she tasted it, the bread was the most delicious thing she ever ate.

One morning Izzie gave Tituba a slice of bread smeared with a jam so sweet, her mouth watered for more. When the cook brought another, Tituba grabbed her hand impulsively and spoke in her Yoruba language. "You take good care of me. Thank you, *Bisi*."

The cook's head jolted, and she looked around the empty kitchen. "Speak only their English language in the house or they will punish you."

"I must know what happened to me."

Izzie whispered while looking up and around. "A sailor attacked you. When the captain and Master Parris returned from dining here at the plantation, they found him hurting you. He was drunk, and when he resisted them, the captain of the ship killed him."

"But…."

"They say the captain feared it might keep him from sailing if the authorities discovered what happened. He paid Master Parris to take you and John Indian, who witnessed the killing, so the ship could depart the next morning."

The story made Tituba' head ache. "I cannot remember it."

"It is better not to remember."

Tituba and Skitôp found mutual comfort and then intimacy with each other while they adapted to the English plantation world of their masters. As love came for the African and the Pequot, they promised each other the English should never know their hearts.

While serving Master Thomas for the next twenty years, Tituba never dreamed of leaving the island. When he died, young Master Samuel rushed home from Harvard College to take over his father's affairs. Tituba expected him to manage the plantation like his father had, without disruption. At first, he did, until the worst pox epidemic in many years, followed by an enormous hurricane that caused the sugar cane market to crash.

For reasons unknown to Tituba, Master moved to the city of Boston. That he had brought Tituba and her family with him seemed to confirm she had been adept at serving both father and son, with her manner of appeasing. Otherwise, their new master would have sold her small family with the other seventy slaves he had inherited.

Alone again in the parsonage with her thoughts and memories, Tituba flushed as if she had been sitting too near a raging hearth fire, but there were only dim coals glowing across from her. She mopped her face with a cleaning rag and added firewood.

Akanni was still chopping and stacking outside.

Tituba drew a small cup of cider and sat near the hearth. The thought—shall I ever persuade Akanni to believe in my manner of appeasing—whispered to her.

She tried to squelch the voice whose tone implied: perhaps never. And failing that, it asked, what if those unreachable mystical powers were the only recourse to protect him?

Then, something else stirred inside her head, another distant memory of Mama's voice: "Show me how much you remember."

Tituba spoke aloud as if her mother were present. "I cannot do it, Mama."

Another trickle of memory came. "You must open your heart to be worthy of what is within you."

Tituba closed her eyes. Perhaps it was not too late. Yes, as soon as Master was satisfied that he has punished Akanni enough. And as soon after Akanni calmed down from his anger at the master… and her.

Chapter Ten

For almost a week Tituba traversed the stairs and ladder so often her legs felt like bags of dried corn. Betty had found no relief and therefore gave none to Tituba. Her cough had changed from dry to phlegmy, and no mixture Tituba made helped the child. This morning she had tried wine cooked with honey and parsley. Hot broths had no effect except to require Tituba to remove and empty the chamber pot more often.

It was no surprise to Tituba when Abigail caught all of what ailed Betty.

Then—not for her benefit, she was certain—Master said both girls should sleep near the main hearth for warmth. Tituba and Akanni dissembled a single rope bed from the loft and set it up in the corner where both girls lay toe to toe. But while Tituba kept the fire burning steadily, it brought them no comfort. All night the wracking coughs and fever persisted. Tituba accepted her duty to nurse them while pining for her son's wellbeing. With every opportunity she checked Akanni, watching his eyes and feeling his forehead. Near exhaustion herself, she concluded work and exposure had worn him out, rather than sickness.

But Akanni's hands were so raw from gripping the ax handles, he could barely feed himself. She tried to bind his wounds with grease ointment, but he pulled away.

Why, Tituba simmered, had Master not become angry at Goody Putnam? Now her son was angry with her. Even if Betty's playing at the beaver pond was her own fault, Goody Putnam was the one responsible for sending her home well before dark. Yet no blame had been attached to her.

Master seemed more concerned with dispensing forgiveness to his white sister than Tituba's son and her. And then another thought arose. Master must be afraid of antagonizing Goodman Putnam.

Akanni came in after the family finished their midday meal. He showed good color from the work outside. Tituba was so relieved she wanted to pull him close. But when he spoke to her, his tone was cold.

"I need to eat."

"Sit on that barrel. I have hot food saved for you."

She gave him a large bowl of hot cider. But after sipping it he snarled. "He is punishing me for something I didn't do. Mama, why have you not tried to stop this punishment?"

Tituba extended a trencher of food to him as she debated whether to answer him. He snatched it from her.

"Akanni…" He deserved an answer, but words eluded her, so used she was to avoiding confrontation. His insolence was as much her fault as his. She had failed to make him understand the danger of disobedience to authority.

Tituba's delay in answering Akanni must have been too much for him, and he whirled away from her with a disgusted grunt. She reached out to him but he already was slamming the door behind himself.

Tituba gave herself a moment to overcome an urge to cry before following Akanni outside. He sat on the wood pile, wolfing down his meal. "You are right. I have done little to protect you from Master's wrath. And this time he has abused you to get to me."

He kept his face down, eating.

"For me, I can bear unfairness. But for you, I need to speak up. I will change," she said.

Akanni finished his food and stared at the empty pine wood trencher.

"Do you believe me? I am sorry."

He handed her the trencher and nodded. "Yes, Mama."

She was unconvinced he believed her, but his terse reply would do for now. She could bear his anger for a while longer. He was justified, wasn't he?

Akanni returned to his task, and Tituba went inside to her work. The splitting and stacking sounded louder. She listened to the repetitive ax blows on wood and allowed herself a momentary wish for mystical powers to lift them all away from this place. She absentmindedly tended the hearth fire, while thinking of that day before Mama died, during the march to the coast and the English ships. The fire reminded her of the blaze Mama had conjured to help them run for freedom.

The two kidnappers were arguing, and the small man was saying, "We have no time for hunting."

"I must have fresh meat." In a moment he was gone.

Mama waited for hours as Tituba endured thirst and unending mosquito attacks. Then she tugged at her daughter. "Shh. Watch and be ready to run."

Mama found her feet, grimacing. And then, oh, she seemed so brave, she called to the remaining man at rest near the smoldering campfire. "You are a weakling!"

He stared at her through hooded lids.

"You must be very afraid of your big brother."

"I fear no one. And you least of all." He picked a branch of firewood and threw it carelessly at Mama.

She caught it in midair and flung it back so hard she made him duck out of the way. "You have the penis of a monkey." She spread her legs; arms akimbo.

A growing smile showed him rising to her taunt. "You should sit with your child and be quiet."

"You should worry about the flames behind you, monkey."

Flames flared, bursting up from the dirt of the forest floor. He whirled, caught up inside leaping flames, stamping at them.

Mama leaned on Tituba's shoulders as they scampered behind a thick tree trunk. The man was cursing at the circle of fire around him, preparing to leap through it. Tituba had trouble drawing breath into her small lungs.

That was the moment an enormous she-leopard dropped from above, landing mere feet away from the mother and child. Tituba clawed around Mama at the sight of the dripping fangs and golden eyes seemingly fixed on her.

The small man shouted, "Come back or—" He did not finish because Mama had flicked her head toward him and the leopard snarled like thunder and charged toward the man.

"Go!" Mama pushed her, hobbling behind, gripping Tituba's wrapper as they crashed into the bushes. The melee of the leopard's roaring and the man's screaming followed them as they ran.

Twenty yards further into the forest, Mama pulled her to a stop. She bent over, wheezing from either pain or lack of air. "Mama, the leopard obeyed you."

"There was no leopard."

Before Tituba could challenge her, Mama turned Tituba away from herself. "Run that way! Keep your back to the setting sun and I shall find you—"

"No!" Tituba shouted, and whirled to see Mama's slack face looking up and beyond her.

"You should have run, foolish girl." It was the leader man.

Tituba's heart kept thumping long after he drove them back to camp and tied them back to back. They had nearly escaped. Nearly. Mama had stood up to that other evil man like a warrior, throwing the branch at him with such force, starting the fire and sending the she-leopard to hold him at bay.

"Mama," she whispered. "That fire. And the leopard."

"They were images created from my thoughts."

"Why…?" Tituba lowered her voice. "Why did you not kill these men with your thoughts?"

"I cannot do what the ancient law forbids." Tituba felt Mama's body shaking as if from sobs. "Above all else, my daughter, we can never use our powers to hurt others, even evil men such as those. Remember this always; the penalty to ourselves — the loss of eternity in the plane of the stars."

Tituba had swelled at her mother's agonized tone and still shaking body. She would never forget Mama's bravery, or her refusal to hurt with her powers even at the price of losing a chance of freedom from captivity.

During the most horrid days and months and then years after Mama died Tituba looked to the stars above and called in vain for Mama to come back.

Tituba drew a cup of cider and sipped at it. With Mama's magic or without, there seemed no way to escape the Master's domination. He looked in on Tituba, and she froze, bracing herself, thinking he might be cross about the wood banging against the house. When he left without speaking, Tituba relaxed and dug in to her chores, choosing the monotony of making a fresh broom of wheat straw than confrontation with Parris. Near the end of her task, she could no longer avoid the demands of her promise to approach Master for Akanni's sake.

But first, Tituba stoked the kitchen fire and moved an armful of wood nearer the hearth for fuel to cook the next meal. The kitchen seemed too quiet. She cocked her head to listen. The racket from Akanni splitting and stacking wood had ceased.

But he must continue working or risk some new punishment! She ran out the rear door and searched the barnyard, but he was not there.

"Akanni!" Her call into the dark barn got no answer. Where was he? Scratching her head hard enough to draw blood, she trudged back indoors.

Half an hour later, the Master came into the kitchen from the main room, startling Tituba from her worry.

"If you are searching for your son, do not bother. I lent him to Deacon Ingersoll, who has foul work for him, and after, he will then go to any others requiring the same."

Tituba was heating water over the fire when Master came in, and as it simmered, she was ready to speak. It had to be now. A simple question. How much longer must this go on?

"Master—" her throat closed. He glared at her—no, it was more than a glare, his eyes were gleaming and Tituba took a step back from him, her mouth dry as ashes.

"Well?"

Tituba twisted her fingers. Her jaw was rigid.

Master seemed to sneer, inviting her to say something when he knew she had never done so before. His certainty showed on his face. And he was right.

He was mocking her.

At once the water pot suspended from the wood lug pole, bouncing up and down as its low boil climbed to a hard fast one, snapped the lug pole. The pot filled with scalding water ricocheted on the fire.

They both yelped, but before he hopped backward, boiling water arched to his legs and steaming water saturated his boots and pants. Tituba stifled an urge to offer help as he cried out. Perhaps his god sent a message. She did not believe it, but took a small pleasure as Master tiptoed away, holding his soaked serge pants away from his legs. Tituba cleaned the mess, disgusted with herself. She had not spoken up. Not a single word for her son.

Akanni, she thought, obey Ingersoll and the others and I will try again. I promise.

The next morning, when she awoke, it was raining. A dream was fresh on her mind. In it she had confronted the Master. She told him Akanni did not deserve his punishment, and Master had thanked her for speaking up.

She would do it, today.

But time got away from Tituba, and Master and Mistress left for the meetinghouse. Yes, Tituba repeated, she would speak up when they returned.

Later in the morning, she ran through the rain to the barn for fresh eggs, and inside, shook the water off her cloak. A shuffling noise drew her attention. Must be a small animal caught stealing eggs. She shouted, "Howa! Scat from here!"

The chickens flapped nervously at the shout, but settled and strutted about with no apparent concern. She crept closer to inspect for broken eggs, still on edge, when she heard an unmistakable ragged human breath.

A stifled sneeze eased one fear and raised another. She knew that sound. It was Akanni, and he was crouched in the farthest empty horse stall. Tituba's heart thudded at the sight of him.

"Why are you here?" She rushed to him and dropped to her knees, drying his face with her apron.

"Goodman Ingersoll lied to make me follow him. He said Father was injured. When I discovered his trick, he locked me in his cellar. This morning, he came to make me work, I struck him and he used a cane on me. I could not think, Mama. I fought harder, and after he fell away from me, I ran."

All youthful bravado had drained from his voice. She pulled him to her breast, not wanting to hear another word. Nothing good would come of this.

"What will Master do, Mama?"

How could she know? She thought of Akanni's smooth back, and the scars that might remain from a public lashing. The rain was driving harder now, water dripping through the fractured roof, running across the hard-packed barn floor. She caressed his face, her son, almost a man but still foolish.

"I hate *all* of them, Mama, like Father does."

Tituba ground her teeth. Mama's powers…, but there was no time for such yearning. She had to gather her wits.

Master arrived outside the barn. When he opened the door and led his horse inside, Tituba and Akanni froze in place. Master tied his horse without tending it and left for the house.

Tituba hugged Akanni and kissed him. "Wait here."

Inside, she found the Master in the main room. She waited for him to signal he knew about Akanni, but instead of speaking, he went up to his study. She followed him a minute later. He seemed already in prayer.

"Master, my son—"

"Do not bother me."

"He is in the barn… he struck Goodman Ingersoll. But he…."

Master turned to face her, and she saw darkness, the evil in him… and from somewhere inside her, faces from long ago arose. The kidnapper who killed her mother in Africa, the sailor Bill, his malevolence peering at her splayed beneath him. Master's face and their faces were all the same.

Tituba could not break away from the ugly look on Master's face. But she had to say something: give a good reason Akanni was back, explain why he had hit Ingersoll.

Lowering her head, Tituba screamed to herself; speak up. Akanni was facing more punishment, and perhaps he deserved some, but he also deserved to be defended.

Tituba felt herself waver before the task. No! She gripped her hands together No, begin, now!

"Master, please permit me to speak."

He thumbed his holy book closed. "There is nothing to talk about. I have decided Akanni will go first to Salem Town…"

Tituba tried to swallow. Salem Town?

"… before going to Boston, where I shall sell him to a new master."

He could have seized her throat and thrashed her around the room, and she would not have felt it.

"We shall have no more insolent looks at me, nor disobedience." He returned to his holy book. "Or, soft gazes between him and my niece. Now, leave me! And speak nothing more of this or it will be worse for him."

Tituba went down the stairs—she might have fallen for all she knew how she got to the kitchen. She found herself standing next to the cutting table, staring at the wood grain, picking at it with a kitchen knife. When Master's face appeared on the tabletop, she raised the blade as if to stab it. But even the symbolic act was beyond her. All the years of appeasing him and his father before him, not just for her, but to keep her family together. They fared better than all the plantation slaves he had sold, but this was what she got?

The mistress called Tituba for help with something and she hurried to her, thinking: Mistress will understand my agony. In their bedroom the mistress finished feeding her child and held her out to Tituba. "Change her soiled napkin."

Upon finishing, Tituba handed the bundle back, knowing the mistress heard every word of the master's decision.

"Mistress, I have… Is there no other way?" She dared place her hand on Mistress' arm, hoping to see a glimmer of compassion. She found none. Her eyes were those of her husband's.

Tituba begged. "Please, Mistress. I ask mother to mother!"

But she was wasting her breath.

Tituba rushed to the barn, scouring her mind for another way to keep Akanni with her. On seeing him, she almost tripped. He was waiting for her and seemed to know from her manner the master had made a fateful decision.

"He has sold you," she sobbed.

Akanni turned his head and spat into the dirt. His defiance terrorized her.

"Wait, son. We shall find another way. Your father…" But what would Skitôp be able to do? He was off working somewhere unknown to her.

Akanni stared at the barn floor, shaking his head.

Tituba needed him to say, yes, Mama, I know you will find a way. But his silence said he would not wait any longer for her.

Oh, Mama, Tituba prayed for her aid, knowing it was futile. Come tell me what to do.

Tituba stayed in the barn with her Akanni, touching his face, smelling his skin, as if by doing so she might keep him with her. She could not stop, knowing she was helpless to stop the fate racing toward her.

This would not be a final parting, she told herself. There had to be another way to keep him. In frustration she raged, unwilling to permit despair to take her. And through the rest of the night Tituba waited for Skitôp. He would help, wouldn't he? He must have known what happened at the tavern. But when the sun rose, she discovered not Skitôp but the factor riding up to the parsonage.

The sight of the stranger dressed in fine city clothes, tying his horse with its great pillion saddle to the post, made it clear beyond any other possibility that Akanni was leaving. Tituba rushed to gather a sack of food for him, but her hands shook so hard she could not manage it.

Tituba ran back to the barn to steal final moments with her son.

They had bound Akanni to prevent an escape, and she sat with him. "Obey your new master." She sobbed openly, no longer afraid of reproach. "Please obey…."

"I shall, Mama." He softened, and she saw he was trying to ease her suffering, thinking first of her rather than his own peril. "And I am sorry for the things I did to hurt you. Rest easier, Mama. I'll obey them as you wish."

The factor's voice came nearer. "No, Mr. Parris. I shall be fortunate to move him for more than a few pounds. It is winter and few buy unskilled slaves before planting season."

"Do what you must," Master said without entering the barn with him.

The factor led Akanni to his horse. But when Akanni could not mount the pillion saddle with bound wrists, Tituba rushed to help, her hands lingering on her son.

Tituba forced a smile, hoping to comfort him while her soul was melting from a sorrow far beyond any other she had experienced. And compounding her sorrow, she loathed herself for missing the chances to speak up to prevent this monstrous act from happening.

She tied and untied her cloak, then reached to touch Akanni where he sat in the saddle. "Remember!" she said, "Remember your promise."

He smiled at her, as the factor spurred his horse, and Tituba convinced herself he would do as she asked.

Tituba remained in place and covered her face with both hands. She whispered, "My son." Hers yet no longer hers.

The next morning, Skitôp drove a horse cart to the parsonage. When he entered, Tituba dropped her work and held her arms out to him. "Do you know?"

"I know everything." His eyes were wet and red, his lips curled under as if to stifle any emotion. "How was he when they came?"

"Your son behaved as you would have."

Skitôp glanced around, then whispered, "We cannot talk here."

He raised his voice, and she knew he wanted the mistress to hear. "We must leave for Goodman Porter's farm up Wenham way. He has hemp seed to boil in milk for the girls' coughing. Master made a trade with him. You are to bake bread and prepare a week of food for Goodman Porter until his wife becomes able. I shall work outside until you are ready."

Hours later, they rode away in silence until well out of hearing by anyone. "And now our son is gone." When he heaved a sigh, Tituba's heart pounded in her ears; she needed to know what he was holding inside, and to tap, if only for a while, his anger.

"Their holy book says, eye for an eye, tooth for a tooth," He kept his eyes on the reins. "It says wound for wound…" He glanced at the blue and yellow swelling on her cheek bone where the master had last struck her.… "bruise for bruise."

Tituba's chest tightened. Despite her stirring anger, Skitôp surely would not ask her to do as the English holy book commanded. Akanni had said he would obey them as he left, and that would give them time to find another way without violence.

A hard jolt from the wheels hitting a deep rut almost bounced her from the cart. If she refused him, would Skitôp leave her?

Tituba keeled forward off the bench seat, toward the horse's rump, powerless to control herself. As she slumped, Skitôp shouted and seized her with one hand, yanking her back on the wagon seat.

"It was my fault this happened, husband. I failed Akanni, and you, in more ways than I can say."

Skitôp pulled short the reins and wrapped his arms around her. When he said nothing, Tituba knew to her core he agreed with her..., even if he would never say so. And his confirmation of her failure tore her doubly, convincing her to dig into her soul with greater vigor, refusing to accept this wrenching calamity until she found some hidden power to overcome it.

Chapter Eleven

Both girls were feverish, exhausted by constant teeth-rattling chills. Betty had avoided looking Tituba in the eye since they took Akanni. Tituba wondered if remorse over his punishment after the beaver pond incident had affected her. She never mentioned the return of her lost mitten. Tituba thought less of the child, believing Betty's silence to be the sad hardening of the English sense of privilege.

But Abigail's illness had flared after they took Akanni away that morning. She was resting in the loft after what must have been a better night of sleep when Tituba brought breakfast up to the girls. Afterward, Abigail was weepy at the slightest provocation, asking several times when Akanni would come back home.

Tituba softened at the child's misery. Abigail was the only one in the Parris family who missed her son. She was sorry at having suspected her of impermissible behavior with Akanni, when all they had shared was the first flickers of young love.

The hemp seed elixir did nothing for their hacking coughs. And Master shifted the household routine again, ordering Tituba to sleep with the girls in the loft.

"Tend them until the fevers break."

Tituba stayed with the girls longer than necessary, not caring about unfinished or sloppily done chores. The recent disparagement from Master over the repetitive, tasteless meals meant nothing to her. If only she could see Akanni from a distance. More than once Tituba stopped amidst some toil, hoping blurry vision from tears, or a sudden darkening when the sun hid behind clouds, were preludes to locating him. She needed to know he was well until she got him back home.

Master announced his intention to escort the mistress to Goody Holton's farm with a basket of food, since she had given birth the day before. Left alone in the parsonage with the children, Tituba bustled about to complete the list of tasks they left for her.

She was tending the children in the loft, while thinking about Akanni, and she jumped in surprise when little Ann Putnam poked her head through the ladder opening in the floor.

"My father wishes to speak to you."

Tituba followed her to the main room. Thomas Putnam was warming himself at the hearth. "Your master and mistress are off somewhere, I see."

"Yes, Goodman." She lowered her gaze, smoothing her apron.

"Tell them I have brought my daughter here to help with chores and such until sickness leaves this house."

"Yes, Goodman."

"She may stay here during the week until Saturdays. Then send her home for a day of rest with her family."

After Putnam departed, Tituba noticed a fresh mark on Ann's face, and the child winced when she took her by the arm into the kitchen.

"Have you eaten?"

"I ate with my father at the tavern on the way here, but I am thirsty."

While Ann sat on a stool and sipped a cup of milk, Tituba tried to divine what was really going on. Kindness among the English neighbors was not unknown, but sending Ann? She knew enough of the child to suspect she had little interest in working. And the child showed it was true, slacking off on the first chore Tituba gave to her. Twice, Tituba had to search for her, and each time found Ann chatting with her friends in the loft. By afternoon, tired of the chase, she allowed Ann to remain with the Parris girls. Her task was to report any change in their condition.

Tituba was reaching for the bellows, to prime a waning fire, when a twisting sensation from her stomach forced her to grab the cutting table for support. The feeling was more than the festering ache of melancholia over missing her son; it was a hard grip. As she fought against it, the pain mushroomed, and she dropped the bellows. The kitchen floor seemed to liquefy, the walls turning dark and limitless, as if she were tumbling into a deep cave. Dizziness forced her onto a nearby stool.

The smallest spot of light, like a lantern a mile away, captured her attention. It enlarged as if approaching her. In the blossoming image she saw Akanni riding away on the factor's horse. But unlike that day, he turned and waved to her as if to say, I'll see you soon.

Tituba said his name as the image faded. To her surprise she felt euphoric, believing what happened just then to be an omen of something good.

From the loft, Betty called, "Tituba."

She gathered her skirts and ascended the stairs, feeling lighter, on the verge of smiling.

As she approached the girls, Tituba heard them talking. Ann was telling the other two how Elizabeth Hubbard knew a way to use white magic to find a husband. "I saw Elizabeth drop a raw egg into a cup of water. She can peer into its shape and tell who you will marry someday."

Tituba shook her head at their folly, but held her tongue while watching the other two giggle and whisper boys' names. Abigail said, "Bring Elizabeth to us, and Tituba can get us an egg and cup."

"I will do no such a thing!" she said. But the girls apparently did not hear her, for they did not bother to try cajoling her into their game, as they had so many times before.

Ann went to the loft opening, forcing Tituba to step aside for her. She shouted downstairs, "We need you to come, Tituba."

The shock of her invisibility lasted a blink before Tituba found herself back in the kitchen—on the stool she had never left. A fresh wooziness surged through her as she tried to stand. How could she have seen them as though she was with them?

"Tituba!"

Off balance, she tripped while trying to stand, but she recovered her balance and, gathering her skirts, once more managed the stairs and the ladder to the loft. With each step she repeated to herself, hide your feelings, hide them, hide them.

The girls saw her this time. Each of them smiled as if asking, "Yes?"

"It is time to nap. All of you." Tituba wiped at the sweat draping her forehead.

She could have none of their protests. They must be silent to let her think. "I shall stay until you all are snoring!"

After a while, she tested them, whispering, "Girls."

None stirred.

Beyond simple confusion, Tituba's mind raced. How? How had she seemed to be among them, but still be in the kitchen, two places at once? Was this how a mother lost her mind? How women shattered after losing one child after another to sickness or accident? She knew she was not mad.

If this were madness, she was determined to verify her sanity. In the silent loft, she counted and recounted her daily tasks to keep from screaming. A woman losing her mind could not function as she did each day, could she?

Loneliness, loss and fatigue were morphing at the edge of her growing panic, and she fought it, repeating the list of the tasks she had to do until the words became meaningless. She labored to keep her eyes open. It was not long before she succumbed to the comfort of sleep.

When the front door opened, Tituba popped awake. The shuffling of people entering.

"Yes, gather around and we shall pray."

Tituba swallowed, resetting herself. Mistress' voice. She cleared grogginess from her head and descended the loft ladder warily. On the second floor she met the mistress.

"Prepare the girls to come for prayers."

"Ann Putnam is up there with them," Tituba said.

"Oh? Well enough. She may join us." The mistress lowered her voice. "There are some brethren from the congregation here to pray for the girls. But a few, I know, want to gather information for village gossip. Make the girls put on clean clothes and fix their hair."

"Yes, Mistress."

"The master is with them, and after Psalms and reading from Scripture we shall need refreshments. I shall call for the children then."

Tituba did as she was instructed. After combing the girls' hair and adjusting their white linen caps, she told them to behave themselves in her absence.

When she came downstairs, the main room was sweltering. Someone had built up the fire and at least twenty-five bodies stood packed together. As Tituba went to the kitchen, she passed two women whispering. "Each day this sickness remains, I am fearful for their lives."

"I wonder, could there be more here at work than common illness?"

When the time arrived, Mistress brought Betty and Abigail down to sit on a bench beneath warm blankets—and the adults' scrutiny. Betty seemed groggy and Abigail listless. Ann Putnam stayed upstairs in the loft, likely to escape any order to help with the guests.

After an hour of singing Psalms, the heat in the room was stifling, and Betty swooned to the floor with a loud thump. She broke down crying, startled by her fall, but calmed under her mother's hand. Several parishioners thanked the Lord the fall did not hurt her further.

The last of the visitors was leaving just as Reverend Nicholas Noyes and Reverend John Hale of Beverly arrived. Master invited them to stay for dinner. After eating he kept the girls bundled on the bench as the ministers joined in new prayers. Tituba thought this was curious. They must believe their new offerings were more powerful than the prayers of the departed congregants.

As they stood around the table, a loud knock on the door interrupted the proceedings. Three elders, men from the congregation, had arrived, drawn by the visiting ministers. Mistress invited them in and summoned Tituba. "Take the children back to the loft and make them ready for bed. They have been observed enough for one day."

Tituba drew them together when Master pulled her sleeve and whispered, "Stay with them and give each a draught of wine to calm their coughing and help them sleep."

She filled a cloth sack with a small clay cup and a jug of wine with enough in it for her, too. Soon the prayers from the men downstairs drifted up through the floors.

An hour elapsed. When Betty began coughing raggedly, Tituba gave her a cup of wine, then poured more for Abigail and herself. On impulse Tituba poured a second cup for herself and allowed Ann a few gulps from it.

When the coughing subsided, Tituba smiled. She dozed at the monotonous voices imploring Jehovah to have mercy on the children until a thump yanked her awake. The girls were no longer in the loft. Her first thought was how much punishment she might receive. Another thump and another sounded as if they were leaping from the steps to the floor. The men's voices shifted to rough murmuring.

Tituba stumbled as she hastened to find and gather the children. At the bottom of the stairway she discovered the master pulling Betty from beneath the table and into his arms. She had vomited on herself and was squirming and coughing again. Tituba wondered if the girl would ever inhale again in peace.

Abigail was lying in an unnatural repose beneath a bench. She alternated between giggling and crying. Ann shouted at Abigail, laughing at her as if no one else was in the room, exhorting her to come out.

When Betty turned her head, Tituba could see her eyes were glassy. A long string of drool slid from her chin and she fell backward into a faint.

The mistress and two elders were backed against the wall, staring at the wild behavior in astonishment.

One elder exclaimed, "Dear God! Save these innocents!"

Tituba thought, what have I done? They had only a cup each! The room reeked of spilled wine.

Mistress found her composure first and showed the elders to the door, crisply thanking them for their prayers.

Betty languished in her father's lap like a newborn lamb. After a choking intake of breath, she asked in an exhausted, raspy voice, "Shall I die of this, Father?"

Abigail joined her in a higher pitch. "I shall die, too!"

Reverend Noyes said, "Bring her nearer, so I may question the child."

"Over what?" Master's comment shot out, unmistakably irritated.

"The cause of their behavior!"

The children had lapsed into exhausted states of semi-awareness, and Mistress interrupted. "Please." She looked at the three men for an objection as she led the girls to the stairway. She and Tituba took them back to bed.

After settling them, Tituba returned to the first floor to clean up. She listened as Reverend Noyes sat in the master's chair with a fresh cup of wine in his hand.

"We think…" Noyes looked to Reverend Hale, "it is time to call Dr. Griggs."

"Brothers," Master said, "they have been ill for some time, and this behavior was shocking, but I will admit I prescribed an ounce of wine to settle them, and the wine and the effects of a very trying day may have led to what we just saw."

John Hale spoke up. "I think an ounce or two of wine would not cause what we saw in a healthy child. We know your concern, brother, but tonight's behavior will be told and retold within the village and beyond by sunset tomorrow."

Master nodded his head, for everyone knew the power of gossip.

"And in truth, we already planned to strongly encourage you to enlist Dr. Griggs. Do we want our brethren to worry if something under the parson's roof has brought on some reproof from—"

"How dare anyone suspect me?" Master exploded, slapping the table board, making the cups jump. "I—I…"

Mr. Noyes held up his hand. "They can suspect what they will." He stepped nearer to Master. "You must do everything to help them recover and soon. Else, someone of your parish will be tempted to start a rumor to disrupt your ministry."

"But Griggs is barely more than a midwife, and perilously hard of hearing—"

"Disruption from gossip over the cause of illness in your family gives Satan pleasure, brother Parris. Move on this now."

After the ministers took their leave, the Parrises discussed the frank suggestion of Reverend Noyes, at first in excited utterances, mostly from Master, but gradually more calmly as Mistress soothed him.

"So, we have no choice but to bring in Griggs?" Master said.

"As they said, husband. There can be only gain to it, and I can hardly bear our girls' suffering."

Tituba backed out of sight as the master pulled his wife close, lowering his voice, though she could still hear him. "What have we done to deserve this trouble?"

Tituba cared little about their search for blame over it. As for the cure, she dearly wanted it for them, hoping the success of the village doctor might give Master cause to reconsider Akanni's banishment.

She ascended the stairs and the loft ladder, wishing she had the secret of healing. Tituba was paying little attention to the talk below until the master said to his wife, "You do not think Tituba has brought a curse from the black ones in Barbados, do you?"

Tituba reeled at the absurd thought. He does not know how powerless I am, nor that I would not waste my power on anything but to bring back my son. When she reached the top of the ladder, Abigail was lying on the rope bed, staring at her. And Tituba knew the girl had heard her uncle's question about her and Barbadian curses.

The next afternoon, Skitôp arrived at the parsonage unexpectedly. Tituba did not hear him and jumped when he touched her waist to turn her around.

"You should not be here," she said, looking into the main room as she pushed him out through the doorway and over to the side of the house.

"Our son," he whispered. "Two days ago, he escaped the factor. They cannot find him. He is free."

Free? How? She bit on her knuckle. Where? In her agitation she tore her skin and tasted blood. "But they will find him, won't they? Could we find him first?"

Skitôp was smiling, and she, unable to match his mood, answered her own question. There was no way to find Akanni before the English owners.

"What more do you know?" She labored to ignore the look in his dark eyes that said how much their son's rebellion pleased him. "How long can he stay free, husband? He knows nothing of survival."

The mistress called out before Skitôp could answer. "Tituba, fetch the children. Dr. Griggs is here to examine them."

Tituba held Skitôp's sleeve, grimacing. Always they needed something, always before her needs.

"Tituba!" Mistress raised her voice from inside the lean-to kitchen.

"Leave," Tituba said to Skitôp, "lest Master discovers you have left your work. Come back tonight. Bring me news!"

He hugged her and trotted away as if unworried anyone might spot him. He was not afraid for Akanni either, and she took no solace in his manner. Tituba hurried inside to Mistress.

Seventy-one-year-old Dr. Griggs completed his examination of the children as the mistress and Tituba watched. "Dose them with this potion, for the sleep will do them good. I can treat them, but it is God who heals."

Dr. Griggs thereafter sent his seventeen-year-old niece, Elizabeth Hubbard, with a fresh vial of medicine each day. She was a tall girl and more heavily freckled than the others, likely so from doing more outdoor work. The older girl stayed with the children long enough to give Tituba a few hours of respite and time to complete the most pressing chores.

After a week, Elizabeth brought a clear glass bottle of a dark liquid. "Uncle says they must take this purgative, and I am to stay the night to see the result."

She reported back to Dr. Griggs the next morning, and he arrived soon after, shaking his head. Tituba concluded the treatment was not going well.

"We shall continue the present treatment until there is a change in their condition. Any change is a sign we should move to the next treatment. And then I shall have to bleed them."

By the start of February, Elizabeth Hubbard was a frequent visitor. When Betty and Abigail writhed in convulsions, Elizabeth seemed fascinated rather than repulsed by them.

"I am grateful for your help," Mistress said to Elizabeth.

"Nothing at all, Goody. And truth to tell, tending your children is more to my liking than doing all manner of chores at my uncle's house."

With the added help, Tituba kept a nervous watch for any sign of Akanni, looking through the window openings, in the corners of the barn, even inside her thoughts for a far-off sense of him when she had an extra moment.

Why had Master not yet mentioned the escape? He must know, mustn't he?

Still there was no word. And Skitôp had not come back. Perhaps he had told her all he knew.

On Sunday morning, Master directed Tituba to bring the girls to the meetinghouse for the morning service. But instead of seating them with the other children in the gallery, he placed them in front of the women's section. A few women sniffed displeasure at losing the primacy of their regular spots, but they accepted the change. Ann Putnam soon joined her friends.

Two hours into the worship, the girls were fidgeting so much that they distracted a good number of the women sitting behind them. When Betty convulsed, Abigail succumbed seconds later, as though suffering the same attack. Ann fainted at the sight of her friends' torment. Tituba rushed from the gallery, watching her steps down the narrow stairs as one girl—who it was Tituba could not tell—shouted, "I feel a pinching pain!"

Tituba and a deacon carried the Parris girls all the way from the front to the rear of the meetinghouse, and out the doorway. In hoisting one child, she glanced at Elizabeth Hubbard still in the gallery, taking in the disruption with a look almost of envy.

The convulsions were the final straw to Dr. Griggs. He huffed his way to the parsonage, and when Master and Mistress arrived at the end of a truncated service, he was waiting for them.

His voice quavered as he spoke. "I have seen epilepsy before, but never more than one stricken simultaneously."

He closed his eyes as though searching for a word. "Reverend. Mrs. Parris. It is not from a cause in this world that their suffering comes. I fear it is by acts of witchcraft that your girls, and likely little Ann Putnam, are suffering.

"This is a gospel house!" Master shouted. "How can you presume knowledge of the Devil's work here or elsewhere?"

"I can draw no other medical conclusion." Griggs reached the front door. "Yes, diabolical means, I am certain of it."

Tituba and the girls heard every word through the floorboards.

Chapter Twelve

The next day, Ann Jr. arrived in the kitchen. She seemed unaffected after the onslaught in the church. Ann helped Tituba carry breakfast to Betty and Abigail without a complaint.

"Last night after Father brought me home," Ann said, "my mother complained that you are afflicted children. Mother said bad spirits from the Devil are waiting to hurt us. She has feared such things for a long time."

Ann glided her finger around inside a small pot of porridge like she was waiting for a reaction. Betty, under triple blankets, lifted her head off the mattress. "Why should we be afflicted? We are good girls."

Ann produced a horsehair poppet and twisted the stiff arms. "Mother says to look for a stranger, a short man in a black coat."

"A strange man has no business with us. We are good girls," Abigail affirmed.

Ann tittered, "Father says most everyone will go to Hell, even some saints among us." She dipped her fingers into the food and flicked a particle at Abigail.

"We shan't go to Hell, shan't we, Betty?" Abigail retorted.

Betty's chest whistled as she labored to breathe. A coughing spasm ended the discussion.

Hours after she cleaned up after breakfast, Tituba looked in on the children and lit a fresh candle. Except for Ann, the other two had eaten little.

"I have brought you fresh bread and butter with honey. You must eat to regain your strength."

Betty was still in bed, with her hands clasped above the covers. When Tituba looked more closely, she noticed the child was wringing her hands.

"What is it, Betty?"

"I had a dream. A great black man came to me and he said, if I abide by him, I should have whatsoever I desire, and go to a Golden City."

"Abide by him? Does that mean, let him take you away?"

She had no answer.

Ann fed bits of bread to Betty. "I saw that old beggar woman, Sarah Good, at our house this morning. She brought along her lousy daughter Dorothy to help her beg."

"Their clothes are full of holes," Abigail said.

Ann wiped Betty's mouth with the corner of her apron. "Some say she was once a witch and killed her first husband, and God made her base on account of her sin."

Tituba tut-tutted. "Why do you talk of Goody Good that way? To me, she is only a beggar."

"She looks like a witch."

Tituba played along for a moment. "If that is the only reason, there are others who look the same. Like Goody Osborne. My friend Candy says she summoned a wild dog, and it turned into a man dressed all in black." She smiled to invite them to giggle, but she felt a small pleasure at seeing them frightened by the fantastic story. "She bade it harm a woman she disliked, and he caused her to sicken and die."

They gaped at her, wide-eyed, as if thinking if Tituba said it, so it must be true.

Tituba did not disabuse them of the notion that someone in the village might be a witch. The girls remained silent until Tituba reached the main room, and she was glad to escape their chatter for a while, hearing only the walls creaking now and then from freshening gusts of wind.

Tituba returned with more doses of a concoction from Dr. Griggs that they already knew was ineffective. At least the girls thought it helped them, that was worth the bother, she thought. Elizabeth Hubbard had delivered it and she was right behind Tituba as they arrived in the loft.

"Betty," Abigail whispered. "Why do witches hurt people?"

Ann answered first, "They hurt people for the Devil since he cannot do it himself. He promises them anything they wish for becoming his familiars. Also, they make people sign the Devil's book in blood or they keep hurting them."

Tituba was tiring of their unending fears and ignored the comment as too foolish to acknowledge. Who would make children sign books in blood?

Abigail was whimpering, and she rocked from side to side on the bed. "I do not want a witch to hurt us."

Tituba once would have soothed the child, but not today. She had enough of the children's cares. To divert herself, she picked up a needle and thread to darn the heel of one of Betty's socks.

Betty wheezed. "If we suffer from Satan's familiars, my father will bring the whole meetinghouse to greater prayer and fasting. He will drive the Devil back to Hell."

Elizabeth knelt next to Abigail and brushed her hair. "Perhaps he will, or perhaps Satan will summon more of his kind and return for a great final battle."

Enormous tears flooded from Abigail's eyes, dripping off her chin and plopping on the floorboards. "Someone must find the witches. Else, we shall never be well ever again."

"We can find the Devil's familiars and stop them from hurting you," Elizabeth said. Her face became grave. "It would be good if someone catches them, but it is very dangerous to seek them out. Satan will bid new ones in their places to hurt more children, and even our parents."

Betty gasped and Elizabeth took her hand. "But I will help you if you wish."

Betty struggled to clear her raw throat. "Father knows Reverend Mather. He fought a witch of Satan's in Boston. And he wrote a book about dogs and cats and how the Devil makes them talk. Plus, yellow birds that suckle sustenance from those doing the devil's work."

Elizabeth chimed in, "And they drink blood and eat red bread for communion." She reached to smooth Betty's sleeping shift. "They say the afflicted children in Boston ran through the house screaming and flapping their arms like geese trying to fly."

Ann raised her arms like wings and said, "Like this?"

Abigail cringed and Betty said, "Yes, but Mr. Mather saved them."

Elizabeth straightened her apron. "I know something more." She waited until every eye was on her and then scratched her nose. "Goody Sibley can make a cake to find a witch who hurts you. If you send Tituba to the Sibley farm, she will tell her how to do white magic."

Tituba shook her head. "I do no magic."

"If you help us, I will tell you where to find Akanni," Ann blurted out.

"What do you know!" The words came out stronger than she intended. How could Ann know his whereabouts?

"Father knows where he was the day he ran away. He says they know where to find him."

"Tell me now!" Her hands trembled, and she put down her needle. If there was the smallest chance, she had to discover where he was.

"When you come back from Goody Sibley."

A surprising urge to slap Ann across the face arose, but of course that was out of the question, and after a long stare Tituba agreed to their summons and left for Sibley's farm at the base of Thorndike Hill.

When she returned from the errand, she demanded, "Now, tell me, now."

"No. She will tell after we make the cake," Elizabeth Hubbard said, joining with Ann.

Tituba held back the impulse to shout at them, even though she had never been so close to screaming at anyone. She must play along if she wanted to learn what they knew about Akanni.

She began, reciting Goody Sibley's instructions. "First, Betty and Abigail must piss in a cup. Then mix in rye flour to make dough and bake it as hard as a field stone."

To fulfill another task, Tituba sent Elizabeth Hubbard out to catch one of the wandering dogs that frequented the farms searching for scraps. "We must give the cur this cake, and if he eats—"

Elizabeth cut her off, "If he eats it, any witch hurting you will be forced to come out in front of us."

Goody Sibley had said the same thing, and Tituba wondered that even children like Elizabeth knew how to find these imaginary witches. Still, she played along in order to finish this game and learn of her Akanni.

The result wasn't promising. The dog, though its ribs showed, wanted nothing to do with a cake made with the urine of sick children. Their attempt to unmask a spiritual follower of their devil had failed.

That did not relieve them of their promise to tell Tituba what she wanted to know. She knelt in front of little Ann, waiting for her answer. The child would not look at her until Tituba begged, "Where was Akanni seen?"

"South of Salem Town. That is all I heard."

Tituba nearly doubled over, wincing to hold back tears at the vagueness if not the bald-faced lie of the child. How could she have not expected it? But if the report was somehow true, anyone else hunting for Akanni would have no better idea where he was than she did. She repeated to herself; if no one knew his whereabouts either, perhaps he was safe.

That night and for several more days Elizabeth Hubbard slept at the parsonage. With the extra help,

Tituba sloughed off on her nursing duties, resentful that she let a child dupe her.

At last, one night Skitôp arrived after stealing away for a visit. His touch almost stopped her heart when he crawled beneath the blanket with her. After they made love to each other, she asked if he had any news.

There had been nothing new since he first learned of Akanni's escape.

"Master has said nothing of Akanni here," she said.

"He knows. He stops at the tavern every day for a fresh word of the search, making smoke and fire at his loss. No slave means no money."

It seemed as great a fear for the master as going to his hell.

Skitôp touched her cheek. "We must hope for the best, until we learn elsewise."

When Skitôp laid on wood for the fire, and pulled the blankets over them, Tituba consoled herself. He was likely right. She would know in her heart if Akanni became ill or injured. A mother feels those things in moments of danger. But she denied the notion almost as quickly; after living in dread for days on end, how would she sense anything through her constant yearning?

"How many times I could have cut the master's throat," Skitôp mused.

"By now I have begun to doubt the wisdom of forbidding you to do so." Saying that, what she never allowed herself to even think, made her feel righteous. Her worry for her son had peeled away the outer skin of caution.

In the warmth of the kitchen, with Skitôp sleeping next to her, Tituba drifted into a restless slumber. She awoke hours later to Skitôp snoring. She poked him to roll over and relaxed on her back, eyes closed, listening to the embers crack in the hearth.

Like a breath of air, a word flew past her. *Tituba.*

Tituba could not comprehend the strange sound, and she dismissed it as a product of her imagination.

Again, it came. *Tituba.*

Yes, it was her name, and she opened her eyes widely. Mama?

This was no dream. Here she was!

Looking the same as she had when Tituba was a child, Mama said, *My little Tituba. We may speak as we did before, for no one can hear our thoughts.*

Tituba felt both an urge to cry and a desire to burst with joy. *Mama? Will you stay with me?* She peeked at Skitôp to verify he was still asleep. *I am so weary from this crushing sorrow. Why have you come so late? Akanni, your grandson, is suffering on my account. I must find him.*

I am not come to you for your present need.

Mama, I must find Akanni.

He is meeting his destiny as we speak. There is no need for you to help him now.

Give me the powers, Mama, or I shall search for him without them.

I cannot give what you already possess.

Tituba sat up on her mat, ready to shout at her mama with words no one else could hear.

Yet her mother gave Tituba no time to speak.

You have already begun to find the secret powers.

Tituba was ready to discharge her fury like a gun when her mama's declaration struck her. She had found noth…. She remembered the day in the loft. The day she seemed to be with the girls, but they did not see her. Had she made it happen?

Mama nodded. *Yes, and more before that day.*

But I have tried to imagine Akanni, Mama. And still I cannot make it happen.

He is safe. That is enough for you now. Mama's image flickered. *You need to give yourself permission to summon your powers… our powers. Accept this truth from me, and you will discover more in time.*

Tituba tried to grasp her mama's hand, but her fingers passed through her mother's as if they were smoke.

Keep yourself ready.

An ember in the fire popped, drawing Tituba's attention. The ember died out just as she spied it. And quickly as that, Mama disappeared.

Tituba drew a deep breath. If she could do as Mama wanted, become strong enough, she might shape her future, find Akanni, take Skitôp to him. And as one family, they could disappear from the English colony—without a trace.

When the daylight arrived, Tituba believed, as certain as the pouring rain outside, her mother had come to her in the night. Mama was neither a dream nor a hallucination. Mindful of her mother's words, Tituba relaxed. She had no choice except to wait with an open mind, ready for whatever was to come.

But she did not expect events to erupt so rapidly.

Tituba was in the lean-to, dressing a fresh fat turkey for the spit, when Master burst in upon her.

"You will ruin me!" His dripping wet black broad-brimmed hat flew across the room before hitting the inside of the hearth, where it fell to the edge of the fire. He seemed not to care if it burned, nor did she dare fetch it.

"God's flesh, you are worse than a cunning woman." He slapped his hands on the cutting table and leaned forward, shouting into her face. "The witch cake! I know about the witch cake."

The nearest object to him was a wooden trencher, and he struck her with it full in the face. Tituba did not feel herself fall to the floor. But she found herself lying on her side. Master stood over her, rain, sweat, or both dripping from his face.

A distant roll of thunder and a renewed wave of hard rain hitting the roof preceded his words. "They will ask why the pastor permits magic under his roof! And they will condemn me for it. They will wonder if he seeks to hide the afflictions of the girls. They will answer by saying I brought on God's displeasure for allowing an abomination under my roof."

Tituba scrabbled out of his reach, fearing he might strike her again.

"You have brought the Devil's work here, and you shall suffer for it."

He undid his leather belt and cracked it across her back and shoulders. Tituba submitted, bent forward, and covering her face. The master's thrashing paused; the mistress appeared in the doorway. He turned to her, gasping from the exertion. "The people will believe divine disfavor has fallen upon this house, and they will lose their faith in me!"

Master raised the belt, and Tituba held her breath to take the blow, but he held back. "This scandal will finish me here." He turned from the women, hiding his face, but it was clear he was wiping tears and trying to stifle them. He whirled toward Tituba again and reared back with the belt, but once more he paused as if he realized whipping her further would not ease his own pain. Dropping the belt, he fell to his knees, and called toward the ceiling. "That conjuring witch cake is the means the papists use for their perverted exorcisms. O, Lord, what a mockery of me who preaches prayer and fasting to save our dearest children."

Then he stood, and grabbing Tituba by her linen collar, dragged her from the kitchen into the main room, heedless of her choking. "How long have you been a witch?"

His face was purple as he hovered over her. "I am no witch, Master," she gasped.

She dared not resist as he pulled Tituba to her feet and drove her up the stairs under a volley of slaps and pushes. Then, like a man himself possessed, he ransacked the small storeroom closet on the second-floor landing, throwing bags of dry goods and such into the hall, clearing enough room to force Tituba inside.

Tituba remained mute throughout, stifling her urge to cry for mercy, afraid to bring on more of the same. After he slammed the door shut, she struggled to draw a deep breath, paralyzed, fearing the next unknown.

Tituba was trapped inside the storage closet for two days without food or water. And during those long hours, enduring cramped arms and legs that would not allow sleep, with her head on the floor and her mouth open to the space beneath the door, sucking for fresh air, Tituba waited.

In isolation Tituba heard the rain beating on the walls and roof of the parsonage. She imagined her first act outside the closet, standing and stretching while taking the deepest breath to fill her lungs.

After an interminable time, Tituba recognized Goodman Putnam's voice downstairs in the main room. She could not hear at first, but his voice got louder as he continued talking. His wife, Ann, would not stop crying out that she sensed evil spiritual forces mounting an invasion. And she said it as plain as possible. "The pastor was a target of them."

From the quietness, it seemed like the master was searching for the right words. Then he said, "Brother Thomas, rest easy. I understand her fear. Our faith will bolster us against Satan. And if you are referring to my, eh, problems, worry not. They will succumb to more prayer. We fight with prayer and soon our entire congregation will hear the Lord speak through me. And we will drive any possible demonic uprising back to Hell."

"My daughter said there was talk about Sarah Osborne here in the village. She has been troublesome for twenty years hereabouts. She birthed a bastard child and dared any to call out her sin. Her bad example follows her, even at meetings. They say she once conjured for sick-headed people."

"Our Father will protect us if we have faith. Worry not, brother." He offered Putnam a cup of beer. As the men drank together. Goodman Putnam must have calmed down because Tituba could not hear their conversation.

After Putnam departed, Master climbed the stairs. Tituba tried to make herself smaller inside the closet. But when he opened the closet door, the look on his face told her that some of his fury had dissipated.

"You will cook and clean, but I forbid you to speak to the girls." He descended two steps before he stopped and shouted up at her, "I shall decide on a fit punishment for your sinfulness."

Tituba dared not move until he went all the way down and out of sight. What more could he do to her? He had sold her only son to a distant life of servitude. No further punishment could be worse.

She had been inside the closet for so long, Tituba's legs were numb and useless. She crawled through the small doorway, extending her legs inches at a time. She paused to catch her breath and hearing a single horse arrive outside the parsonage, she rested.

It was Deacon Ingersoll, and he shouted, "Mr. Parris," before dismounting and pounding the front door. Tituba scarcely cared why he had arrived with such urgency, but she waited to hear.

Master opened the door to him and Ingersoll stepped inside from the rain. After some muffled exchange, Goodman Ingersoll said. "Shall I help you bring her down?"

"No, leave her up there."

She peered over the top step to pick up what news Ingersoll brought.

"I am told, there was no way to stop him."

Stop him? Stop… who? She lifted her head.

"He refused to obey after they caught up with him."

A fresh clap of lightning and thunder were no match for Tituba's deafening heartbeat. She knew. She knew her son was…

"Your Akanni's dead, Mr. Parris."

Dead.

The awful word, like an anvil dropped from a height, crushed Tituba. After frozen seconds, she screamed denials, heedless of the master's response, sucking frozen air, burning her lungs as she fed her howling. Tituba began slapping herself, punching and scratching to come awake from this lie. After exhaustion stilled her, Tituba accepted the truth. My baby is dead.

A gauzy sense, her instinct to blame herself, picked at her, but she rejected it. And with the rejection of her habitual nature, a cold clarity came. She had done nothing to cause this.

When grief washed over her again, Tituba bit the hem of her dress to stifle her urge to scream anew. But the grief, like a wave receding lessened, and was itself overcome by a new wave. He killed my baby! He branded a scar on her heart and seared a vow by Tituba to never forget *he* caused her suffering. Nor would she allow that suffering to be quenched. For Akanni's sake she would strike back. Justice must be meted out to her English master and all the people like him—they were all vile. She did not know how to make it happen, but she would not rest until she dispensed it.

Tituba rocked side to side, giving in again to grief. Sometime later, Skitôp arrived to care for her. She found herself in the barn with him. They lay upon a thick mound of hay, under blankets piled high, which did little to muffle their mourning

Chapter Thirteen

Tituba awoke at first light inside the barn, with a clenched fist in her mouth.

Skitôp was smoothing her blanket. "We must wait for Akanni to come."

"What?"

Her first thought—how has my child come back? — was shattered as he said, "For them to bring his body back. I heard the master tell them to go fetch… him."

She wondered at her calmness but she could see that there was no way to change what happened. Yes, she told herself. We must wait. For a last goodbye.

"Master wants me to go back at the tavern to work, but I shall refuse."

They were worth only the money they made. Why should Parris care if she had to face this agony alone? "No, husband, obey him." And she told herself—for a while longer.

The days of heavy rains had ended, replaced by unremitting days and nights of bone-rattling cold. Inside the parsonage, Tituba fought whipsawing emotions, trying to keep her thoughts from plunging into deepest despair. Just concentrate on what is right in front of you. When an avalanche of dark emotions loomed, rather than allowing them to frighten her, Tituba let them come, and shortly they melted away.

In their place came a starkly clear awareness. All the terrors she had spent a lifetime suppressing were not caused by her. Not one of them. She was *innocent* of her mother's murder in Africa and the horror she had endured during the voyage to Barbados; the captivity of callous insensitive masters, the whippings, the perpetual servitude, and the long estrangement from Mama.

The true cause was the unrelenting need of the English to control others.

She would no longer appease men such as Parris, men who prized hard-heartedness to carve out their paradise, willing to sacrifice kindness in service of their pitiless god. They understood unrelenting cruelty, and she would give it to them.

As she awaited her son's body for burial, no one bothered her when she slacked off to indulge in sorrowful musings. She heard the family depart for Lecture night services. And they did not disturb her when they returned and went to their beds.

After the house fell silent, Tituba set the fires in the main room hearth and the lean-to. The crackling from the burning logs relaxed her. She would find the power to complete her mission from among the secrets Mama said were embedded inside. Serenity enveloped her, and she lapsed into a dream state. The first vision to appear was Akanni. She recoiled as she saw his wrists were bound behind him as he rode in back of the factor on the pillion saddle. Akanni's face was bruised and swollen. This was not what she wanted to see.

Tituba roused herself. She opened her eyes to keep her thoughts from dwelling on Akanni's suffering, but he remained in front of her no matter where she turned.

He and the factor rode in open country. Tituba saw Akanni stand on the saddle somehow, and although what she saw had already happened, her stomach lurched as he tried to leap away.

Sensing the escape, the factor swung around and grabbed for him but too late, knocking Akanni off balance as he launched himself into the air.

He hit the ground head first… his neck snapped with a sound like a brittle stick.

Tituba remained fixated, staring at Akanni motionless and crumpled on the ground. Her old instinct was to blame herself, if only she had better taught him how to cope, to say "yes" and "sir" with a smile. She caught herself, raging at the baselessness of her guilt. No more.

The English were guilty for what happened. She would make the guilty pay.

Did she wait another day, or a week, or a month, for the body to come home? Time had become meaningless. An hour was a minute, a minute… a day. She bided her time, feeding her waxing and waning fury.

The mistress looked into the kitchen to inform her of Skitôp's whereabouts. "Deacon Ingersoll sent word; John Indian is coming by cart with…."

She felt no gratitude for the news, as she once would have. Tituba shuddered to think what Skitôp might do upon returning. Losing him on top of …. No, she could not permit that. Worry for him distracted her for a while.

She was picking firewood from the stack outside the parsonage when she spotted Skitôp approaching in a two-wheeled cart. Tituba knew his cargo immediately, and she waited, not wanting confirmation of what she already knew. When he pulled up ten yards from the parsonage, she rushed to him.

At the rear of the cart, he took her arm so gently she worried at his tranquil manner. "Is there something else, husband?"

"The master tried to make me believe it was an accident. When I denied it could be so, he grew angry. 'No one was responsible but your son,' he said."

Skitôp was shaking his head, looking at the wrapped cargo in the cart bed. "He went on, 'Mind me, John Indian! If you make trouble, I shall ship you to Barbados and the cane fields, where you will die. Tituba will have no one.'"

Skitôp pursed his lips so hard, they looked like pine knots as he denied himself tears. She drew him into her arms and waited for him to release a breath.

"I would have killed him right then, but I had no weapon."

Again, he stopped himself, frozen like his emotions.

"Am I less of a man for agreeing as he demanded?"

Skitôp's chin fell, his eyes seeming to bore a hole through his chest. And Tituba hoped her silence told him he did the right thing.

He soon recovered and carried Akanni's body into the barn. As Tituba followed, she could not help a glance at the horse stall and remember she had found Akanni hiding that day. A dirty canvas shrouded the corpse, the cover stiff from the cold, and she felt a knife at the thought of him beneath it like a butchered side of beef, frozen hard. Skitôp tried to hold Tituba upright, but she wrenched away from him and fell to her knees next to Akanni.

They buried Akanni on the back acreage of the parsonage. Skitôp spent an entire day chipping rocky ground for the grave. It was after dark when the master appeared with a torch and his Bible.

Tituba kept watch on her son's father gripping the handle of his shovel, twisting it hard enough to shred the wood. His black eyes glittered in the torchlight, and Tituba worried he might strike Parris. She feigned collapsing so Skitôp had to drop the shovel to hold her, and the dangerous moment passed.

After Parris read his bible god's words, he left them without a kind word of his own. Why kindness from the monster who killed their son?

It was time to part with Akanni, and Tituba would not allow Skitôp to lower him into the frozen earth by himself. Once they lowered their son tenderly into the hole, she could not release her grip on the canvas shroud. Lying on the ground, her arm extended, Tituba held tight, ignoring Skitôp's soft cajoling. When she was ready, Tituba arose, not bothering to brush the dirt off her clothing.

While Skitôp scooped from the pile of earth to refill the grave, she stayed by him, scooping dirt by hand until the aching cold climbed to her shoulders.

Finally, all emotions drained, she watched Skitôp finish. Her child would soon be forgotten by the village's godly people, but never by his mother and father.

Skitôp pulled the cart horse by its lead as they walked back to the parsonage. Each stumble on the unplowed field jolted Tituba, reminding her that the grieving must end. She had new work to begin. She gripped Skitôp's arm as they left their son behind.

Approaching the parsonage, she turned back toward the grave site, trying to make it out in the darkness. She battled a surge of self-pity. For now, she would let him rest. Tomorrow she would set about taking revenge.

Deep into the night, Tituba wrapped her arms and legs around Skitôp, her mouth pressed against his shoulder. The feel of him strengthened her against the doubts she could succeed in her resolve. Eventually, loosening her grip, she slept. She woke when he worked free of her, and pretended to sleep as Skitôp fetched his skinning knife. In the light of the diminishing hearth fire she watched him. The blade was pitted and notched after he used it to chip out the grave, and he honed it, the sound joining with the fire sounds. Grrish, pop, pop—grrish. He sharpened slowly until he had a smooth edge.

Upon sheathing the knife, he came back to her and spoke into Tituba's ear. "We must run from them, but not before I put this blade to *master* Parris' throat."

Tituba kept her eyes closed, afraid she might blurt out her plan to exact revenge.

When Skitôp lay down, she listened for his breathing to even out, the sound punctuated by the crackling fire.

Tituba briefly thought of calling for her mother's counsel. Instead, she set her jaw and resolved never to call for Mama again.

She was ready to find her occult powers by herself. And use them.

In the dim firelight, as Skitôp slept, another surge built within and she welcomed it by opening her mind. She listened to the sound of her breathing, in and out, in and out, until a visual aura traced red and purple zigzags and straight lines before her, coalescing into darker, almost black circles as an image of the Parris children, with Ann Putnam and Elizabeth Hubbard, emerged. They seemed to be soundly asleep.

Tituba inhaled more deeply. The air was thick as if filled with smoke, but it caused her no pain. Sinews and bones and muscles relaxed as she arose from her body like a leaf in a soft puff of air, willing the current by her thoughts, to carry her to the girls.

The sensation did not surprise her as she arrived above the children. And as she watched them, she turned inward. Her mind, like it was a key, unlocked a door inside her head, opening it for her to follow a pathway to a second door, behind which she found what the ancients had taught.

She discovered a new soul sense beyond the ordinary ones of touch, taste, smell, sight and hearing. The first of the new senses was the power to absorb and enjoy the essences of life waves of every thing or being. She swelled at the pleasure it gave her. Tituba moved on to another door, behind which was the power of reaching a lucid state at will, to see and hear from great distances, as well as the secret of ethereal manipulation. She did not understand these senses with words, but she understood their power.

There were more doors, and likely many other powers beyond them, but Tituba felt no need to search further. She had enough to begin her mission.

She turned to the girls, slowing her breathing, then her pulse, meandering into their heads, circling their dreams: angels and God's grace, paradise forever among protective parents and family. Friendships and favored newborn lambs and stolen moments of puppy love. These predominated, but also deep-fingered fears of devils and witches, bringing depraved temptations into unknowable sins great and small.

They would be her first tools for vengeance. She exhaled slowly, forestalling anger, reveling in a new confidence. They would have no more pleasant dreams if Akanni had none. Nor would the rest of the English have them.

With merely a thought she dipped into the girls' realms again. Betty's fear of damnation for one so tender. Abigail's heart was laid bare and Tituba saw her pure sense of loss over Akanni. It weakened her, but she steeled herself. No exceptions.

Ann Putnam's thoughts centered on pleasing her parents and avoiding punishment for her impulsiveness. And Elizabeth Hubbard, the oldest of them, yearned for a man who loved and respected her.

One after the other, Tituba fed the insecurities that dwelt within their dreams, reminding them of how feeble their lives were, the way the adults constantly preached. Someone was waiting for them, someone they knew already, to force them if need be to renounce God and join the Devil.

Tituba felt coolly indifferent, hardened by Akanni's death, as she infiltrated their souls, until she left the girls moaning in their sleep.

In the morning, Tituba awoke refreshed, and content in a way she had never felt among the English. After building the fires to warm the rooms, and then her usual first duties, Tituba gave Elizabeth Hubbard a small pot of pompion stew to carry for the girls' breakfast. No more of their favorite foods would be coming from her.

She heard them chat, half-whispering to each other, while she rested in the kitchen. Her activity during the night left her physically sluggish, and she strained to eavesdrop on their talking.

"We must find the witches," Ann said. "No one else has helped us."

"If Tituba is a witch like Uncle Samuel said, she must have helpers," Abigail said.

Tituba started at the mention of Parris' accusation. Then she calmed. And if they charged her? So what? It mattered little, now.

"My father says they come together for hellish worship."

"How do you know?"

There was no answer to that question, and Tituba smiled. They soon enough would know many things that made the skin crawl.

Betty spoke to Elizabeth. "Can you think of one who might be a witch?"

"One day Goody Good came begging to my uncle Griggs, like she does to everyone. She snarled at him when he said we had short rations during the winter and tried to shut the door on her. She said, 'A man of God ought to remember his charity.'"

"Did she curse him?"

"I think she might have. I heard her say, 'You will get your just deserts someday.'"

"What of Goody Osborne?" Ann asked Elizabeth. "My uncle Edward says witches beget witches. He said she kept her first husband's inheritance from his children, and then she married her indentured Irishman."

Yes, Tituba nodded. They were giving her fresh seeds to plant.

"My uncle says the yeomen at the tavern say we have strange black dogs roaming and talking pigs. One of them said Sarah Osborne's dead mother was a witch many years ago."

That night Tituba returned to the girls for the next assault. She entered their dreams and stirred their memories with the gossip of Goody Osborne and Sarah Good, painting them in colors of red and black. As they thrashed, Tituba roused them awake in the dark loft and presented herself as a gossamer image of Sarah Good sporting a ghastly distorted face, cooing for them to come with her.

As the girls shrieked, Tituba became a glowing image of Goody Osborne, and she swooped toward them, pinching them and pricking with a glistening straight pin.

Betty yelped as though a wild animal had gotten to her until at last her father clambered up the ladder to them. They babbled about Sarah Osborne and Goody Good and pointed into the corners of the loft where he could only see darkness. "Their bodies were shimmering and gauzy. They laughed as they pricked us with sharp pins."

They would not subside until he promised to sleep among them. "No, I shall not leave you. Let us say another prayer, together."

After first light, Elizabeth Hubbard begged to return home. She had to help her uncle Griggs, she said. "I shall return to help the children, but I must see if he is well." Tituba knew she was going to spread the story to anyone she met. Yes, child.

After his breakfast, Parris left for some duties but he returned, slamming the door as he entered. The parsonage shook and the baby awoke bawling.

Tituba knew his walk when he felt burdened. Samuel Parris soon would have more of a weight than he ever expected.

Parris thumped up the stairs and plopped on the bed next to his wife and baby. "I know not what to say, it seems impossible. But at Ingersoll's some men are talking of witches seen here at the parsonage!"

Uncontained, his voice carried to every room of the house.

Tituba nodded in satisfaction. Those gullible fools will help with their own undoing.

She went back to the girls to do more grim work that night. There was no need to enter their heads as she morphed her thoughts into the visible specters of Good and Osborne.

It took little effort to set Betty to screeching, and this time she tumbled down the ladder as she fled the specters, coughing the entire way, her nose streaming snot. One apparition had spoken to her, she cried. "It said, you will join me, and you will give me your blood."

The other girls kept up a din as well. "There she is! Hide! No, get away. Someone save us!"

Parris bolted back up the ladder with a stick in one hand and Betty in the other. He almost dropped them both upon seeing Abigail and Ann cowering behind the wooden rope bed flipped on its side. Tituba's specters had backed Elizabeth Hubbard in a corner of the gable roof, and she was gaping at the rafters of the loft, swinging her arms at something Parris could not see.

He tried to assure the girls there was nothing to fear. "Say your prayers."

But they continued to wail until his voice hardened. "Tituba!"

She called back, "Yes, master."

"Come up and attend these girls."

"Yes, master."

The fruits of her work exhilarated Tituba, but the mental labor exhausted her. She hid both feelings and made her way to the loft with a pitcher of weak beer and a sack containing cups and a loaf of bread. "There, children. Drink and eat a bite for me."

The girls slurped from the cups.

"Tell Tituba what happened."

The girls babbled, talking one over the other, describing the demonic faces and vicious attacks by the two ghostly women. Tituba dabbed their tears and nodded until they finished.

"I believe you, children."

Chapter Fourteen

The shocking story of the ghostly attack spread, and Thomas Putnam sprang into action.

"Griggs was right," he shouted to Parris. "We must do something more while you continue calling on the Lord."

Putnam, with his brother Edward, Joseph Hutchinson, and Thomas Preston put together formal legal Complaints and filed them with the Salem Town magistrates. The men accused Tituba, Sarah Good, and Sarah Osborne of hurting Betty, Abigail, Ann and Elizabeth Hubbard by witchcraft.

Parris returned to the parsonage with the news. "Have you heard of the Complaints?"

Elizabeth put down her sewing. "I have, husband."

"How…?" He was pacing. "Witches! We all know they await Satan's call; I have admonished our people of it. But our Betty and Abigail bewitched by those three women? I've confessed to you my concern it could be more than a lingering sickness, but I am yet to be convinced anyone might be using demonic powers. And our Tituba. That mouse accused of hurting them?"

He slapped his leg. "What are the Putnams doing? Their impulsive actions get the horse before the cart." Tapping his chest, he said, "And for us, he presumes to act on our behalf! He has no right." He paced. "No longer will

I see a few wary looks from the pulpit as I teach. No, soon they will openly pass rumors of whatever they hear. And, and, the stories will grow with each exaggerated telling."

"What shall we do?" Elizabeth asked.

He shook his head. "I cannot… I can't think. One thing demands attention, then another and another."

Parris bit on a fingernail. "Noyes and Hale are eager for this reckoning, I know it. But…." The thought flew from him as he crossed and recrossed the room without speaking.

Elizabeth exclaimed, "Please sit, husband."

The rope bed creaked as he sat next to her.

Biting once more on his fingernail, he said, "We might profit by sending our girls away until this visitation passes us. I know Stephen Sewall will take them in as his own."

She stared at him open-mouthed.

"You must listen. Do you understand the burden of caring for our sick children without Tituba's help if they arrest her?"

"Husband, do not talk of that. They are too young. And I cannot live separated from Betty. No, not either of them."

She was holding her breath, as if expecting his demand for obedience. At the sight of her ashen face and searching eyes, he abandoned the idea as quickly as he'd first thought it. He took her hand, needing to steady himself as much as reassure her that perhaps this was premature. "Very well. I shall wait awhile on this."

Elizabeth withdrew her hand and busied herself on a torn pair of breeches. He couldn't endure lingering despondency in her over losing Betty and Abigail, but he had these other problems to address, too.

"Perhaps I shall consult Cotton Mather."

Parris composed an urgent message and dispatched it. But he couldn't overcome a nagging worry. Mather might not answer soon enough. Already, a fresher uncertainty begged for answers he did not have. The charge of witchcraft was a civil *and* an ecclesiastical matter. What if the magistrates hearing the Complaints call on him to preside over some portion of the proceedings, or at least give theological advice? The idea raised a cold sweat and Parris crossed his arms to warm himself.

Finally, he succumbed to nervous energy, unable to wait for his dispatch messenger to make a trip and then hope Mather had time to answer. He had to get out of the house and *do* something. And so, he rode for Boston to visit unannounced. Five hours later, rider and horse arrived, both in a lather.

Parris banged on Cotton Mather's front entrance and the housekeeper led him into the parlor, whereupon his hope for advice re-formed into a lump in his stomach. His patron was reclining in his armchair and he looked very unwell.

Mather seemed older, dressed in a long white sleeping shift, leather slippers, and bundled in an enormous shawl. He wore a fox fur cap pulled down past his ears.

"Pray, I beg pardon, sir," Parris said. "Here I am interrupting your distress with my troubles. I shall come another time." As he spoke, Parris mentally begged for the man to overcome whatever ailed him, give him answers, and *tell* him what to do at this terrible juncture.

After an extended moment, Mather hawked and spat dark saliva into a pot near his chair. He waved a limp hand for Parris to approach. "Nothing at all, brother. Is this about your little church on the frontier?"

For the next hour Parris unburdened himself. After finishing, he was staring at his hands. When Mather did not respond, Parris inspected him. It seemed like he was asleep, and Parris reflected back, searching for the last acknowledgment from the divine, a "yes" or a "go on."

He was debating whether to sneeze or cough to arouse him, when Mather, eyes still closed, stirred and exclaimed as if he was in the pulpit. "It is so easy to teach of God when plague hits or Indians attack..."

The sick man rubbed his belly and grimaced. Parris leaned forward and touched his arm, ready to help. But Mather brushed him off and continued to speak though still with his eyes closed. "More of our churches report covenanted members do not attend lesson days, and worse, avoid coming to communion on Sabbath Day."

"I have preached on this time after time in Salem Village," Parris responded. He needed Mather to address what he'd just explained. "But, but Mr. Mather, I need advice on the practicalities. The upsetting witchcraft accusations in my village, and the threat to my leadership as pastor, and my children's suffering."

Even now, sitting with this man in confidence, he hesitated to say with certainty they were afflicted by witches. "And as I was saying, they accuse my servant Tituba, and they will call my children as witnesses against her and other two women."

"Go on."

"I don't know what to do."

"I am sure you do, my son. Some ministers equivocate when they see troubles among the flock. They forget how to stir the people. The Devil is our tool, Mr. Parris. He comes to tempt our people whenever spiritual lassitude pulls them from God. It has always been that way, even in times of plenty." Mather coughed into his handkerchief. "But there, in your village, I see a message from our Father in heaven. He wants the people to see how Satan disrupts our lives by His, our Creator's, permission. Satan's wiles serve to remind us we need Divine Providence. If witches abide in your vicinity, we shall make the most of the opportunity."

"I do not follow." *Opportunity?*

Mather frowned as he struggled to lean closer. "If they suspect witchcraft in your village, do not fear it. Recognize it. And use it!"

"But my family—"

"The Father permits your troubles at home so we can search out the combinations of demons in our air."

"But my ministry—"

"Yours and mine will prosper beyond our due once we manage this matter in the public eye. Allow it, brother. We shall bring our energies to saving your poor afflicted ones as we did with the Goodwin children here in Boston. And if they bind those women over for trial—"

"But—"

"With Providence, we shall go further than the law courts to recover the souls of sinners in league with the Devil as his familiars." He coughed. "If they confess, we can lead them once more to God's love and forgiveness."

Mather leaned back in his chair and rubbed his eyes. "Go back to your village, Samuel. As the legal process continues, encourage it. Take part in it. Pray for the afflicted ones with renewed vigor. Our people will follow your example and will glorify God all the more."

Riding homeward from Boston Parris juggled Mather's guidance. On the one hand, he feared Mather did not understand a single word he said. On the other hand, Mather knew spiritual matters far better than him. He had done battle with the demons afflicting those Goodwin children and vanquished them. Perhaps he needed to have more faith in Mather. And besides, he owed Mather for helping him gain the pulpit.

Parris struggled against a momentary wish he had remained a merchant in the city.

As weariness bent him forward in the saddle, Parris resolved to follow Mather's lead.

Preaching against the Devil's relentless temptation was, after all, an essential duty for Puritan ministers. And, perhaps, on account of his children he'd slacked off that duty but no more. He would go beyond preaching, by offering to help the magistrates in the upcoming trials.

And, as he thought about it, there was another benefit to the plan: if the women were convicted of the charges, he might avoid suspicion that his sinfulness had brought on the children's sickness. That thought, at least for the moment, diverted him from Mather's notion they should also recover the lost souls of the witches.

By the time he crossed into Essex county Parris had drifted into a tranquil certitude, knowing what he would do. And if God willed that he loses Tituba, so be it. The lost investment would be bearable if it brought peace of mind.

When Parris approached the village, he aimed for Ingersoll's and a nice pint of beer. A dark first floor window showed the place was closed for the night and seeing it, he slapped his leg so hard it sounded like the crack of a whip. As he turned his horse toward the road again, the window shutter above the tavern entrance opened and Ingersoll popped his head through.

"I have been waiting for you. Your wife said you went to Boston. Wait a moment, I'll let you in."

Ingersoll poured them both a measure of hard spirits after setting a bayberry candle on the battered tavern table. The pleasing scent of it wafted against the stale air of the low-ceilinged room.

"An expensive candle, deacon."

"My wife demands it." Ingersoll shrugged his shoulders. Then, as if remembering what he wanted to discuss, he leaned closer. "Thomas Putnam tried to question your Tituba today in your absence. We persuaded him it was improper and to wait until you returned."

"Thank you, deacon." This latest development at first was like a poker thrust; once again Putnam was nosing into his private affairs. But Parris calculated for a moment. How should he respond, given his new course of action? Thomas Putnam had come to his home and demanded access to Tituba, his property. There had to be limits. Yet, Putnam had been more of a friend than most of the others. And he had sided with Parris on his shorted pay and the never-ending battles for firewood. No. He would not cause a stir, especially since Putnam had not gotten his way. But still. The man had his nerve.

He would interrogate Tituba with his ministerial brethren, Mr. Noyes and Mr. Hale. They could uncover more details before her day in court arrived.

"What of Thomas Putnam?" Ingersoll said.

"I do not know, my friend. Perhaps he should attend to his own family and allow me and the ministers to do our role in battle with the spiritual world."

When Noyes and Hale responded to Parris' call, they met in the parsonage. Together they interrogated Tituba, though Noyes did most of the talking.

"Did you make the witch cake?"

"Yes, but—"

"What other magic tricks do you have?"

"Only what my mistress in Barbados taught me."

Parris' mother had been one of Tituba's mistresses. It was impossible she could have ever been a conjurer! He kept his face free of expression and raised his voice, hoping to divert their attention from Tituba's words. "Do not lie about your present actions. We already know of Sister Sibley's involvement and your foolish use of witchcraft to, of all things, find witches." He turned to the two ministers to gauge their thoughts before continuing. "If you do not speak the truth to every question, I shall beat it from you like this."

Parris forced her to kneel, and driven in equal measures by a need to expel his own suffering and a need for truth he used his belt on her until Tituba sobbed, "I will, master. I will tell all."

As soon as Tituba spoke, she fainted, and no amount of shaking or shouting brought her around.

When the visiting ministers pulled on their coats, Parris was not sure if they wanted more time with her. He relaxed when Reverend Noyes tugged on his hat. "We shall watch to see how she answers Magistrate Hathorne at her public examination."

* * *

On the Sunday morning before the day set for the public hearings on the three charged with acts of witchcraft, Parris was on edge. He had labored over his sermon, writing and rewriting it without satisfaction. There were the usual admonishments and lessons he often taught, but he also had to address the rumors and the realities; there were some among them who may have joined with Satan.

It was undeniable that familiars of the Devil were his tools to inflict pain on people. But it was almost unbearable to believe Satanic means were hurting his girls. He had his duty, though. He must warn his flock of the dark dragon's presence and the danger to their souls. Then he will soothe them by explaining how civil justice would be swift and sure to deal with the ones guilty of doing witchcraft.

Parris pulled on his face as he climbed the pulpit steps. It was time to confront the Dragon not in theory but reality. His hands shook as he took his place.

When the last arrivals claimed their seats, he gazed toward the elders nearest him and then up at the gallery holding the children and servants. They all settled.

He drew a deep breath, swelling his chest, and proclaimed, "Satan has come to our village." He surveyed the pews again and saw some heads nodding agreement. "One of our community used sinful means to make a witch cake. And once used, demonic specters have shown themselves as torturers directed by the Prince of Hell.

"Grievous sin has opened wider the door for Satan as he searches for them who will reject our Lord in Heaven. Make no mistake, Satan is prowling among us, within arm's reach, in every room, waiting to steal our right to heaven.

"Against this present calamity, we must pray, begging our Father to shield us from Satan's rage while we call our accused sisters Good and Osborne, and Tituba to answer for their sinfulness. If we do these things to our Father's satisfaction, we shall send Satan back to the bowels of hell empty handed. If we do not, there will be no end to our peril from this demonic attack."

It was another hour before Parris finished the lessons, but every minute of his sermon fueled greater fear of damnation unless they dealt with the witches. The meetinghouse was as quiet as the fields after a heavy snow. Parris surveyed them from his perch. What secret sins had these people done to bring on this calamity?

Please, Lord, let there be no others.

Parris closed the worship by leading the congregation in The Lord's Prayer. Churchmen considered it a true test for discovering witches because no witch could repeat the prayer word for word. Their collective voices sounded especially earnest.

Upon dismissing them, Parris watched men and women whispering to their neighbors as if enquiring who might have stammered the words of the prayer. What unknowable evil was still lurking among them?

Chapter Fifteen

Tituba laughed aloud as she listened to Parris' sermon from afar. Not sure which pleased her more, her ability to eaves drop, or the fear she saw growing. He had ordered her to remain in the parsonage to avoid distractions. Little did he know there was no benefit to confining her, nor any protection. She gloried in her power, sensing she possessed an unstoppable force.

Salem Village's congregants, though, had reeled under Parris' Sunday afternoon sermon. Within hours, the more devout neighbors gathered outside the parsonage again, to pray for a release from the Devil's meddling. They knew God would only intercede after He deemed them worthy.

Tituba lay on her mat that night, thinking they would take her to the village's wooden jail tomorrow. She had heard talk of chaining the accused women's hands and feet to the walls so they could no longer fly. The idea made her chuckle. How earthbound they were to think such a crude remedy would work.

Mirth turned to sadness, however, as she looked at Skitôp's unused sleeping mat next to the hearth. She yearned for him. If she must dwell in jail, Tituba would only see him from afar, and he would not know it.

From the loft above, a sound like that of a child falling out of bed punctuated her thoughts. But she was not rushing up to check on them. So many times had she lit their fires and cooked their meals and nursed them, only to be paid back with cruelty. Now she would stoke the fire they feared above all else, the fire of damnation.

She remembered a part of Parris' sermon to his sheep: "There is no end to the Evildoer's design until he takes the souls of every one of us."

She would use every part of her being to make his words prophetic.

* * *

Ingersoll's Ordinary filled beyond its seating capacity. The magistrates were ready to examine the three accused women. Their task was to determine if true cause existed to bind them over for further proceedings and a capital trial carrying the sentence of death by hanging.

Parris stood nearest to the tavern's kitchen, leaning against the limed plaster wall. The perpetually leaky ceiling had stained the whitewash with overlapping streaks of brown.

He pulled at his broad unstarched collar, for the room was stifling. Besides the observers massed together under the low timbered ceiling, a rare sunny day was baking the roof.

Aside from the heat, most of the men seemed at ease in the close confines of the tavern, less so for the women. Smells of hard apple or pear cider mixed with the malt scent of beer.

Mothers with children took seats next to old men snoozing on their canes.

At the rear wall, yeomen who had abandoned early season field work lolled with mugs in their hands, joshing each other while they waited. Parris wondered how their idleness profited anyone. He resigned himself to God's desire for everyone to hear at least part of the interrogations of the Devil's handmaids and see security reestablished.

Parris prayed, *Father, if it is your will, see that these lambs of Christ so tortured for their faith receive justice.*

He hoped Mr. Hathorne and Mr. Corwin would be diligent, unlike the magistrates in Boston who never seemed on his side when he needed to collect debts owed to his business.

Thomas Putnam had assured him John Hathorne, the senior magistrate, possessed many years of experience and knew the families of Salem farms well. Some said he was impatient on the bench, sometimes demanding admissions against interest by a witness to force a case to settle.

Jonathan Corwin was a well-to-do merchant of Salem Town, reputed to be a thoughtful magistrate and devoutly literal in his faith.

Neither of the men, however, had ever presided over a case of alleged witchcraft.

Nathaniel Ingersoll squeezed his way through the tavern crowd, carrying empty tankards. He pushed past Parris on his way into the kitchen. Parris followed him. Inside, Mr. Hathorne and Mr. Corwin were chatting.

"Mr. Hathorne?" Ingersoll nodded his respect over to Corwin. "There are too many here. They already stand around the table reserved for your bench. There is no room and twenty more are pushing to get in."

Hathorne turned to Parris. "Reverend, this morning I took refuge in your meetinghouse to think and pray for guidance. It can hold twice the number as this tavern. Can we not slide the communion table in front of the pulpit for our bench and give the public their right to observe?"

Before Parris could express himself, Ingersoll agreed. "If we move, accommodating everyone would be easy. And it's just four hundred yards down the road."

"Mr. Parris?"

Remembering his commitment to follow Mather's advice, he assented with a nod.

"Very well!" Hathorne summoned a constable and gave orders to hold the prisoners in the tavern kitchen. "After we arrive, send them first before permitting all the others to follow."

Corwin spoke to no one in particular. "What of the afflicted children? Will you make room for them near us?"

Parris frowned at the idea of his children appearing in court with the accused women. Last Sunday, before her arrest, Goody Osborne had surprised the congregation by taking her assigned seat in the second row. When the four afflicted girls reacted upon seeing her, several elderly members became upset, which made the girls' squirms and random thrashing worse.

While looking at Betty and Abigail, Parris said, "Can you not rely on depositions rather than present testimony?"

"No," Hathorne said, "I shall hear them certify the averments and examine them."

Parris had labored to write statements out for the girls to sign by mark. Who knew what they might say now, in open court? But he had no authority to object.

"Mr. Parris?"

"Uh, yes, yes."

After the magistrates and their assistants took their places, they permitted Parris and his wife, and Goodman and Goodwife Putnam, into the first row in the meetinghouse.

They ushered the afflicted children to stand a mere five feet from the bench of the magistrates. The deacons arrayed rough wooden benches in an orderly fashion across the floor and in the gallery. Someone took every place and all the floors seemed to be creaking under the packed weight of the nervous villagers and chattering visitors. Many sat not ten feet from the afflicted girls.

On account of the dim light of the meetinghouse, Hathorne ordered more candles. "To observe for truthfulness as they testify."

At last, they were ready to begin.

Mr. Hathorne called through the rear door, which was standing open. "Constable Locker, produce Sarah Good. Keep a close watch on the other two. No one is to come near them, and if you must, blindfold both." He rapped on the table. "We shall maintain proper order throughout these hearings."

As Reverend Noyes said opening prayers, Parris watched the prisoner. He asked himself how anyone could question whether God had frowned on the ragged dirty woman standing between him and the magistrate. He smoothed the collar of his shirt.

Sarah Good half bowed to the magistrates, shifting her weight from foot to foot, scraping the soles of her boots, her leg irons rattling. She had the profile of a cornered rat. Yes, a form the Devil takes.

The assembled girls huddled together, seeming almost like normal children. Parris wished they would stay that way. He allowed himself an angry flare as he thought of the suffering they had endured. And their families, too.

Parris prayed for the Lord's blessing on the magistrates. The end of his troubles depended on their judgment. Then he prayed for his girls, and then the other ones.

The victims told their stories of tortured visitations and convulsions. And worse, most recently how Good and Osborne hurt them again. "Just this morning, before we came from the parsonage, Sarah Good came to us even as she was in jail."

Elizabeth Hubbard cried as she continued. "Her fingers dug into me. See, these are the marks and I still bleed from them."

Magistrate Hathorne addressed the chained prisoner. "With what evil spirits have you familiarity?"

The room filled with a collective gasp followed by silent anticipation.

"None, sir. And I will tell you I have hurt none of them girls even if they deserve it for their false accusations. I scorn any claim I have done it."

"What creature do you use to carry out the commands of the Devil?"

"I use nobody." She coughed up phlegm and wiped her mouth. Her hand was trembling

Mr. Hathorne pointed to the girls, who had bunched tighter together. "Look at them!"

As she turned her rheumy eyes to meet theirs, Betty, Abigail, Elizabeth Hubbard, and Ann writhed. Who could deny they were in excruciating pain?

"Stop your torture of these innocents!" Hathorne thundered.

And at that moment the crying and writhing stopped.

Parris closed his eyes, *Thanks be to God*, convinced Sarah Good had obeyed the magistrate's command.

The accused woman searched the faces of the magistrates, then the court helpers, the constable, and him. Parris looked at his boots.

"I am guilty of nothing other than worshipping the God who made heaven and earth," she said.

Hathorne shot a look to the assembled people. "William Good? Husband of the accused, stand if you are present."

An unkempt young man Ingersoll once had pointed out to Parris as a drunk, one of those who talked too much in the tavern, stood slowly.

"Have you ever seen your wife perform witchcraft?"

William Good pushed back thin blond hair from his face. "I saw her do a few things with me abed."

Nervous laughter from the room drowned out her sobbing denial. Hathorne turned again to the accused. Through her tears she swept the crowd for a sympathetic face. Her toothless mouth opened and closed like a fish suffocating out of water.

"Tell me then, how came these children to be thus tormented if not at your hand?"

She did not answer. And he raised his voice, demanding one.

"What do I know? You bring others here today, yet you charge me with it."

"Who are the others?"

"The two you keep outside the door."

"Who? You must give a name.

"It was Osborne." Sarah Good's face flashed bright red through the dirt smudges.

Hathorne smirked to Mr. Corwin as though proud of himself for getting her to accuse a fellow witch. "And so, who do you serve? What God?"

"The One who made heaven and earth, you foolish fat man. How long must you punish me? I am sick and with child, sir." She stood up straight, clasping her hands as if in prayer to her Savior. "I have little to gain and nothing to lose to you or those simple-minded children standing there."

"Blasphemer!" an anonymous voice declared.

Hathorne rapped the table with his knuckles. "That is all from this one. Take her away."

The room buzzed and Parris held his wife's hand as everyone watched the constable escort Sarah Good out. The murmuring continued while the next accused woman hobbled before the assembly.

Mr. Corwin administered the oath to Sarah Osborne to speak true, as the Lord God, Jehovah, may witness, while Hathorne rapidly drummed the table with his fingers. He seemed to relish his role of probing for witchery.

When she faced him, he said, "Goody Osborne, upon examination, do you deny that you used witchcraft, or hurt any of these children?"

Elizabeth Hubbard stiffened at the question, shuddering as if chilled. Ann Putnam reached out in her direction, but rather than giving support, she fell to the floor, where she rocked, hands over her ears.

Abigail rubbed her arm vigorously and wailed, "She is stabbing me with pins! Look!" She was rubbing both arms, where red blotches had bloomed for all to see. Parris looked from her to Betty and back, holding his breath at what, in her pain, she might say next.

Hathorne barked at the constable, "Bring the children closer to the prisoner." At three feet of distance the four girls began to babble, disheveled hair streaming from under their untidy white caps in blond and ginger red wisps. The accusations at Goody Osborne seemed to come in a single voice.

"She hurts me as well!"

"Stop, Goody!"

"Please, God save us from her."

Parris barely drew breath as his girls passed beyond shivering fits, clasping each other, crying and wiping away each other's tears, and gasping for breath as if their lives were forfeit. He rushed from his seat in the first row and scooped up his daughter, heedless of Hathorne's demand he back off. Parris gripped Betty with one arm and took Abigail's small pale hand.

Magistrate Hathorne called a ten-minute recess. After he reconvened the hearing, the tortured innocents had settled somewhat.

"Now, Goody Osborne, with what evil spirits have you familiarity?"

She denied the question by shaking her head and looking at the magistrates as if saying, how could you ask me this?

The girls whimpered.

"Why do you hurt them? How do you hurt them?"

"I am not hurting them."

"What familiarity have you with Sarah Good?"

Murmurs swelled across the entire room, and Parris strained to hear what the accused woman would say.

"I have not seen her for two years and then only one day a-going to town when I said how do you do."

"Sarah Good said it was *you* that hurt the children."

Osborne wavered, seeming on the verge of crumbling. She reached out for balance but there was nothing to grab. She steadied herself and stood to her full five-foot height. "I do not know if the Devil goes about in my *likeness* to do any hurt."

Hathorne ordered the children to turn and face the witness. "See if you know this woman."

"Yes," one of them said. "We have seen her in the habit she now wears. We even saw her this morning before coming to this place."

Osborne turned from the girls, pleading to Mr. Corwin. "It is more likely *I* am bewitched than to be a witch."

"What makes you say so?"

"One time I was frighted in my sleep, and I saw, or dreamed I saw a thing like an Indian all black, which pinched me in the neck, and pulled me by the back of my head all the way to the door of our house."

Hathorne half-closed his eyes, clearly suspicious of the witness. "Did you see nothing else?"

Goody Osborne wiped her face and paused as though considering what more to say.

A woman's voice from the rear of the meetinghouse shouted faint support, "She said she would never believe that lying spirit anymore."

"What lying spirit is this?" Mr. Hathorne had inclined his head toward her. "Has the Devil deceived you and been false to you?"

"I do not *know* the Devil, nor ever saw Him. It was a voice I thought I heard. It said I should no more go to meeting, but I refused and went to the next Sabbath."

Hathorne had a ready question to follow up. "Why then did you yield to the Devil by never going to meeting except once of late?"

"Alas! I have been sick and not able to go."

After asking the prisoner several ways, but getting no nearer an admission of guilt from her, Mr. Hathorne dismissed Goody Osborne.

The court adjourned two hours for the midday meal.

In the parsonage, Parris lingered at the table as the magistrates ate and discussed the morning sessions. He kept his head down, cutting off a slice of cheese, when Corwin said, "Are we agreed that sufficient evidence exists against Good and Osborne?"

"Aye, of having served the Devil by hurting those innocents. If we fail to bind them for the grand jury and trial, they may feel the license to kill someone."

Parris felt his heart beating as he listened. He swallowed, tempted to say his slave woman would never kill, being meek as she was. But then they might wonder if he was trying to save a faithful servant from justice for a personal reason. Dismissing the idea, he cut another piece of cheese and chewed in silence.

After a while Corwin spoke to Hathorne. "Do you worry if our proceedings will comport with the laws of England?"

Hathorne shook his head. "Not at all." He patted his colleague on the shoulder. "Continue to follow my lead and we shall do our duty. Once we find cause to move those wayward sisters and the heathen toward trial, we can return to home and hearth."

Corwin sighed. "Those girls—how they suffer."

"The black one is next." Hathorne stood up from the table. "It is time we return to the meetinghouse. Man's work through God's laws."

Chapter Sixteen

Jonathan Corwin, being younger and less corpulent than his partner, arrived first at the roadside door of the meetinghouse. Parris was with him. As they entered, all present quieted down.

When Hathorne joined his co-magistrate behind the communion table once more, he nodded to Marshal Herrick to bring in the prisoner. He spoke privately to Corwin. "Soon you and I shall return to our homes, done with our business here."

They had chained Tituba like the preceding two. Black dirt soiled her blue skirt and waistcoat. Parris suppressed a wince at her filthy appearance. Yet again, he thought, no one could judge him for her dirtiness now that she was a prisoner.

Tituba's wrist and ankle chains clanked as she walked, and the children, who hours before had been wracked by pains and bent joints, remained calm until Abigail burst into a loud squeal. Parris stared at her, hoping to catch her eyes and settle her somehow, until another girl near her screamed, obviously in pain and soon little Ann joined in.

Elizabeth Hubbard wailed, "Oh, no. Keep her away. Do not hurt us."

Betty was covering her ears, but not otherwise moving. Parris watched as she and Abigail moved behind the other girls, hugging each other. Neither looked at Tituba.

Parris opened a folio of documents and pulled out a sheet of loose paper. He sat alongside the scrivener. He'd forgotten to record the earlier hearings for Mather and began jotting what he remembered.

As he wrote, some in the audience murmured nervously until one woman up front hawked and spat toward the prisoner.

"Order." Hathorne banged his hand on the table until the room quieted under his authority. Rather than beginning his interrogation, he stared at Tituba as if daring her to look him in the eye, measuring her.

Parris approached the magistrates and handed over a sheaf from his folio. "The prior statements of the children about this accused, sir."

"Thank you, Mr. Parris." Corwin glanced over the sheets and passed them to Mr. Hathorne.

Parris' heart pumped in his ears as he watched the magistrate tap his knuckles lightly on the table until he finished reading. What was he thinking?

Hathorne cleared his throat. "Before we proceed, who can confirm the handwriting of these written statements?"

Thomas Putnam glanced to his wife and stood. "I wrote the true words of my daughter, Ann."

"And I did for the others." Parris avoided the magistrate's eyes, hoping he would not be required to explain his method of gathering the information.

"Very well." Hathorne was looking at the afflicted girls. "Let us have Elizabeth Hubbard step forward to confirm her written statement."

Parris' pulse rate slowed. Hathorne was not interested in questioning him, and he hadn't called one of his girls to be the first witness. Reflexively he offered Hubbard a smile of encouragement, but she did not respond.

"Very well, then." Hathorne searched the paper sheaf of statements; he pulled one out and ran his finger down the page to a point. "Did you ever see Tituba with the other accused women?"

"No, sir."

He flipped through more pages as though surprised at her answer. "Have you? Have you... seen her make the witch cake?"

"I did not watch it being baked."

"You did not? Mr. Parris said she engaged in the work of the Devil."

"I know, sir. Everybody knows." Elizabeth seemed to labor as she peeked at her questioner. Parris nodded in support at her answer.

"Did you see Tituba pinch or prick anyone, ah... or did she prick you?"

"Yes, once she did." Elizabeth looked at the floor as she spoke. "She choked me once, but not much since that time."

Little Ann remained huddled among the other girls as Elizabeth answered questions. Her lower jaw jutted out, and she stared at Mr. Hathorne brazenly. Parris suppressed a shudder. Where did that come from? Was it his imagination or were her eyes like blue ice?

When the magistrate called for Ann, she marched to the same spot Elizabeth had vacated, making certain her feet covered the first girl's boot marks on the dirty floor.

And Parris imagined her unblinking visage as she faced the magistrates.

"Do you know it is a terrible sin in God's eyes to lie?"

"Yes, sir."

"Have you been grievously attacked by Tituba?"

"I saw the apparition of her who tortured me most grievously by pricking and pinching me most dreadfully." She rubbed her thin arm while speaking.

As murmurs from the floor and galleries began, Hathorne raised a pewter tankard and tapped it on the table. The room settled, and he addressed the constable. "Bring the accused one closer."

As the constable pulled Tituba nearer, Ann called out in a quavering voice, "Make her stop it, sir."

The onlookers seemed to lean backward as if smelling foul odors.

"Please, sir!" Ann begged.

The constable bravely interceded and held Tituba back. Mr. Hathorne ran his fingers through his hair, peering at Ann, the other girls, and Mr. Corwin. "No, bring the prisoner closer!" All the innocents quivered, some crying like infants.

In the hall, foot shuffling and coughs gave way to rough whispers and mumbling for someone to do something, before a woman shouted a well-known remedy. "Make them touch the witch!"

Parris caught Hathorne's eye and nodded agreement. Hathorne said, "Make them."

One after the other, the first two being forced, the next ones hesitantly but by themselves they touched

Tituba's sleeve. Each child seemed to calm, and Ann going last stopped her pleading cries.

Everyone seemed awed into silence until the same voice in the crowd called out again. "The Devil is in this room!"

Others succumbed to their fears, and shouts arose. "Oh, Lord Jesus!" and "Father protect us!" An older married couple stood while reciting the Lord's Prayer, until Hathorne shouted above all the cries. "Order! I shall have order!"

Hathorne's demand quieted the meetinghouse. Parris felt the vibrating fear in the room; some of it, he knew, was his. He needed to keep control of himself and, by example, those gathered in his church. With brows pinched, he surveyed them, daring anyone else to break from orderly behavior.

"Reverend Parris, step closer to give testimony."

When the magistrate called on him, Parris' mouth went parched like dry salt cod. He repeated to himself: maintain dignity. He shot one more look at his congregants. Their earlier reactions had distracted him from considering how to answer if asked to testify what he knew. Tituba had already implicated herself in front of the ministers. What had she said, again?

"I shall not ask you for an oath, being a minister," Hathorne said. "Now, then. I call on you to confirm what has gone on during these examinations."

Someone in the crowd called out, "Make him take the oath. It is what all other men must do."

Parris felt his face burn. "I, pastor of Salem Village congregation," he glanced across the meetinghouse to the person talking out of turn, "swear what I speak is the truth, as God is my witness."

"Proceed."

"I saw the effects of witchery on these blameless children as they screamed and shouted in pain, just as they have suffered here today. I watched them writhe, and stiffen, their thin necks twisted to breaking. Yes… they were writhing into positions—unnatural—positions." The vehemence of the truth overwhelmed him as he stood there. He was in a supernatural war over souls as much as a battle to protect his reputation. "My daughter Betty and my wife's niece Abigail, and Elizabeth Hubbard and Ann Putnam Jr., all of them suffered in Tituba's presence. I just now saw the witch's power to stop the afflictions upon being touched."

Mercy Lewis, Thomas Putnam's maid, and her friend Mary Walcott had joined the afflicted girls in the front of the room. All of them were hugging and whimpering, several dropping to their knees. Every person in the meetinghouse seemed drawn to the wretched suffering as Hathorne gaveled order.

Parris swiped his sweaty upper lip and forehead. God give me strength, he prayed, and save us from Satan's grasping. Ann Putnam's shrieking was the first answer to his prayer. Then Elizabeth Hubbard joined her. At the same time Betty and Abigail pitched forward to Parris' feet. And before he could reach them, they thrashed their arms and legs into abnormal angles that stopped him in place.

Every God-fearing soul watching—the magistrates, the other parents of the afflicted ones, the witnesses in the building, even a few of the children themselves—

succumbed to the scene in astonishment. Lucifer was hard at work through that black slave standing among them.

A man in the gallery wailed, "I feel an ill wind." Another cried, "God, look down on us, save us from this evil!"

If fear could be palpable, stark horror seemed to grip everyone in the meetinghouse. Like frightened sheep carried away by a swollen river, their mouths were gasping, their eyes wide open and darting from one person to the next for reassurance.

Goodman Hughes spoke over the din to a fellow two rows behind him, "I sawr it! In my closed bedroom there was a great light rising above my bed and I saw a white dog and a gray cat."

Hathorne bellowed like a wounded bull. "Silence!" But the clamoring went on until he stood for leverage and hammered the table until the cacophony ceased. The only sounds came from the troubled girls.

"Under the power granted me by our sovereign king, I shall arrest any man or woman speaking without my permission." Satisfied that they believed his threat, Hathorne returned to his seat with a heavy thud.

"The witness will continue." Hathorne tapped a forewarning on the table to anyone daring to challenge him.

"My slave Tituba confessed what she had done." Parris peered at each of the magistrates and debated whether this was the time to point out she also claimed the other two had afflicted *her*. His head was filling with competing versions of what he ought to say and unable to decide, he said nothing.

When Hathorne concluded his examination of Parris, he dismissed him and motioned for the prisoner to come closer. Her scraping chains set off childish sobs.

"Is this one of the people that tormented you children?" Several high-pitched moans answered him.

Hathorne coughed and growled at Tituba. "Captain John Putnam, and Joseph Hutcheson and others, have charged you with violating Massachusetts Bay Colony statutes for the practice of witchcraft, a sin before almighty God, and of aiding and abetting Satan and His cohorts."

Tituba kept her head bowed and eyes toward the floor as Hathorne shuffled papers.

"When first confronted over your sins before several ministers, you claimed to be innocent," he said.

Tituba struggled to control her breathing and an urge to speak. She had to bide her time for the proper moment to launch into her unexpected tale. Her heart was booming.

"Why do you hurt these poor children?" Hathorne asked.

Betty and Abigail started whimpering and then wailed as though lost and abandoned in a forest.

"Now children, be at rest." Hathorne soothed them. "This day will be over soon enough." He returned to Tituba, his tone no longer comforting. "What harm have they done to you?"

Tituba steadied herself. *Wait, a little longer.* "They do no harm."

"Well then, if you do not hurt them, doth the Devil tell you he hurts them?"

She kept her eyes downcast. "He told me nothing."

Hathorne grinned. This meant the evil one had conversed with her... an admission.

"Had you ever seen something appear in some shape or other?"

"Nothing, Lord." Tituba looked at Parris. *Straightaway justice is coming.*

"Now answer me, is it the Devil that hurts them, the girls?"

"It is him for all I know." *Patience.*

Hathorne rose from his chair, his teeth showing through a smirk as if chiding her for thinking she could stand up to him. "Did you never see the Devil?"

"He… he did perhaps come once."

Every child up front fell abruptly silent.

"What appearance… how does He appear to you?"

And now I begin. This was her moment to bring a new level of terror to these fools. "I—I think he is shaped like a man. In the lean-to, I saw the thing, and it said I must serve him."

The girls were unable to turn away from Tituba, mesmerized. She was admitting her sin! The onlookers gasped at Tituba's statement before drawing a collective intake of breath. The room grew entirely still.

Tituba covered her face with both hands and sobbed. "I-told-him-no, I would not—do such a thing."

Several women at the rear stood and hurried from their places. One covering her child's mouth with a kerchief as if sulfurous air might soon fill the room.

"It was Goody Osborne and Sarah Good that hurt them." She shouted so every person heard her next words. "There were two other witches *and* a man with them."

Tituba watched both magistrates' mouths fall open; their faces were white as if stunned by a blow. "They said to hurt the children and then fly far away with them. They said if I did not do it, they would hurt me."

Tituba's new story exploded with the force of a volcano as everyone realized at once there were more witches. This was not an isolated incarnation of malevolence among three village women.

Frantic calls to God for protection washed around the room, sweet sounds to Tituba's ears. *Believe what you hear, you gullible fools. I am your devil's henchman and there are many more of us to come. Prepare for your end of times and see a witch firsthand as none have done before.*

Tituba watched Parris catch Mr. Hathorne's attention and silently mouth, "Clear the room."

He did not hesitate. "Everyone out! Only those necessary for court, the girls, their parents or family. And the minister may remain." He kept shouting, "Keep everyone else out. Ten-minute recess!"

After a complaint from a departing villager wanting to hear more details as they shuffled him out, the magistrate told a constable to remain at the door. "If you have any problems keeping them out, I shall have their names, and a day in the stocks will follow for them."

Twenty minutes later, Hathorne had drained his tankard. Judging that the townsfolk outside had calmed down sufficiently, he began the hearing again. "So, Tituba. They wanted to make you hurt the children, as they have charged you?"

"Yes, but I was sorry. I said I feared God and would not more hurt them."

"Tell us of these others besides Gamer Osborne and Sarah Good."

The magistrate should have known his voice had carried through the walls of the meetinghouse. Outside, more than a few agitated people demanded entry. It sounded like bodies thumped against the door.

Tituba stifled her satisfaction behind a bewildered look as the tumult outside swelled. They were rebelling because of the fear she had already sown.

Hathorne waited for the constable, who, joined by a deacon, finished shouting down the crowd outside, demanding order or face the consequences. He nodded consent when the constable, instead of bolting the door, allowed it to remain open enough for those outside to hear the proceedings. They appeared willing to listen respectfully as a result.

Hathorne picked up his papers then, but was clearly staring at them without reading.

Tituba had to spike the tension higher. Suddenly two, then four pairs of young eyes turned toward the rafters, searching for what Tituba made them believe was up there. There was nothing to see, but she planted the sounds of fluttering wings like small birds only in their heads, making them look left and right as if the birds were flying from one rafter to another. Following their gazes, Hathorne's forehead beaded sweat. "Corwin, do you see anything?"

"I do not," Corwin replied, though he reached for the knife at his belt.

Hathorne shouted at Tituba, "Who were the others?"

"Sir?"

"Those others you say there were…besides Good and Osborne..." He seemed to lose his stream of thought as he scanned the rafters once more.

"I do not know." She would hold back that information for later. Tituba then waited for a moment before raising her manacled hand to scratch her cheek, as if searching her memory. "There was a man came just as I was going to sleep. He said if I did not serve him, he would kill children, at least one, and me too."

She saw bald fear flash from the magistrate and he stammered, "Who—I—in what other form did he appear to you?"

Tituba recalled another detail from the girls' gossiping upstairs. "A big black dog. I was afraid it was going to bite me. The black dog said worse will happen if I do not serve him."

She heaved a deep breath and waited as the scrivener broke his quill tip, trying to record every spoken word. "But still I said I would no longer obey him."

"Have you seen other familiars?"

She expected him to press her for more names of people, and she sidestepped the question. "A little yellow bird stays with the man who has pretty things. Sarah Good has one, and it sucks nourishment from between her fingers. And I saw a cat, a red one, and it was as big as a dog, and they all could speak. Last night they scratched me when I said I will no longer serve the man."

"What service did they want of you?"

"To hurt and pinch children and make them bleed."

Two of the girls furiously rubbed their arms, but Hathorne did not seem to notice. "What has Osborne got which goes along with her?"

Both magistrates leaned forward as if to better hear Tituba, and she lowered her voice even more. "I cannot name them, for she has these things. One has wings and a pair of legs and a head like a woman."

"And what else does Goody Osborne have?"

"A thing all hairy, with a long nose and I don't know how else it looks." She screwed up her face as if searching for words. "It walks like a man, but it is only two or three foot high. The other night I came upon it standing before the fire in Mr. Parris' hall."

From outside, someone shouted through the front door. "Abigail Williams, that lives with her uncle Parris, said she saw the same creature, and it turned into the shape of Goody Osborne."

Hathorne kept his attention on Tituba. "What else?"

"The man bade me to take cats to Mr. Griggs' house, and they made me pinch his maid, Elizabeth."

Elizabeth Hubbard came to life. "Yes! She hurt me by pricking and pinching and almost choking me."

Hathorne banged his makeshift gavel. "Did the man have a book with him?"

"He showed me the book which he had in his pocket."

"What did he say?"

"To set my name to it and I made a mark in the book with red like blood."

"How many marks do you think there was in it?"

"Nine."

Pandemonium broke from inside and outside the meetinghouse. Some begged for immediate divine providence. The past exhortations of the ministers, and their sermons about the Devil, they were all true. How much longer could it be until Satan and his familiars moved to overthrow God's people and their mission to control this dark land?

Tituba closed her eyes and through the walls of the meetinghouse, observed those outside. Sharp looks darted all around, searching for suspects in thrall to the Devil.

The constable and the deacon stood in the doorway to keep them out, and despite their rising calls for entry again, Hathorne continued his interrogation. "Did the man tell you to hurt anyone else?"

She nodded solemnly. "He said they would hurt me if I did not take a knife and kill someone. Goody Osborne and Sara Good wanted me to kill Thomas Putnam's child, that girl there, Ann."

Thomas Putnam bolted to his feet. Red-faced, his voice cracking, he screamed, "Neither you nor your henchmen of Satan will hurt my Ann! I will find the others who hurt our children and you will all hang!"

His wife seized his arm and used it to help her stand. "Is this enough for you magistrates? Affliction is not enough, now they want our child dead!" She shrieked. "We shall find this other spawn of Hell's prince and bring them to holy justice!"

That woman's daughter was directly responsible for what had happened to Akanni after the dallying at the beaver pond, and her suffering gave Tituba particular joy.

Hathorne called another recess to permit the Putnams to gather themselves. Before convening again, he went to the door to address the panicky people outside. "As you have been obedient to my order, I shall allow you reentry so long as you maintain respect for this proceeding."

Tituba wanted to thank him for making that impossible bargain. She would do her best to inflame them to new heights.

After the room filled again, the afflicted girls began their agonized contortions. Right on cue, Tituba thought. She would have never guessed that the girls she knew so well were capable of such hysterical behavior.

Hathorne spoke to Tituba. "What do you see now? Who comes to make those innocent children howl in pain even as we speak?"

A shout interrupted from nowhere. "Oh, the Old Dragon is at work here. God bless us, Lord Christ deliver us!"

Hathorne's face slackened as if he had lost the strength to continue presiding over bedlam. He repeated his last question with more force. "Do you know who comes?

Tituba noted the frenzied pitch in the room and decided this would be a good time for the hearing to pause so these English could scatter and spread the word of the black witch's new disclosures. "I would tell you if I could..." She rubbed her eyes. "Oh, my lord, sir, I cannot see. I am struck blind."

She covered her eyes while Hathorne hammered repeatedly on the table to quiet the assembly, to no avail. "This is enough. We shall adjourn until tomorrow morning. The prisoner will return then for further examination."

* * *

Later in the day, after the astonishing revelations by Mr. Parris' slave during the hearing Yeoman Sam Sibley called on Dr. Griggs for help with a persistent carbuncle on his leg. He found Elizabeth Hubbard dozing before the hearth when he entered their house.

She smiled timidly while crossing the room toward him before freezing midway.

Tituba had willed the specter of Sarah Good to hover above Sibley's head. Good was already in jail after her own hearing, but this was proof even witches manacled in prison could do mischief.

Elizabeth moved her mouth as if trying to speak, unable to look away from the apparition.

"Goody…?" Elizabeth gasped.

"What is it, Lizzie?" Sibley asked.

The spectral image floated closer and spoke so only she could hear. "I will, as my heart beats, set upon you until you are dead."

Elizabeth's wits fled, and she started screaming. Hands waving, she tried to step away from a bare-breasted apparition of one of the accused women. She tumbled to the floor and from her knees she begged for help. "Sam, strike there," she pointed, "Goody Good comes to kill me!"

He had his walking staff with him, and he slashed over and over in every direction as Elizabeth cried, "There. No, here. No, over there!"

In her jail cell, Tituba knew as word of this visit spread, the village fools would see witches where there were none. She dissolved the image. Exhaustion overwhelmed her, sapping her pleasure. It had been a busy day. She settled under her thin blanket from home, to gather her strength for what she must do next.

The next morning, March 2, Tituba appeared once again before the magistrates. The group of girls near the front had swelled as youthful supporters joined the afflicted ones. Many onlookers from the prior day had returned, but a horde of newcomers crammed in with them, packing the makeshift courtroom tighter than before.

She stood in place for twenty minutes, head bowed and eyes closed while men prepared the room to go into session. The soft talk among the anxious onlookers provided new information as Tituba listened to them. Of particular interest, Martha Corey had badgered her husband, Giles, to avoid the nonsensical hearings. A mature woman of experience, she often gave opinions, and some felt she had a good sense about her.

She might need to deal with Goody Corey to prevent her from sabotaging Tituba's mission.

Joseph Putnam took his place at the side table with quills, ink and loose papers. He had agreed to take down the next testimony and nodded his readiness to the chief magistrate.

Hathorne brought Tituba back to the moment. "We must review your prior testimony." He perused a sheet of paper. "Was it six weeks ago, when Betty Parris and Abigail Williams fell sick, that the Devil first came to you?"

"Yes. Then he offered me some fine things, but I said to him I would not believe him a god unless my master says it was fine."

"What did he say?"

"He said we must meet all together—"

"Stop!" Hathorne sensed new evidence. "*Who* must meet all together?"

"He said next Wednesday we must meet at my master's house, and that night I saw all of them—"

"Stop, I say. Answer me! Who are they? You said there are others."

She ignored him and continued to ramble. "Yes. But I would not hurt Betty and Abigail." An enormous tear ran down her cheek. "He wants me to sign in my blood."

Hathorne was sweating, and he wiped his forehead. "Tell me of these *others*, you hag."

"He came again the next week. He had his book."

"I want to know what other names are in this book!"

"Yes, many, many names, and marks in red and yellow. I could not read them, but he said Good and Osborne was in there."

"How many ink lines did you see?" His intensity swelled, and his face was purple.

"I do not know—"

Hathorne slapped the table, and it sounded like a clap of thunder.

Tituba blurted out, "Nine, sir."

Hathorne and Corwin did not realize their mouths were hanging open again. She bent her head forward to cover the smile trying to escape. You and all the others, wait, she thought. There will soon be more than nine.

Hathorne recovered his composure and demanded order amid the shrieking children, and the terrified cries of men and woman. "What day did you next see this, this man, this Devil?"

"He came to me in prison and told me to say nothing to you, sir. He said if I tell you anything, he will cut off my head. Please keep me safe, sir." She sniffed her nose to stop a stream of mucus and trembled for good measure.

"If you tell us the truth, we shall keep you as safe as prayer permits."

So, they will pray for me? Hah!

"I have heard of witches that ride rods in the sky."

Amid the clamor that erupted, Hathorne asked, "How many of them came to you on flying rods?"

Tituba wiped her nose. "At first he did not show me the others. I only saw Good and Osborne. Another time, we saw a man, a dog..., ah, a red and black cat, and a strange imp. A hairy imp that was the monster I told you about before."

Tituba marveled at the magistrates' gullibility. Their faces showed no doubt about her descriptions. They did not realize that a slave heard their superstitious talk amongst themselves, which she now was handing back to them.

Mr. Corwin was writing, scratching out mistakes and rephrasing as he did. Hathorne spoke to him. "You wish to examine the accused?"

Corwin shrugged his shoulders.

"No? Well, I shall continue. Did the man ever show you where Good and Osborne put their marks in the book?"

She followed his lead. "Yes, he showed me their marks in the book, and then he said I must serve him along with the two women who came from Boston."

"Boston!"

Tituba nodded, avoiding eye contact.

"I will ask you this, and by God and Christ the Savior in heaven, you will answer me. Of those nine others you spoke of… did they live in Boston?"

She wondered if he wanted to pass the responsibility for the hearings to other magistrates. "Some in Boston, sir, but some here in this town."

"Who *are* the ones here?"

"He did not tell me who they were."

Hathorne slammed his hand on the pile of loose papers on the table. "I need hear nothing more. The hearing will stand adjourned *sine die*."

Chapter Seventeen

Both magistrates remained in the empty meetinghouse with Parris after the adjournment.

Hathorne said, "Mr. Parris, please lead us in prayers and some words from Scripture."

Parris' heart was not in it, but he obliged with several Psalms that had no obvious connection to the day's events. After a closing prayer, he invited the magistrates to the parsonage for the midday meal. As they walked, he waited for either of them to comment, fearful they might ask what he thought about the proceedings. Parris was relieved when they walked the entire way without talking; the magistrates seemed as awestruck as he was.

After a silent meal together, followed by fervent prayers for guidance, Parris regained his composure from the shock of the legal proceedings. He had to know if Hathorne considered him at all culpable for his children's afflictions. And just as much, as Mather requested, he needed to stay close to the person meting out justice. When Hathorne excused himself to take a stroll, Parris accompanied him.

"I apologize for our simple fare. My wife has many skills, but cooking is not one of them." If only that was my worst problem, he thought.

"Not at all, Mr. Parris. After several days like we have endured, who can think of food?"

Walking eastward, they stopped outside the blacksmith's, where a group of men were idling. One young man tipped his hat as the pastor and magistrate walked by, but the others were in animated discussion. More witch stories, likely. At the sawyer's, the laborers were working at a faster pace than usual, and the owner hailed the strollers as they approached.

"Mr. Hathorne. Quite a few days, aye?" He nodded at his work crew. One or two glanced back at Hathorne and Parris.

"They are good lads, working hard on my promise to let them go home early to be with their families. But what good that will do them against evil spirits, I do not know."

"Tell them to pray, Sawyer," Parris said.

More than a few villagers were still milling outside the meetinghouse as they walked past it. The two men stopped at Ingersoll's, but the tables were crowded and everyone was chattering. There was no doubt of the topic. Who could think of work after the revelations?

The magistrate and the pastor stayed for a drink of strong water and left.

"They look as if they are unprepared for Judgment Day, Mr. Parris."

Parris thought, who of us are?

On the return route to the parsonage, they once more passed the meetinghouse. "I think your church will overflow this Thursday, parson."

Parris tried to lighten his mood. "Aye, there will be no need to ask Christ to send out the angels to bring in sinners."

As they walked, he got no further insight from Hathorne. And on the last leg, he mulled over his problems. If it was providence that the Beast was so active, the Creator must have a role for him. But was it to face a punishment or to find an opportunity for his advantage? The word from these hearings traveled at high speed through every part of Essex County. Cotton Mather would want to hear it first from him. And perhaps a trip to Boston would give him a chance to get more guidance from his mentor.

When the strollers returned to the parsonage, Hathorne bade the Parris family farewell. Upon discovering he intended on going to Boston the following morning, Parris asked to ride along with him.

They left in Hathorne's two-horse cart with Parris' chestnut mare tethered behind them. En route they discussed the Bible, and the fragile economy, the Indian threats and the weather until there was nothing else to talk about except the specters in Salem.

"It must seem more than you can handle out here alone," Hathorne said.

"We do what the Lord demands."

"Yes, we all do. But your children afflicted, your slave accused among the many other responsibilities in your parish."

Parris felt a rush of warmth that Hathorne might appreciate his station. But it gave way to the rising hair on his neck. Was this man about to castigate him with a qualification? "We do what the Lord demands."

"I had thought perhaps Mr. Corwin and I were going to preside over these hearings with dispatch and be done with them, but now I am not so optimistic."

Parris exhaled at the change in topic. But to make certain Hathorne viewed him in a good light, he complimented him. "Tituba, under your careful examination, disclosed that there are more in league with Satan than our several neighbors in the village."

Parris snuck a glance to confirm the effect of his statement and saw Hathorne nod agreement. He decided Mather was right in his approach to stay close to the hearings and Hathorne would welcome Parris' participation. Indeed, other ministers might view him as a good example for confronting the Devil's plans head-on.

When Parris and Hathorne arrived in Boston, they drove past the jail and saw John Arnold, the warden.

"How now, Mr. Arnold?" Hathorne called.

"Good morrow, Mr. Hathorne. I hear you have been busy down in Essex County."

"We shall send you a few witches to hold, pending trial."

Arnold smiled. "The more inmates, the more money in our pocket. Have they names?"

"Aye, Good, Osborne and Tituba."

"Very well, I have plenty of chain to keep them secure from flying off in the night."

Hathorne slapped the reins, and they moved off with fare-thee-wells to the warden. At Market Street, Parris took leave of Hathorne, who extended his hand to the parson.

He held his grip. "Between us, ask Mr. Mather what weight he gives to this spectral evidence testimony."

Parris agreed to convey the question and hurried to Cotton Mather's home.

Once more he waited in the parlor. But this time Mather called him into his small adjacent study. Mather still looked unwell. After a brief greeting, Parris recalled all the hearing high points from his personal notes of the proceedings.

"Let us see if there are more of the witches in other locales. If it be true, we shall have our opportunity to permanently cement the church's authority by supporting the laws and being part of the next level of proceedings. But we must know what happens in those hearings and encourage the magistrates in their mission of finding every familiar of Satan."

Parris fought a quailing urge. Did his mentor not realize there could be more than three; six, maybe nine! They were active across the county and coming for his people. He wondered if a drowning man waving his arms to an empty shore felt this sense of peril.

As if Mather partially understood Parris' discomfort he offered, "Well done all around, Mr. Parris. You are doing God's work."

Parris welcomed the praise but he tasted bitter with the sweet.

Then Mather said, "This will be the beginning for us, the salutary cleansing of souls lost in sinful obeisance to Satan. Only we leaders can do it before they are sentenced to hang and return them to life among the saints."

Parris sucked in a breath and labored to speak in a level voice. "What if there is a gathering multitude of these demonic forces beyond counting? Sinners can repent, and we have seen it. But the prayerful process of bringing them to repentance is weighed down with uncertainty when the numbers may be so great. Is it not?"

Mather was smiling rather knowingly. "Have faith in God, my son. He has led me to this approach. But first things first."

"With respect, tell me more clearly what you want me to do. I do not know if I can remain tied to the prosecution of them as I have been and still serve the spiritual needs of my people in the village."

"My dear Samuel, I need your firsthand witness if I am to have the clearest understanding of those goings-on. Stay with it. I shall join you at the hearings before long. Until then, make good copy of everything, will you?"

That seemed like a reasonable request. Be a neutral reporter, and wait for Mather. He was, after all, one of the most respected divines in New England.

Before Parris could say more, Mather grimaced, holding his breath. "This belly of mine…" He cleared his throat and swallowed. "My dear brother. We… you and I and all our ministers have the power and authority to strike back against the Devil, and bring contrite sinners once more into the fold. Better to save a sinner's soul than pass him off for the hangman's noose. I welcome this battle with Satan, and I need your support."

Mather let out a long burp and swallowed something bitter. "Think of the glory."

"For whom?"

"God, my good man. God's glory." Another grimace. "The king's new charter likely will seek to limit our influence over general civil governance. Therefore, we must demonstrate our involvement in the administration of criminal justice before it arrives to cut us out."

"As you wish, sir."

When Mather labored to stand, Parris recognized his cue and helped him up. He did not offer anything further since his mentor had given him too much to think about and digest, much less discuss.

As he prepared to leave, he thought of Magistrate Hathorne's request for guidance on using spectral evidence in the hearings. "One more thing, Mr. Mather. Magistrate Hathorne asked me to pass on a question to you. In your opinion, what is the weight to give spectral evidence at the hearings?"

"Tell him I approve of it, unofficially." He took Parris' arm and walked him toward the sliding door of the parlor. "Without such evidence, we might never have the guilty arrested or subject to a fair trial with all due speed."

It appeared another thought came to him when he held up his hand. "If Hathorne needs further guidance, he may send word. I can get the opinion of all the ministers if he needs something in writing. Notify me of all future hearings so I may attend knowledgably and we shall begin our intervention."

"I'll convey your reply and do as you ask. God bless you." He felt lighter, but not completely relieved. He told himself to trust Mather, and release his worry.

Parris tarried overnight in Boston, and the next day he stopped at several parishes as he rode home. He invited the ministers to fast and gather at his home to pray for his children. They came on March 7. All had fasted since dawn, but even after travel, they took no refreshments when they arrived.

And they prayed together, imploring the Creator to turn the tide against Satan in his diabolical attack on Parris' family and the village's afflicted ones. During their prayers, from time to time noises upstairs in the parsonage distracted them.

"It is the children," Parris said. He imagined his face drained of color, unable to even make a weak apologetic smile.

The assembled men, not knowing what else to do, continued praying.

During their entreaties, word arrived concerning Cotton Mather. His wife had found him sprawled on the parlor floor, drooling black blood. The physician ordered indeterminate bed rest and regular doses of his chalky liquid formula. There was to be no preaching, and absolutely no travel to Salem Village.

Parris felt his legs weaken and his mind darted: I am further abandoned. He looked downward so as to hide any hint of his feelings. After another moment, he regained a measure of composure. There was his duty. He'd made his promise to Mather and although deprived of his mentor's presence at the hearings... Parris squinted at a new thought. Mather's absence simplified his life, even if only slightly. One less force whipsawing him every minute of the day.

He offered a prayer of thanks for the modicum of firm ground.

Chapter Eighteen

Tituba sat on the floor of her new Boston jail cell, chained to a sweating stone wall, not four feet away from street water dripping down it to the floor. She could not sleep on account of the pressure of her obsession. Yes, it was an obsession, but more than that, she viewed it as a virtue, a single-minded pursuit, exacting suffering from her targets.

Earlier in the day, when the prison cart carried her from Salem Village, she listened to the driver and his helper marveling over the latest news.

"They heard Goodman John Proctor say there were no witches in Salem Village."

"Many know him to be a smart and able man."

"Aye, but a man who heard Proctor announce it one evening at Ingersoll's tavern over drinks told me it happened."

The driver reined up the horses when a dog darted across the way. Both men stared at it as if trying to determine if it had been a devil's familiar. Tituba nodded in approval. She wanted everybody to be nervous.

"Proctor might've been a bit under the weather, but he said to his mates the antics of the afflicted girls were enough to make a dog laugh. And if he had a chance, he would beat the fits out of them. The same went for his maid, Mary Warren, if she acted up."

Tituba decided John Proctor needed a warning against such talk.

That night, knowing Proctor's wife, Elizabeth, by sight, Tituba conjured the image of Goodwife Proctor and visited little Ann Putnam in her bedroom.

She hovered over the child's bed. When a hard burst of wind rammed the side of the house, Ann's eyelids fluttered open and she saw Goody Proctor pointing a crooked finger at her and cackling like an ancient woman, "Come join us, or suffer pain worse than the fire."

Tituba remained to observe Ann's father rushing to her, trying to still her screaming. Soon Ann's mother hurried in and the parents calmed the child enough to hear how Goody Proctor had threatened their daughter. "I could see right through her body!"

They remained with little Ann until she returned to sleep, in her mother's arms, under her father's protection.

"Husband," she whispered, "Tituba said there were others. Can Goody Proctor be one of them? Is this a visit from Tituba's next witch?"

Thomas Putnam's hand shook as he reached out to lead his wife from the bedroom. With her on his arm, he announced defiantly, "We need to see them all hanged. They will hurt no one when they are dead."

A rush of satisfaction swelled in Tituba. If John Proctor picked up on her warning shot, there would be one less worry of interference from men like him.

Tituba dropped into a sound sleep. Soon she was dreaming of Africa and saw the silhouette of her huge central village tree. So many days she had spent under that tree, playing games with other girls. There were the thick roots growing out and into the soil where they sat and told stories. Tituba followed the dark trunk upward. It was as it had always been, so tall and round, the width of a large house.

She gazed upward further, reaching the dark green leaves; she peeked through at the white clouds floating far above. Tituba inhaled, remembering the sweet scents, and she basked once more in the warmth of her secure childhood.

The peace broke with a sound much like a wooden door being slammed. Just as fast the bottom half of a body dressed in a white shift dropped into sight, snapping to an abrupt stop. It twisted ever so slightly amid creaking rope sounds. A woman's boots extended below the shift of the motionless body.

Tituba snapped awake at another banging and hit the back of her head on the stone wall. A third bang near the cell door drew her attention to a small metal port built into it. A jailor had pushed a bowl of porridge through it so hard, half the contents slopped on the filthy floor. Tituba stretched her leg to draw the bowl closer, whereupon she gobbled down the cold food, hoping it settled her queasy stomach.

Tituba needed to forget the jarring sight of the hanging. Why should she care for someone's execution? It was the English who killed in that manner. She would only help them follow their natural inclination.

On March 12 an apparition of Goodwife Martha Corey pinched little Ann Putnam. When she ran to her father with the tale, he summoned Parris to come over that morning for spiritual support. Parris arrived to find Thomas with his brother Edward and Ezekiel Cheever near the large hearth, speaking to the child. "Could you be mistaken about Goody Corey? You must be certain. Are you certain?"

"It is her. She was wearing a green dress."

Parris drew Thomas Putnam aside. "Your child seems a frequent target of dark spirits beyond the first three witches. I have heard about the visit of Goody Proctor and now this one."

"Do you question her?"

"I—" Did Putnam want the truth? He feared for his ability to confirm his own eyes and ears anymore. Uncertainty was growing everywhere.

"Brother Parris, your children have been as much afflicted, as my Ann. Do you expect me to believe her afflictions any less than you with yours?" He leaned right in Parris' face. "I need you with us."

"I am here to offer whatever is in my power…."

"If anyone thinks I will stand by and allow debauched things, no matter how many, to afflict my family, they will see my ferocity. I will not abide this without a fight!"

Parris searched for guidance within himself. He could pray over this child as Mr. Mather had with the children in the Goodwin family in Boston, and as he had done over his own children. It was all he had to offer.

Parris touched Thomas Putnam's arm. "Sit with your brother and Goodman Cheever while I pray with little Ann."

He placed his hands on Ann's shoulders and bowed his head, asking God to give him the grace to intercede for the child. After a while, he raised his eyes to little Ann and prompted her to recite the Lord's Prayer with him.

After they finished, the grumbling among the men in the room demanded his attention. He inhaled and turned from her, unable to determine whether he had been a help to the girl.

Thomas Putnam waved Parris nearer. "Edward and I have to ride for the Corey farm and Cheever will go with us."

"To what end?" He sensed vigilantism in the air.

Putnam hunched his shoulders. "We must do something. So, we shall try to catch Goody Corey by surprise and question her."

"I… I cannot go with you. I am expected at two other farmsteads today."

Putnam half smiled his disappointment and held Parris' eyes. And Parris knew Thomas was ready to remind him he owed a favor to the man who hired him.

"Our pastor can confront witchcraft in his home, but not elsewhere in his parish?"

Ten minutes later, the Putnams, Cheever and Parris galloped to the Corey farmstead two and a half miles south.

They rumbled up to a crude hitching post. From inside, Martha Corey had to have heard them arrive. She opened the door and shouted, "Is it something with my Giles?" Martha had a sturdy build and she waddled out to the dismounting men.

"Nothing about Giles," Thomas Putnam said.

She placed her hand over her heart and laughed giddily. "I should not have married a man so many years my senior. I worry about him every day."

Then, as if she wanted to joke about the current topic on everyone's minds, Martha said, "I know what you are come for. You came to talk with me about being a witch." She covered her toothless mouth with a hand as she laughed.

Edward Putnam shouldered in front of his brother. "To the point, Goody. My niece Ann spoke of a visit from you last evening." He was not returning her smile.

She at first seemed confused, then her eyes narrowed, and Parris heard in her voice an angry suspicion of betrayal. "What? I cannot concern myself with people talking about me, least of all a small girl."

But then she rolled her eyes sideways as if reconsidering her tone. "I am a gospel woman, everyone knows it."

Parris had planned to remain aloof, but he slipped into reminding her that professions of faith alone could not clear one's name. He checked the other men, who were agreeing.

"What do you wish to ask me?" Corey said.

Thomas Putnam answered her with another question. "Why have you not come to witness the unmasking of the witches at the hearings?"

Martha Corey had a reputation for boldness. And Parris did not have to wait for her to show it. "I had no knowledge there *were* any witches. Plus, I kept my husband from wasting time by attending. And I am sure by this question you know I took off the saddle from his horse so he could not ride."

She turned to reenter her home. But she stopped. "Thomas Putnam, did your Ann say what clothes I wore during the so-called visit?"

The men exchanged glances at each other until Edward barked at her, "How could you know she described your clothes? They are the color of those you are wearing."

Martha ran her hands over the green skirt she wore. Her face lost its color. "But Goodman! I do not know. I have spent every day laboring here, with no time for the foolishness of girls better served with a willow branch across the bottom than willing ears of their elders."

She stopped once more at her doorway. "I shall visit you tomorrow after mid-day meal. Perhaps I might see the child."

She slammed the door, only to open it. "And I shall not come by flying, but in the flesh, by walking!"

The next mid-day Parris was at Thomas Putnam's home when Martha Corey came marching, her head tilted forward. Parris accompanied Thomas as he stepped through the open front door to meet her.

Martha pulled up when she found herself almost upon the men. "Lo, you have been expecting me, wasting time at your front gate."

She seemed ready to battle, fists clenched and jaw locked.

"Good morrow, Martha Corey," Putnam greeted her without a smile. He was in no mood for backtalk from this arrogant woman.

Before she arrived, Putnam had told Parris his child suffered through another bad night. "Nightmares and then a fit after another invisible spectral visitor, an unnamed one this time."

Putnam invited Corey to enter and have her say.

Mother and daughter had been spinning and plying yarn. The child was facing away from the door, and without looking back at the visitor, she gazed upward and pointed. "Look, Mother, it is Goody Corey. She floats among us!"

Martha reacted as if slapped. She looked amazedly at her feet on the plank floor.

Ann screeched, "And look. A yellow bird is suckling between her fingers and now it comes for me." The child twisted away as if avoiding the invisible bird in flight and almost fell into the hearth fire.

Corey held up her hands. "Am I the one bedeviled? I am right here, not up there somewhere!"

A shrill voice from the kitchen drew Parris' attention. "God forgive you, Goody Corey." Mercy Lewis, an eighteen-year-old indentured maid, rushed in carrying a broom upside down. She swiped the broom overhead as if to strike the invisible bird while Ann pointed to each place it flew.

"Mercy Lewis, you girls are distracted," Corey shouted. "Nothing is there!"

Mercy fell to her knees, and bent forward gasping for breath. Her eyes had sunken dark rings beneath them, like one who had not slept well for months. When she struggled to her feet and raised the broom again, little Ann squealed, "Do not approach it, or you will suffer as I do." Ann thereupon fainted and Mercy did the same.

As Parris gained his senses, Thomas lunged at Martha Corey. Parris got between them and held Thomas by both arms until Martha had time to back up and run from the farmhouse.

"Thomas, even if she is a familiar, you still dare not touch her without risking retribution by the law. We do not countenance vigilantism."

Once Parris was satisfied Putnam would not pursue Martha Corey on horseback, he led the family in a short prayer. He stayed a while longer before going home.

* * *

No sooner had Parris returned to the parsonage than a visitor arrived with news. Goody Putnam had collapsed and did not respond when they tried to rouse her.

"Goody?"

"Aye and they said it happened shortly after her child and their maid fell afflicted today.

"From what cause?" He had just left them and was afraid he already knew the answer.

"Did you not know, Mr. Parris? She is pregnant again."

Surprised and relieved since he had not known of the pregnancy, Parris protested to his wife, "Goody Putnam had lost her seventh in a row only four months ago!"

"I should fear for a new child in a house under affliction."

The following Sunday morning, Martha Corey kept her head bowed in church. The newest rumor that she had visited Goody Putnam turned into the widespread belief she had demanded Goody Putnam sign the red book of the Devil.

Parris searched for Martha's husband, Giles. The older man was in his assigned seat, but not ogling the attendees, as he usually did, nor was he looking at his wife.

Reverend Deodat Lawson was assisting Parris that day, and as he climbed the three steps to the small wooden pulpit, the two men squeezed past each other as the pastor stepped down.

The church was soberly awaiting Lawson's first words when a sound like a shot came from the gallery. There, among the other village children, servants, and visiting worshipers Ann Putnam had banged her boot against the half wall and railing at the front edge.

The mass intake of breath at the interruption preceded a unified exhalation of relief as one of Ann's mates giggled.

Parris located Martha Corey again. She was holding a handkerchief to her face. Who could have expected the claim against a regular attending church member? They said she feared no one, having survived the reprobation of the community after she bore a black child. But this morning she seemed to cower under the glares of her fellow parishioners.

Ann had remained standing in the gallery after causing the disruption, and she edged closer to the railing. She pointed up to the rafters. Her movement seemed to catch everyone's attention as if they were watching her with peripheral vision. Betty and Abigail, attended by Elizabeth

Hubbard, crowded next to little Ann. They leaned together, whispering and following Ann's hand as she pointed.

"Yes, there. Yes, I see it," Abigail said.

Goody Pope, sitting at her place on the first floor, shrieked and collapsed almost unnoticed as everyone else searched the rafters for a spectral invader. The room fell out of reverential order amidst many fearful whispers.

Giles Corey barked out a disdainful laugh, and multiple hard stares turned his mirth into a fit of coughing.

"Look there! Goody Corey sits on the beam," Ann shouted. Abigail intertwined arms with her, and the girls took up the call, shouting at the specter of Martha Corey only they could see, until Ann screamed, "She suckles her yellow bird. There it is."

A long while later, after the ministers and deacons had reestablished a degree of respectful behavior, the congregation vacated the church posthaste.

Parris stayed after the last person left. He prayed even as he wondered whether he still believed in the power of prayer. All alone, he comforted himself. Had Job not suffered this way? He would withstand his own trials—if only they would end soon.

Two days later, they jailed Martha Corey under a criminal complaint signed by Edward Putnam and Mr. Cheever.

Everyone knew the charge.

Chapter Nineteen

Elizabeth Parris greeted Reverend Lawson. "Good morrow and welcome." She led him to her husband's wooden armchair in the main room of the parsonage. "Let me tell him you are here."

Parris had already started down the stairs, and he summoned Lawson up to his study. Inside the tiny room, they sat knee to knee in the cramped space. Reaching from his chair, Parris closed the door. He had invited Lawson to visit, hoping his brother minister might agree to help manage the parish during the crisis.

"Brother Lawson, how have you fared of late?"

"After seeing the bedlam in our worship service the other day, I needed to clear my head at home." Lawson glanced at the Bible lying on the small desk. "But Martha Corey's examination tomorrow drew me back."

"I shall be there, too." He leaned forward to ask for help, but sensing the visitor had something more on his mind, Parris retreated.

"Last evening I took a room at Ingersoll's."

Parris nodded.

"I wish I had not done so." He pushed on the door as if making sure it was tight. "Brother, have you something to drink?"

Parris opened the door and shouted. "Elizabeth, if you please, a pitcher of beer for our guest and me."

After their beverage arrived, Lawson took a long draught. "Last evening, I intended to sleep after my prayers. I was dozing until someone outside my room made a sound."

He drained his cup. "I opened the door to find young Mary Walcott, and her face told me she was troubled. It embarrassed me to see her outside my door, given the time of night."

"What did she want?"

Lawson lifted his arms to the sides. "She said, 'Please, Mr. Lawson, I must speak to you.' And I tell you, Samuel, for the briefest moment, in the flickering of the candlelight, she looked like my dear late wife."

Was his brother about to confess he had fallen into sin?

"When she stepped forward, I backed into the room. I said, 'Pray, leave the door ajar, child,' but she closed the door until only a slim crack of light remained. As she took a seat on the stool, I saw her crying. She was shaking, and little did I know I was about to do the same."

"Lawson, to the point, man."

"She cried, 'Oh, Mr. Lawson! I heard one of the afflicted say Martha Corey has admitted that she had a diabolical hand in the death of your wife and child, two years ago.'"

Lawson's eyes went dead. The candle in the small study dimmed, making the walls seem to draw closer. Parris needed air—and a moment to think. He knew the story of Lawson's family tragedy. Wife and child both had died of natural causes, which meant no one knew why.

Lawson revived. "For two years I have struggled to let go of their deaths."

Parris refilled their cups, spilling beer over the tops.

"But a diabolical agency?" Lawson drank half the cup. "Could it be that one parishioner, someone you or I may have counseled, caused…" He sobbed into his hands.

Parris barely suppressed his surprise. Oh Lord, could there be one of their parishioners had done murder in league with the Devil?

Lawson pushed forward. "If even a scintilla of proof exists that the Devil's familiars attacked my family, we must expose them for judgement."

Parris swallowed to ease the lump in his throat. How could he ask for Lawson's help with parish business after this appalling news? As much as he needed help to address his needs, Lawson's own seemed as demanding. Unable to speak, he let the other man vent. And Lawson spilled out his fears again, magnifying them as they both labored for breath in the tiny study. When the guttering candle puffed out, Parris banged the door open and heaved in a gulp of cool air.

The next moment he heard his wife's urgent call from the main room. "Please, Samuel! Come! We need you…" Her tone was like a child calling for absent parents.

Parris bolted down the stairs, answering, "I heard nothing. What—"

He first saw Elizabeth rocking Abigail as they sat on the floor in front of the hearth. The sight of burning firewood caught him next: smoking embers were strewn inside and outside the hearth. He kicked several smoking pieces off the plank wood floor.

Parris looked his wife and niece over once more, thanking God neither was suffering some present torment. Elizabeth seemed in control, more so than he, and she said, "This sweet girl is just now calmed, husband. She was throwing firebrands from the hearth and clambering in as if to fly up the chimney."

Abigail's eyes were docile, those of a weak lamb, and her hands black with soot. Elizabeth's eyes were filling with tears. "I called and called up to you in the study, but you must not have…"

Parris strained to follow what she was saying, his thoughts spiraling backward, before these days of parrying Satan. That night Abigail had stumbled into the blazing hearth as he led them in prayers…. Had his new life been under attack from Satan then? Had the poor girl's affliction begun then?

Feeling as blasted as the smoldering bits of wood scattered on the floor, unable to catch his breath, Parris wanted to shut his eyes to escape—everything. Unable to stand there another instant, frozen and impotent he gasped, "I—I cannot think, nor deal with this." His usual defenses against appearing weak were near to collapse, and he scrambled up to the shelter of his study.

Inside the study, Parris clasped his hands, and bit his knuckles, searching for a prayer for relief. He heard Lawson downstairs offer help to clean up the mess.

After some while of seclusion every minute of which he dreaded interruption, Parris heard all of them ascending the creaking wooden steps, and when Lawson opened the study door to rejoin him, he saw with relief his wife and niece going into the bedroom across the hall.

Alone again with Lawson, Parris unburdened himself. "Brother Lawson, these weeks have drained my soul." *How to keep from sobbing in front of this man so deep in his own suffering?* "I have neglected too many of my duties... It has been so... long since I visited the sick with the message of salvation." He laughed ruefully. "Or even merely written the ordinary doings of the parish in my record book." He reached across the desk and put his hand on the large open Bible. "I am failing in so many ways."

He noted the irony; Lawson was now waiting for him to further open his heart. They sat in silence until Parris decided he had nothing to lose by bluntly asking for help. "Can you stay in the village to teach for me this coming Lecture Day?" He wanted to ask for more, but the words would not come out.

Parris felt his face burning for ignoring Lawson's own need of pastoral aid, but in his state, he had nothing to offer.

"Brother Samuel. I can take the pulpit for you on Thursday if you wish. And if we work together, we may discover what truth there is in the Walcott girl's story about my family's murder by witchcraft."

Lawson extended a hand to help Parris stand. "Let's to the tavern. I'll buy us a measure of a strong drink."

As they walked, Lawson retrieved a stick, breaking off bits of the end. "But this matter of Martha Corey." He tossed the branch. "She always acknowledged God's providence and never missed a trip to Salem Town for Sabbath Day communion. She could be guilty of the sin of pride, but guilty of murder?"

Parris could not summon the energy to reply.

At Ingersoll's, more people had gathered than usual—sitting or standing and drinking. "Have they no productive work to do?" Lawson remarked.

"Who can make them when this—this thing has confounded us?" He straightened, knowing other patrons of the tavern would be watching him.

Among the tavern patrons the talk was the same as everywhere. Who might have joined with the Devil to hurt the girls this way? Why would anyone become a witch familiar of Satan?

Parris caught sight of Giles Corey sitting in a corner, talking with another older man. They were both going deaf, and their loud voices carried. Giles groused, "It may be better to accuse a suspect yourself, and be seen as one afflicted, rather than wait for someone to charge you as a witch."

After their drink, Lawson said, "On second thought, I shall not attend Martha Corey's hearing. Instead, I'll take the time to contemplate God's will and my part in His plan."

He must have read the spike in Parris' apprehension by the flush of his face. "And I need time to prepare myself for Thursday. I will not let you down."

"You are a good man, brother. I am more than grateful, especially since I must attend the imminent hearings." Parris thought, more grateful than Lawson could know, "The law needs my witness as it searches for the truth." As did Cotton Mather.

But Parris did not attend the hearing either. He kept to himself inside his study after telling Elizabeth he wanted no distractions. But in the silence, he could not steady his thoughts as they bounced from one transitory fearful idea to the next. Use the law. Use the church. Stand with Mather. Or run to flee this mess.

He could not escape knowing the hearing was in session as he remained in solitude, drumming his fingers, laying his head on his arms and napping, begging God to let this chalice pass from him.

In late afternoon, Elizabeth tapped on his door. "Another attack! Goody Putnam was greviously abused during Martha Corey's hearing."

"And?"

"You should go to her."

"What of Corey?"

"The magistrates bound her over for trial. The examination is finished."

He put his head back down.

"Husband, the afflicted ones need your ministry."

There was no rest from this business.

When Parris arrived at the Putnam farm little Ann let him into the house. He noted she looked paler than her normal sallow complexion. From the second floor, Thomas called to him. "Samuel, my wife had a sore fit not two hours ago."

He found Goody Putnam lying in bed. She raised her head as he approached and said, "God's praise, Mr. Parris, stay and pray with me whilst I am sensible."

They prayed together, but before they finished, she lay back on the pillows abruptly, stiffening. She called out, "What? Who is it?"

The poor woman glanced in every corner of the room, avoiding Parris' face, yet speaking to him. "Stay not, pastor, you cannot pray here on this occasion."

He ignored her raving and knelt next to her bed, though his insides were shaking almost as much as she was. When she broke into thrashing, tossing off the blankets, he backed away as Thomas lifted her from the bed to take her on his knees like a child.

Goody Putnam was so stiff, Thomas could not bend her at the waist. When she relaxed, she devolved into what seemed like a state of supernatural vision. Such a vision, were it from God, had not happened since the saints of the early church and so it had to be a manifestation of evil then, not of God.

Parris was powerless to assist his friends as Ann disputed with an invisible something or someone. He knelt to the side of the couple, clasping his hands and wordless. Again, a fit seized her, this time shaking her body like a rag poppet. When it released her, she blubbered. "I see you, Martha Corey. And you, too, Rebecca Nurse." She screamed. "I shall not sign your red book, and you shall not tear my soul from my body!"

She closed her eyes as if to shut off sight of the specters. "They tortured me so many times today I cannot express it." She turned her head to face Parris and he froze as she fastened her eyes on him. "And all because I would not yield to their desires."

When she exhaled, almost like a dying woman losing her last breath, Ann stared vacantly at the ceiling. Thomas meekly carried her to bed. He tucked her covers and turning to Parris, offered him a drink. Parris refused, fearing he might choke on it.

They bade each other terse wishes for a good night and Parris left the farmhouse. He approached his horse on wobbly legs and struggled to mount. En route home, he peeped this way and that as he rode, despising himself for it, yet terrified at the prospect of meeting Ann Putnam's demons in the twilight.

While Parris sat the saddle, listening to every creak, he fell deeper into his personal darkness. The supernatural events were coming at him like hammer blows.

After he got home, Parris described what happened to Elizabeth. "She succumbed in front of me. That vacant stare between fits… I have seen it before among disturbed survivors of Indian attacks, and the people suffering from isolation on the frontiers during the long snowed-in winters. Some go on that way for months, sometimes years."

"We can only pray that our afflicted ones do not give in to the foulness of despair and join with Satan."

"I… fear I understand their temptation to hopelessness more now than ever."

* * *

Tituba rested in her cell. She had followed Parris to the Putnam farm earlier. Somehow, Goody Putnam's afflictions had exploded with spectral visions without Tituba's prompting. At first, she was pleased to see it, and unconcerned. On reflection she was puzzled. Not one part of Ann's suffering was her doing.

No matter, she decided. If hysteria was contagious, it suited her plan.

Nevertheless, she decided to return to Putnam's and observe Goody Ann. She found Putnam relatives and a few close friends had arrived to give Goody comfort. The visiting women went to the bedroom upstairs with Ann, reviewing her horrible afflictions earlier in the day. The men relaxed around the table in the main room, drinking and discussing the feuds between them and neighboring farmers.

Tituba smiled at what she heard downstairs. "The Topsfield men are still at it, Thomas. When will our claim over the timbered land be called for hearing again?"

"Our appeal is pending until the proper court is formed. We have no choice but to wait until our new governor arrives."

"I'm sure Isaac Esty is already thinking to challenge us with a new grievance, no matter who wins in court."

Tituba felt angry heat rising in the men.

"The Topsfielders are spreading new lies on us. They're saying we passed the last village resolution using trickery to disadvantage them." There was laughter. "Can you imagine we should do such a thing?" There was more laughter.

Tituba thought the mirth was driven by meanness and it was no surprise to her.

Thomas Putnam nearly shouted, "I am near the end with their scheming. They are united against us by marriage or kinship. The Wilds, and the Hows will never let us rest."

Another man said, "Don't forget Mary Esty or her troublemaker sister, Sarah Cloyce."

"And both of them sisters of Rebecca Nurse, the grand dame."

There was bad blood here. And with Goody Putnam's tendency to fly into fits, Tituba sensed opportunities to exploit the animosity. She repeated the names. Nurse, Cloyce, Esty, and Wilds. Her next targets. And why not?

Putnam and his kinsmen would follow wherever she led, seizing on any fantasy about those unmanageable women and their contentious families. They were more than ready for manipulation.

Tituba decided Rebecca Nurse would be the next spectral familiar of the Devil. She had seen the old woman before, but did not know much about her except that Rebecca was regarded as a Puritan paragon of virtue. She was a perfect target to demonstrate their devil's reach.

That night, in her jail cell, Tituba planned her next steps. If Rebecca Nurse, the head of a large and prominent family, fell to Tituba's revenge, anyone could be a suspect.

Tituba leaned against the wall of her cell, savoring the idea, when an image popped into her mind. She envisioned Rebecca Nurse struggling up a gallows ladder and being shoved off it with a rope tight around her neck. A crowd of onlookers watched as the old demon swung alongside Martha Corey's lifeless body. Enjoy it, you fools, for your judges will deliver my fury tenfold.

Chapter Twenty

On March 24, at seven-thirty in the morning, Mr. Hathorne and Mr. Corwin sat at the front table in Ingersoll's Tavern. Parris walked in, ready to escort them to the meetinghouse for the next hearing. Rebecca Nurse already awaited them, wearing iron chains.

He took a seat across the table from the men, determined to serve them in any fashion they wished. But as they chatted before beginning another day in combat with the Devil, Parris remained occupied within his own struggles. It had already been a difficult morning.

His wife had more faith they could weather these afflictions inside the family. But a week ago, without telling her, he decided Betty and Abigail were in too much danger to remain here.

The villagers needed to find witches. And afflicted girls visited the parsonage constantly, talking among themselves, learning about each other's afflictions and who had visited them in the night. What retaliation might Satan come up with?

He had convinced himself that one of those witches Tituba described could appear at any moment and do greater harm to his girls. Deodat Lawson seemed ready to believe his wife and child were murdered by diabolical means in their parish. And Parris could not prove otherwise.

Parris, in a rush, gave in to an unstoppable impulse to protect the girls and he secretly dashed off a letter to Elizabeth's cousin Stephen Sewell in Salem Town. Could he take the girls?

Yes, came the reply, but only one of them. For the good of the family, Parris chose Betty.

"Why, Samuel?" Elizabeth Parris had cried. The betrayed look on her face, when he told her Betty was going away was fading after the first shock of it. Her eyes were turning icy. He realized if she refused him, he might lose Elizabeth's support.

Tears welled from him, a man who boasted of never crying. "I don't see a better way to protect at least one of them.

"How will this protect her?"

He had no clear answer for her in this confusing miasma so he offered his best hope as a reason. "She will be better able to find peace far from this turmoil."

Elizabeth closed her eyes and shook her head. "I shall worry for her every moment she is there."

"And I am sick of worrying for her here. I cannot carry on my duties to our people with her illness weighing on me." He wanted to add, on top of your poor health, but bit his lip. "I must push on with my work and help root out the witch infestation as the Lord wills."

"Then I shall go with her."

"No. I must have you with me; else I shall be lost. And besides, Abigail remains. She will need you as a comfort and a model for her behavior."

Elizabeth had never failed to follow his guidance as God's appointed leader of the family. But he was not confident she would if he expressly demanded obedience. Thank God she consented.

Parris broke from his musing and returned to the present, overhearing Mr. Corwin speaking to Hathorne. "We likely will have another full house today, and we must be on guard against trouble. Our friend informed me that many from Rebecca Nurse's family and friends do not believe she could ever join with Satan."

"Who are they to presume there are no sinners among those whose piety is well known?" Hathorne said. He seemed to be considering a further response but instead drained the last of his beer. "We shall see."

They departed for the meetinghouse.

The constables had become more efficient. When the magistrates took their seats, Rebecca Nurse was already standing before the communion table. Even after several days in custody, someone dressed her as if she would attend Sunday services.

When she reached for Marshal Herrick, grabbing his arm for support, Parris fought an urge to leap to her aid. At seventy-one, Rebecca stood tall, but she was fragile and thin. Her attire draped from her shoulders without an untoward crease or bulge.

She had not looked at Parris or the magistrates when they entered. And he was grateful for it. She kept her parchment-like hands folded while she murmured a prayer.

Parris gave the invocation, asking for divine guidance for the magistrates and petitioning Him for grace upon Rebecca so she would speak true whether innocent or guilty. As he took his seat, Parris reminded himself: in all these cases he also had to trust in God's unfathomable will. He pictured Cotton Mather nodding approval.

Hathorne rapped the table for attention. "Rebecca Nurse, wife of Francis Nurse, you are charged for detestable acts upon the bodies of Ann Putnam, Mary Walcott, Elizabeth Hubbard, and Abigail Williams, on the complaint of Edward Putnam, and Jonathan, son of John Putnam. How do you answer?"

She looked at the marshal beside her. "I cannot hear all of his words."

"Answer that you are not a witch," Herrick said.

People still pushed in through the doorway, and Hathorne craned his neck to see if they left any room. "Constable, split those outside into groups of ten. Every hour remove ten from the rear bench and bring in ten more."

To Parris, Hathorne said, "Since it is Thursday and Lecture night, I will make certain we vacate the premises in time for you to clean up for services tonight."

The meetinghouse door closed with a thump, and Hathorne perused the four afflicted girls to his right. As usual, one or two were in constant motion, whispering, touching back and forth and bursting out babble at inappropriate moments.

He tapped the table and addressed the afflicted ones. "What do you say, children? Have you seen this woman Rebecca Nurse hurt you?"

"Yes, she beat me this morning," little Ann cried out.

"Oh, and she hurts me now!" said Abigail.

When Abigail collapsed, Ann pointed at the accused woman. "It is Rebecca Nurse who afflicts me."

As the room erupted, Parris sensed the marvelous ways of the Lord to use a child such as Ann Putnam to turn out unseen forces of evil. She spoke so convincingly against the first witches, and now boldly accused a woman considered saintly by many.

He noticed Hathorne was not stifling the outburst. The pouches under his eyes seemed darker, and his shoulders were slumping. Instead of asserting control as he had done throughout the hearings, he allowed the crowd to react after little Ann's outburst. At last, he tapped for order and addressed the marshal while pointing at Abigail on the floor. "Herrick, take her outside for air."

The taciturn marshal carried Abigail Williams like she was a royal. The other children watched without a whimper.

"Goody Nurse, there are two, Ann Putnam and Abigail Williams, who charge you with hurting them. What do you say to it?"

Goody Nurse cupped one hand over an ear and reached for support again. But she was standing alone.

Parris hoped the magistrate would be gentle with the matron. She was a delicate witness, and not to be abused in the dock. But he was as much or more worried about any reaction in her defense from her supporters present in the room.

Mr. Hathorne repeated the question with more force.

"I can say before my eternal Father I am innocent."

"All in this assembly desires it. But if you be guilty, pray God we shall discover the truth."

Some of Rebecca Nurse's supporters started shuffling their feet and grumbling.

The magistrate waited for them to settle before continuing with his interrogation. "Not only these children, but the wife of Goodman Thomas Putnam accuses you by credible information of tempting her to iniquity and hurting her."

"It cannot be, for I have not been out of doors for more than a week."

Hathorne shuffled sheets of paper. "Edward Putnam, are you among us?" Putnam stood to show his presence. "Have you seen with your eyes these children call out the prisoner's name?"

"Aye, I have. She tormented them."

Rebecca Nurse shrugged her shoulders and again cupped a hand behind one ear.

Hathorne pointed at the afflicted ones while raising his voice. "You can see these who accuse you; is it true? Or are you an innocent in relation to this witchcraft?"

Tituba was following the proceedings from her jail cell. She had contented herself to listen rather than watch from afar or attend. It required less energy and she needed the rest.

But Hathorne's last question had captured her attention, and she joined them from afar. The soft expression on his face confirmed her worry. He seemed to suggest the old woman should answer with a believable alibi.

Tituba could not take the chance the village's prominent citizen might make a case for her innocence. Rebecca had to fall. And so, Tituba made a hasty decision to attend the proceeding, ready to intercede and manufacture whatever proof was necessary to show Goody Nurse was one of Satan's familiars.

Tituba took the appearance of a farmer and blended in among the people watching, taking a place along the rear wall of the courtroom. She waited like a leopard ready to ambush its prey.

When Goody Putnam, sitting in the second pew burst out, "Goody Nurse, did you not bring the black man with you? Did you not bid me to tempt God?" She shrieked, "How often have you ate and drank your damnation?"

Every eye turned on Goody Nurse to observe how she answered and they saw an old woman seemingly unwilling to speak in her own defense.

Tituba's coiled tension eased as she realized Ann Putnam's mind, whether filled by wild imagination or deep melancholia, helped to damn Rebecca.

She relished the unwitting help, supposing Ann might be driven by fear for her daughter's safety. She knew how a mother of an afflicted child might feel.

Tituba shook her head to clear any inkling of sympathy. None of them had cared for Tituba's anguish at her son's fate.

She would make further use of Goody Putnam to stir the pot of credulity among those English. The woman had proven herself a convincing witness.

When Ann Putnam retched as if to vomit, her husband asked permission to escort her home.

"Permission granted, Goodman."

The assembly hushed as if in reverence for the unhappy soul as she left them.

Tituba knew Parris' mannerisms as he tried to hide his emotions, dabbing his eyes only when he thought everyone was watching Goody Putnam. At the sight of him Tituba's anger spiked. Where was his milk of compassion for her and Skitôp during their son's misery and senseless death?

Parris and the magistrates, every one of them, were eager for the safety of the precious afflicted English children. But they dismissed any feelings of compassion for the accused women, assuming their guilt. She eyed the assemblage contemptuously, willing as they were to sacrifice their own to appease their god.

A large man sitting among the Nurse family spoke to the stilled room. "This interrogation concerns the least likely one to act witchcraft." He stared intensely at Parris and the magistrates as if to emphasize his judgment of them as simpletons.

Tituba kept the large man in view, alert for the smallest sign from him or any others that she needed to intercede.

Mr. Corwin summoned Parris to the bench and whispered to him and Hathorne. "That one carries a petition signed by forty people swearing Goody Nurse is no witch."

Hathorne cleared his throat and banged on the table. "There will be time after the hearing to consider the petition in proper order." His stare dared anyone to talk back.

Fear retook the floor when someone shouted, "She hurts children." Rebecca Nurse collapsed as if she'd been shot dead.

As she lay there, another person yelled, "Stand her up to face justice, Mr. Hathorne."

Grumbling was rising as the marshal came back into the room with Abigail Williams in hand. He helped revive Rebecca and helped her stand.

The old woman held up one hand. "Oh Lord, help me!"

She repeated her prayer, "Help me." And her feeble voice provoked further unsettled expressions in the room until Hathorne demanded silence.

"Now. Mary Walcott and Elizabeth Hubbard, come and stand before me."

Then to Rebecca Nurse he said, "Listen to these two grown persons who accuse you."

Walcott rubbed her arms. "Help me! She is biting me, pinching and… I cannot breathe." She fell hard to her knees. With a breathy voice she said, "There, a black man whispers to Goody Nurse whilst her yellow bird suckles on her."

Elizabeth Hubbard stepped forward. "Goody Nurse came to me this morning. She pinched me with pins, and she demanded I write in her book or else suffer death at her hand."

Elizabeth staggered toward the magistrates. "She hurt me most greviously. And—and—and said she need but look upon me to strike me down. She made me watch as she hurt Goody Putnam and Mary Walcott and Abigail Williams!"

"Rebecca Nurse," Hathorne said, "it is awful for us amidst these agonies to have you, a professor of our faith, charged with doing work for the Devil. But here you stand with dry eyes where so many others are crying in sympathy."

"You do not know my heart. The Lord knows… I have not hurt them."

Parris was shaking his head as he wrote as if denying the truth of the old woman's statement. And Tituba knew he had convinced himself Goody Nurse was lying and had committed evil acts in front of everyone.

Hathorne shouted at Nurse, "You know whether you are guilty of becoming a familiar of the Devil, and now these afflicted ones testify that a black man is whispering in your ear, and there are yellow birds near you. What do you say to it?"

When she bowed her head, he shouted again. "Give me a forthright answer. Have you any familiarity with these spirits?"

"No. I have none but with God alone."

Rebecca's eyelids hooded her watery blue eyes, but they opened wider as if she came awake to her peril. "It is all false. I am blameless." She raised her hands to her lips, trying to stop their quivering.

Hathorne gave her a moment to recover and his tone became soothing. "Is it possible you may have been led aside by temptations?"

Tituba tensed again, ready to act.

"I have not."

From the near part of the room, a shuffling noise drew attention to Bathshua Pope. She was red-faced and sweating so hard her face was dripping despite the chill that made others wear coats. "I have been to each examination, and those children speak true. I feel evil is here."

Bathshua Pope stood on her assigned pew, brandishing her shoe. She threw it forward. It sailed in a lazy arc and hit Rebecca Nurse flush in the face.

As Pope dashed from the stunned room, Tituba wondered if Goody Nurse's supporters might rise at the further indignity. But they remained in their places, seemingly waiting for higher authority to intervene.

How like sheep they are, she thought. Ready to be led to slaughter.

Hathorne's voice pulled Tituba's attention back. "Tell us, Gamer Nurse, have you had visible appearances of the black man?"

"Never."

"Do you think these afflicted here accuse you falsely?"

"I cannot tell."

"That is a strange reply. If you think they speak falsely, you must look upon them as murderers of you and the others!"

"I cannot tell what to think of it—"

A fresh accusation shot down from the gallery. "Look, she calls them murderers!"

Rebecca's composure broke, and she cried, "All I say is I cannot *tell* what to make of that conduct." She reached for the magistrates as if to touch their hearts. "Please, can I go from here, sir? I am so fatigued."

"First tell me. Do you believe these children are bewitched?"

She lowered her outstretched arm. "I think… they are afflicted, yes, by an evildoer, not me."

Tituba suspected Hathorne might see reasonable doubt that an old sickly woman could sneak around, afflicting people in person. To help him plow on, Tituba planted a thought in him to address the spectral attacks.

"When this witchcraft came upon the stage, there was no suspicion of anyone. But it was their apparitions did the mischief: and why shouldn't you also be guilty if your apparition hurts them, too?"

"Would you have me contradict myself? I can only speak the truth!" Rebecca wiped her eyes and clasped her hands. "I am as innocent of this sin as an unborn child." She paused and seemed to be searching for an answer. "Perhaps God has found some unrepented sin in me, that He has laid an affliction on me by these accusations."

Stillness settled over the room. It reminded Tituba of the earth after a storm. Rebecca's answer that she was in peril because of some unknown sin, sank into the roomful of people like rainwater soaking into the ground. They glanced around at their neighbors. Who among them could be without sin? And if God willed they should be accused, it was the divine order of things. Tituba felt a kinship with their god, as she considered the foolishness of their illusions.

Hathorne regained their attention. "Reverend Parris, read this statement from Thomas Putnam relating to his wife's recurring affliction."

Parris' face glowed. He cleared his throat and read with emotion, dramatizing the statement. "Goody Putnam says, 'Martha Corey and Rebecca Nurse descended on me and pressed the breath from me a week ago. Except for the grace of God, I should have died.'"

Parris glanced up from reading the statement like he did when reading God's word from the pulpit, to confirm he was being heard. "The following day the apparition of Rebecca Nurse again set on me in the early morning, dressed only in her shift. And she brought a little red book, urging me to write my name in it. But I did not yield, even though she threatened to tear my soul out."

Hathorne spoke to Goody Nurse. "One more time, Rebecca. What think you of this and other accusations? Is it your apparition hurting people?"

"I cannot help it: the Devil may appear in my shape."

With this statement Hathorne and Corwin huddled for a moment. He turned back to the accused woman. "Upon hearing the aforesaid, and seeing what we then did, together with the charges of the persons present, we have no choice but to commit Rebecca Nurse, the wife of Francis Nurse of Salem Village, unto Her Majesty's jail in Salem." He banged the table hard. "If she is saintly, a jury will set her free of the charges."

The end of the hearing thrilled Tituba. Was there anyone whom she could not capture in service to her needs? This power to enslave them swelled her sense of wrath—and satisfaction.

She almost returned to her cell to gloat, but for a reason she could not explain, she stayed to watch the elderly woman hobble away in her chains. At the doorway Rebecca stopped to allow a four-year-old Dorothy Good into the meetinghouse.

The child was leading a vexed-looking guard who said, "Mr. Hathorne, this is Dorothy Good, presented for examination. She is the daughter of Sarah Good, already in custody."

Tituba had forgotten about Dorothy Good, having done nothing to arouse suspicion of her. The elation of only an instant ago drained away.

The guard took the child's hand and held her in place before the communion table.

A lurch in Tituba's stomach told her not to watch, but she could not help herself.

Hathorne spoke to Ann Putnam. "Come forward, child, and testify again."

When Ann approached, Dorothy said, "Hello, Annie."

"I was abed in my room and Dorothy appeared. She pinched and bit and choked me. She begged I should sign her mother's book."

Mr. Hathorne turned from Ann and spoke to a matron in the front row. "Did you find a mark from the Devil on Dorothy?"

The matron stood. "We searched her and discovered between her ring and little finger a red swelling showing a witch's teat."

Dorothy interjected. "A little snake bit me."

"Where did you get this snake?" Hathorne said.

"Mother gave it to me."

Mr. Hathorne gaveled for order. "Witches beget witches. She travels and hurts by specter and has indicia of a familiar of Satan."

Hathorne continued questioning for a while and then bound her over to wait in jail with her mother, as coolly as a butcher gutting a pig.

A wave of revulsion lapped at Tituba, but she squelched it viciously. They had taken her child, hadn't they? Why should she care for this girl's fate?

Chapter Twenty-one

When Parris entered the meetinghouse, it was pitch dark outside. The magistrates had finished late, and an elderly deacon was sweeping loose mud and dirt to prepare for Mr. Lawson's lecture. The guest minister was sitting on the first step to the pulpit, head in hands. He looked up at Parris and they acknowledged each other with a nod.

Parris arranged a dozen fresh candles to illuminate the service, checking his fellow minister as he read his lesson notes.

"How goes it, Brother Lawson?"

"I have been praying for help that I shall be faithful to Scripture for today's lecture, but I confess my discovery of the murder of my wife and child… Samuel, I want to seize each suspect and shake them until they confess."

Parris took a seat in the first row of the benches as Lawson continued. "I once read words of Cotton Mather, 'And if innocent persons be suspected, it is God's providence as the Supreme Being and Satan's malice. Be at peace with the will of the almighty Creator.' But how elusive is that blessed peace?"

Lawson stared at Parris as if hoping for an answer to the eternal question. But Parris, so filled was he with his own issues, was not inclined to offer an empty platitude in reply.

After long moments, Lawson continued. "Tonight, I shall tell them whosoever among us sees diabolical happenings must speak out against the satanic operations with the greatest force so we may punish the guilty."

"Aye, brother. The greatest force will lead to peace." A window inside him opened a crack. And a tease of incoming air offered the possibility of clearing his doubt over God's will, and his role in carrying it out.

Parris remained with Lawson in companionable silence. How sweet if the sermon tonight brought him closer to God's will.

When Lawson returned to making several notes on his sermon, Parris left to fetch his family and return in time to open the meetinghouse door for the faithful.

Reverend Noyes and Reverend Hale along with the magistrates arrived first, and they sat together just beneath the pulpit. After covenanted members claimed their pews, nonmembers from the village and beyond took the remaining places.

Each week since these troubling times began, more had come for services seeking answers, and tonight prayerful people filled every inch of space. The size of the crowd pleased Parris, and he tried to memorize some of the new faces. He'd visit them after these upsetting days were past.

When Lawson began, he preached for an hour with measured control until he faltered for a moment.

Parris tipped his head forward; did his friend need help to continue?

Lawson nodded to Parris as if to show he was still in command. "It is amazing to me that anyone gives their name to serve the Devil.

"But if you join with the Dragon, our all-knowing God will thunder, 'Depart from me. You are cursed into the eternal fire prepared for the devil and his angels.' Matthew twenty-five: forty-one.

"There will come Judgement Day sooner than you might wish. So, hear me, now. If you have not confessed and returned to our love, you will spend eternity in the fire of Hell."

He then turned attention to the victims. Their suffering and pain must be recognized as they fought off the witches' physical attacks. "God commands us to give compassion to those afflicted persons. They endure the Devil's assaults by Divine permission though it may seem impossible to understand."

From the first row of pews to the last, heads nodded agreement. No one doubted the suffering children.

After a long pause, during which every eye came to settle on the preacher, Lawson held both arms out to the assembly. He almost shouted as he continued. "And so, today I am commanded by God to sound the alarm. Arm yourselves with vengeance! Take up the sword of God to better serve Him. Admit no fear of doing justice to those who do evil."

This was righteous. Lawson knew these parts far better than anyone in Boston's high pulpit. This exhortation laid out the solid ground Parris needed. Admit no parley to end this grief. He inhaled deeply at the relief he felt, resolving to follow Lawson's route until they overpowered the invasion. We must not suffer witches to live. Exodus twenty-two: eighteen.

And then Lawson leaned forward, looking directly at the officials in the front row. "Honorable magistrates here to inquire into truth and falsity, you have a sacred duty beyond the king's business. Permit me to suggest you also have a duty to act in harmony with God's demand. Bear the righteous sword of heaven as you check the forces of darkness and end the suffering of every afflicted person."

Yes, Parris would join them. They will vanquish Satan with the might of the law. He would keep faith with the Almighty by helping the magistrates find and punish every familiar of the Devil. This was his chance to lead his flock once more with certainty.

On Sunday morning Parris was ready to build upon Deodat Lawson's inspired preaching. When he took the pulpit, the room was silent as he opened his great Bible and read from it. "And Jesus answered them, 'Have not I chosen you twelve, and one of you is a devil?' John 6.

"At this moment, our Savior knows who the witches are, and they are now awaiting our revenge!"

Parris squinted at those seated below him and then slowly gazed across the main floor and up into the galleries to draw every eye. His confidence returned, a fervent pastor once more. He looked at the empty seat reserved for Rebecca Nurse. "Even a saint can become a devil."

Sarah Cloyce, Rebecca Nurse's sister, was sitting in her pew with Mary Esty, another Nurse sister. She said something meant only for Mary while rising to her feet and then rushing toward the door of the meetinghouse. She heaved it open so hard, it tore from her hand and banged like a gunshot upon hitting the wall and then again as it slammed shut.

"How dare she interrupt the pastor," Bathshua Pope declared. But Parris accepted the exit as a sign his words had struck home as he intended. Yes, there are devils….

At the end of the service, before dismissing the congregation for their midday meal, he called forward Mary Sibley. Cotton Mather had advised him to show the church's power to recover lost souls and he had promised his benefactor to offer forgiveness when appropriate. Although Mary's sin did not go so far as a pact with the Devil, he could say he'd offered her forgiveness for her role if Mather asked.

Parris descended from the pulpit and stood next to her. "Everyone knows some in our village have been tormented. The suffering progressed without us suspecting it, before Mary directed a satanic method to discover a witch. Since then many specters have arisen and worked the Devil's business."

His anger swelled, and he welcomed it. This fool Sibley, no matter the original pettiness of her offense, he was living with the present chaos.

Parris swallowed his disgust at the simpleton and kept his voice modulated. "Now, Sister Sibley, will you beg Almighty God and your fellows of our covenant to forgive you?"

Mary tearfully begged forgiveness, and the church voted to accept her back into communion.

Was Mary Sibley's renunciation of her sin a first step to reaching the more debauched souls and reclaiming them? He doubted it. For those who hurt others and tempted them to renounce God, the hangman seemed more and more the best solution.

In jail, Sarah Good, Sarah Osborne, Martha Corey, and Rebecca Nurse might have found a renewed hope for forgiveness had they known of the leniency shown to Mary Sibley, but they knew nothing. Nor would it have mattered because they could not admit to what they were at a loss to explain.

In the darkness of the unheated cells they remained on meager rations of food and water and subject to strip searches at all hours. The jailor's wife and her matron helpers looked for signs of witch's teats, proof the accused ones had suckled Satan's familiars. The humiliated prisoners returned to their cell, limping, dragging the eight-pound leg irons hopelessly.

Tituba was chained among them, though she avoided meeting anyone's eyes. She shielded herself from their troubles by keeping her head bowed and remaining silent. They wanted nothing to do with a black slave, in any case.

Lately, she had been feeling a heightened sense of sorrow, a melancholy riding in alternating waves between her greatest loss, Akanni, and something else she could not place. Each time her distress arose, she steeled herself against it. Her tasks demanded an icy heart and unbending fury. Recalling what the English had done replenished both.

The fear Tituba had sown inside the parsonage and then the village was gaining a momentum, not a person could stop talking about the invasion. Yet with that success, she could not help feeling a touch of pity for that kindly old woman, Rebecca Nurse. For the first time, her heart asked, should she better control the spiraling accusations? Was that even possible?

Against her will, she remembered how just that morning during a light slumber, she again saw the feet suspended from the village tree. The hem of the white shift billowed like sails. She had tried to avoid the sight, but the scene expanded into a wider perspective as if she was standing farther away. And she saw four, then five and more swollen faces: eyelids opened to empty sockets, necks bent to the side, their red tongues protruding out of their mouths.

The image shifted to the ground below the bodies. In the shade a child looked up from drawing in the dirt. It laughed and said, "Look at Mama!" The high-pitched laugh changed from giddiness to a shriek as a tiny blue baby descended from a body above, lowered by a shiny blackened umbilical cord. Down it inched until the wrinkled figure dropped free. Tituba squinted as if doing so could give a better view: was it a girl?

But upon hitting the ground, it burst open, covering the child and everything else in a wet sheet of dark blood.

That image made Tituba shudder violently. Immediately, she pulled the slop bucket to herself and retched to vomit. But after emptying mere drops of sour liquid, she talked to herself. Think only of Akanni. The dream meant nothing. She must have been thinking how much the Puritans liked to mete out punishment.

Drowsiness arose from just behind her eyes, where it always seemed to linger, and she allowed it to envelop her.

The hard work of enchantment robbed her of energy, never allowing her to regain full strength, even as she felt the pressure to do more. That must be it; she was tired.

On Monday, April 4, a visitor to Martha Corey, now a fellow prisoner, told them Captain Jonathan Walcott, Mary's father, and Nathaniel Ingersoll, the tavern keeper, had filed complaints against Elizabeth Proctor, the pregnant wife of John Proctor. She had been arrested and was scheduled to appear in front of Mr. Hathorne.

Tituba felt numb as she eavesdropped. Goodman Proctor had failed to back away when she tried to warn him about scoffing at the afflicted ones' cries. He had instead become more vocal.

Perhaps, though she hadn't directly targeted Goody Procter, this blow might make John Proctor keep his mouth shut.

Just then her cell door opened. The jailor announced that an Indian servant had come to see her. All thoughts of the Proctors and the witches disappeared. Skitôp? Here?

Tituba touched her filthy cap to straighten it as her Skitôp entered, carrying a half-filled sack. She held her arms to him as he knelt and embraced her. "Are you well, husband?"

Skitôp answered by squeezing more tightly. Then he dropped a coin into the jailor's hand and the man left them.

"I brought clean clothes for you, and fresh bread."

She struggled to unfasten her grimy blouse, but her vision blurred and the ties were knotted. He helped her tenderly, careful not to tear the worn fabric.

Tituba could not keep her eyes off him. And she thought he looked as if he had a secret to tell.

"This month and last, they have cried out against a total near to thirty witches. Plus, the master says it will not be long before they file more complaints for the magistrates to hear."

He glanced at the other prisoners, but they had scarcely moved since he arrived. The proximity of both an Indian and a slave must have overwhelmed them. "On Sunday last, I joined in with the accusers!" he whispered.

Tituba's joy at seeing him dissolved.

"They are crazy, and they will kill themselves over the witch foolishness. I joined in with the accusers against Goody Cloyce."

He looked at the women chained to the walls. "Can they hear me?"

"No." Tituba caressed his face while shaking her head. A new sensation grew. Panic. Though she did not want to know what he had done, she asked. "Tell me what happened."

"I saw them acting up as they sang the Psalms, and I dove into the center aisle and rolled halfway to the pulpit. I shouted out, 'She bites me! Goody Cloyce descends on me and tears at me as I pray!'" He held out his wrist to show Tituba scab marks where he had cut himself to prove the injury. "And the people called to their holy god for help."

He smiled at her proudly, but she could not muster one for him. How could she have overlooked the possibility Skitôp would find a way to use the spiritual disruptions for his own gain?

She could not allow him to get further involved. Her plan demanded absolute secrecy, and not the least of the many reasons was to keep him safe. If Skitôp got wind of her involvement, he would demand to join her efforts with increased vigor. But if she allowed it, he surely would act without her knowledge or control, endangering the plan and himself. For herself, she did not care, having launched the plot with her spectral creations and admission of witchcraft, but she would not sacrifice Skitôp.

"Soon," he boasted, "every one of them will be an accused witch and in the confusion I shall find you and we shall run."

Chapter Twenty-two

A week before Sarah Cloyce's and Elizabeth Proctor's hearings, word came from the colonial government. They had selected Deputy Governor Thomas Danforth to preside, and he would sit in Salem Town instead of the village. Danforth, a sixty-nine-year-old politician, always sensitive to avoid potential hard feelings, ordered that Mr. Hathorne and Mr. Corwin should sit the bench with him.

On April 11, the afflicted girls arrived at Salem Town's large meetinghouse, having traveled the eight and a half miles together in a large wagon. The passengers had nestled together in the wagon bed for warmth as it bumped over the road in predawn darkness. Tituba loomed nearby as Little Ann poked a snoring Abigail. "Will Betty be with us again?"

Abigail pushed Ann off and squeezed her eyes tight. "I don't know."

"Will she meet us there?"

"I don't know! Let me sleep."

When the girls arrived, Mr. Danforth was speaking to Parris near a large communion table adapted into a judges' bench. "Be certain to record testimony as spoken. Do not summarize. I know some are prone to do it."

Danforth broke off as the marshal escorted the girls into the meetinghouse. "Take them into the small room, there. Keep them sequestered until I call each one."

It surprised Tituba to see Skitôp already in the hall, behind Parris. Her initial pleasure at seeing him gave way to a heightened dread he might interfere. What had he told them, and what might they want from him now? She took a corporeal form and mingled with those crowded in a gallery above and off to the side of the judges, posing as a hooded, disheveled man stinking of pig manure. That visage guaranteed others would avoid standing near her. Tituba overheard people saying that they had come from Boston, Beverly, Andover, even Maine.

Once they shut the doors, Danforth called for the prisoners.

Sarah Cloyce and Elizabeth Proctor entered, helping each other walk as they lugged their shackles. The scrapes and rattles of the metal links seemed to settle the several hundred present in the meetinghouse.

Reverend Higginson led prayers, assisted in part by Parris. Deputy Governor Danforth read the charges aloud. Next, he spoke to Parris sitting at the end of the makeshift judges' bench. "Is he here? Your Indian man?"

"Yes, there." Parris pointed at Skitôp with his quill and returned to writing.

Danforth addressed the witness, dressed in his blue servant's work clothes. "John, who hurt you?"

"Goody Proctor, first."

Tituba's pulse picked up as she leaned to catch every word. What was he going to say?

"What did Goody Proctor do to you?"

"She choked me and brought the book."

"How often did she torment you?"

"Many times. And with Goody Cloyse. They took hold upon my throat—"

Sarah Cloyce shouted, "When did I hurt thee?"

"Many times."

"Oh, you are a grievous liar!" Cloyce retorted.

Skitôp scratched the side of his head, as Tituba knew he did when nervous. The roomful of people stirred at the exchange between the prisoner and the witness, but Tituba ignored it, fearfully awaiting what else he might say.

Husband, say no more, she thought.

Danforth rapped his gavel, and the room quieted.

"What did Goody Cloyce do to you?"

"She pinched and bit me till blood came. At the meetinghouse, and many times before."

Skitôp, do not lie so. They will catch you in it, and they will punish you.

Abandoning her fear of being noticed, Tituba the pig farmer shouted, "We now need savages to bear witness against our white women? They too are from the Devil."

Danforth seemed to consider the remark fair enough, and he squinted at John Indian. "Stand aside for now." He waved his arm. "Bring in Mary Walcott and Abigail Williams."

Abigail held onto Mary's hand with both of hers as they entered, gazing out at the multitude. Mary was trembling and contorted her face, squeezing her eyes shut as she stood before Danforth.

"Mary Walcott, who hurts you?"

"Goody Cloyce."

"What has she done to you?"

"She hurt me and brought the book."

"What were you to do?"

"To touch it and be well." Mary wrapped her arms around herself, shivering so hard she barely remained standing.

Seeing this, Danforth ordered the marshal to take the girl's arm. "Bring her to Goody Cloyce. Have her touch the sleeve of the accused, and let us see if it relieves her."

When Mary touched Sarah Cloyce's arm, to the awe of every soul in attendance, she calmed and opened her eyes. Dark power was in full view and onlookers murmured. Danforth silenced them with his gavel.

"Now, child, tell me. Is she alone in bringing the book to you?"

"Sometimes alone, and sometimes with Goody Nurse and Goody Corey, and a great many I do not know."

As more murmuring arose, Danforth shot the crowd a sharp glare, but then he looked at Abigail Williams standing at Mary's side. "Have you seen a company of people at the parsonage eating and drinking?"

"Yes, and our blood was their sacrament."

"How many in number?"

"Forty at least, and Goody Cloyse and Goody Good were deacons."

Danforth leaned backward in his high-backed chair, seemingly oblivious of the credulous chattering from the pews. The magistrates along the bench huddled around him. And after a tense, red-faced discussion they decided this new mention of a throng of witches demanded deeper investigation.

"Mary Walcott, have you seen a white man among them?"

"Yes, a great many times. He was a fine grave man, and, when he came, he made all the witches tremble." She paused before adding, "We all saw him." She looked to Abigail, who nodded agreement.

"Among them at the sacrament, are any already in our custody?"

"Goody Cloyse, Goody Nurse, Goody Corey, and Goody Good."

Sarah Cloyce reeled as if she might collapse. "May I have a drink of water?"

Mr. Danforth permitted it and someone brought a cup, but before it touched her lips, the girls broke into spasms as though being beaten. One of them cried, "And there is the black man whispering in Goody Cloyse's ear."

The cup of water clattered to the floor and Cloyce collapsed.

Danforth was shouting over the din as he banged for order. "Sit her there on the side pew."

After the room calmed again, Danforth said he'd heard enough about Goody Cloyce. "Bring forward Elizabeth Proctor."

Goody Proctor had been standing just to the side of Sarah Cloyce, head bowed until the mention of her name. As she approached, she looked back past the heads and shoulders of those on the main floor, as if searching. Her mouth hung open until she located her husband standing at the back near the doorway.

Tituba stared at Elizabeth Proctor's hands, which she clasped under her pregnant belly.

"Elizabeth Proctor, look here." Danforth leaned forward across the bench. "What say you to the charge of sundry acts of witchcraft?"

Elizabeth pursed her lips and glanced at the wet spot on the floor from Goody Cloyce's spilled water.

"Speak truthfully!" He waited, but she endured her disgrace in silence.

Danforth drummed his fingers. "Very well, stand there and ponder your answer while we hear from the remaining afflicted children."

When the other afflicted ones joined the first two girls, all of them fidgeted as Danforth cautioned them, "You must speak the truth when I ask you, or answer before God another day."

Suddenly, John Proctor caused a commotion from his spot in the rear. Two men restrained him.

Danforth ignored the brief ruckus. "Mary Walcott. Does this woman hurt you?" He pointed at Goody Proctor.

"I never saw her."

Mr. Danforth's bushy eyebrows shot up. "But you say Sarah Cloyce hurts you!"

"But not Goody Proctor."

Danforth took a breath before turning to Mercy Lewis. "Does she hurt you?"

Mercy showed him a dumbfounded face.

"Ann Putnam, does she hurt you?"

She did not respond.

"Doth the Devil stop their voices?" Danforth wiped his face and looked to his colleagues.

Parris got Danforth's attention and speaking to his niece, pointed at Goody Proctor. "Abigail, does she hurt you?"

Abigail stared at her uncle and the men on the bench, fingers in her mouth.

Tituba broke her distracted observation of the pregnant woman. The silence of the girls surprised her as much as anyone. She searched for a spectral image to somehow prod Abigail and the others into responding.

Restless feet registered and mumbling arose. Parris addressed all of the judges. "If you might re-call John Indian, he may have something else to say."

Tituba abandoned her hurried thoughts at the mention of Skitôp's name. First, before anything she had to protect him.

Then she noticed Parris' pained expression, and she understood he was grasping blindly for time, to allow Danforth the chance to regain control of the hearing. Tituba relaxed to watch him struggle, enjoying his discomfort as he furthered his own punishment.

How ironic to watch Parris participate in her plan, that vile tormentor who had sold her son into distant slavery and death. It was a bitter pleasure, so much that Tituba momentarily forgot the need to prod the girls, or safeguard Skitôp.

"John, does Goody Proctor hurt you?" Parris prompted.

"Yes, she came in her shift and choked me."

Parris smiled tautly, but Danforth took control of the examination by asking, "Did she ever bring the book?"

"Yes."

At the answer, Danforth scratched his scalp, perhaps remembering the admonition not to rely on a savage's testimony. "What do you say, Goody Procter? Ready to speak?"

"I take God to be my witness that I know nothing, no more than this unborn child inside me."

Tituba shot another look at the pregnant woman's belly.

Mr. Danforth leaned toward Hathorne, and Tituba extended herself to hear. "I am told one, Sarah Good, gave birth to her child in prison, where it died." He squirmed. "For what reasons have I convened this council? To place pregnant women in prison?"

Mr. Hathorne put his hand on Danforth's arm, assuring the senior man of the righteousness of their cause. He aimed a question to little Ann Putnam. "Doth this woman hurt you?" He softened his voice as if to cajole the answer he wanted.

Before speaking, Ann looked over to her father and mother sitting nearby. Breaking eye contact with them, she said, "Yes, sir. Often, and she says she hath bade her maid, Mary Warren, set her own hand to the book." Ann looked back at her parents and then the magistrates with what seemed a half-smile.

Tituba hadn't expected any mention of Mary Warren, nor the conspiratorial look on Ann's face. Mary Warren? Tituba had done nothing to involve the Proctors' maid. What was Ann Putnam's motive for bringing up Mary Warren?

But no matter, Tituba reminded herself. Her avenue was the way of terror, and any way it spread was acceptable, was it not? Tituba rubbed the back of her neck. There it was again, that anxious tingle come to annoy her as it had when she watched the pregnant woman before the magistrates.

Ever since the night Sarah Good gave birth to her baby in the constant sorrow of prison, shushing the infant to a sleep from which it never awoke, Tituba had confronted every inkling of compassion. She could not give up anger to make room for compassion. No exceptions.

After Ann's reference to Mary Warren, Tituba thought back over her recent activities. Not more than a week before, she had considered Mary as a target. What a powerful witness Mary would have made against John Proctor; a servant who saw and heard everything in a household. But Tituba hadn't yet committed to move on Mary. She massaged her neck again.

Danforth's booming voice drew Tituba back to the proceedings. "Why have they not mentioned Mary Warren before today? Did she do anything to hurt others?"

Parris remained hunched over his papers, likely hoping Danforth's question was not asking him for an answer.

No one spoke up. And to no one in particular Danforth said, "Rest assured, we shall return to that question in a moment. But I shall hear more from Abigail Williams. Come forward, child."

Abigail obeyed but kept her eyes glued on the floor.

"Now you tell me, does this woman Goody Proctor hurt you? Does she bring the book to you?"

"Yes," she whispered, "to write in it and I shall be well." And then, as if whirled by a burst of wind she shrieked at Elizabeth Proctor. "Did you not tell me that your maid, Mary Warren, had written in the book also?"

Goody Proctor answered, her tone like a patient correcting mother. "Dear child, it is not so. Remember, child, there is another judgment for everyone."

At the rebuke a sheen on Abigail's pink face glowed. But then she jerked her head toward the ceiling, screaming, "Look! There is Goody Procter sitting upon the beam."

John Procter howled like a man watching a rip tide pull his drowning wife out to sea. He leapt into the center aisle. "Shut your mouth!" he screamed.

Then little Ann Putnam cried out, "He too is a wizard. John Proctor is a wizard."

John Proctor howled louder and took a step toward the bench but two burly men pulled him into their pew.

"Restrain that man in chains if he speaks again unbidden by me!" Danforth ordered. The judge motioned little Ann forward again. "Ann Putnam, who hurts you?"

"Goodman Procter and his wife, and look, they are taking Goody Pope's feet!"

At which, Bathshua Pope screamed and climbed on the bench in her pew.

Proctor shouted again, "I am John Procter and I know not what these—these… whatever they are have spoken. Like *all* those called out I am innocent of this sin, and these silly girls need a sturdy green branch."

Danforth shouted back, "The Devil can deceive us from the apparition, but these children are seeing what you are about to do."

Danforth pounded the gavel, hitting it harder each time until two constables seized Proctor and pushed him from the hall.

Parris stood as Thomas Putnam approached him. The men whispered and Parris addressed the magistrates. "Goodman Thomas Putnam has asked the court to permit his wife to speak."

Danforth raised his eyebrows. "About what?"

"She has news of John Proctor."

Goody Putnam came forward after Danforth granted permission.

"John Proctor has most greviously tortured me by pinching and choking me, urging me to write in his book. Also, today I saw the apparition of John Proctor afflict Mistress Pope. And he and his wife and Goody Cloyce all scared Elizabeth Hubbard dumb to stop her from speaking."

That testimony prodded the deputy governor to declare his mind as duty required. In response to the swirling charges. The other judges nodded agreement as he spoke. "This special tribunal has no recourse but to commit Goody Proctor, and her husband and Sarah Cloyce, for trial upon the charges made. We remand the prisoners into the custody of the Boston jail until further notice."

As the meetinghouse emptied, a voice inside Tituba's head said, you are sending another woman to prison to have her child and lose it.

Tituba shook off the voice. What was she to make of Mary Warren, the Proctors' maid?

She felt empty of answers about Mary until a yearning for Skitôp arose… along with a question. Was he feeling as alone as she?

When she dissolved her image in the gallery, no one noticed.

* * *

A week later Magistrate Hathorne returned to Salem Village with Mr. Corwin. He had signed warrants for the arrests of Abigail Hobbs, daughter of William Hobbs, of Topsfield; and Bridget Bishop, wife of Edward Bishop, charging them with diabolical crimes. A few people wondered why he accepted charges against Giles Corey too. The elderly man had spoken up against the recent arrests despite his prior testimony against his wife, Martha.

The villagers knew young Mary Warren had been implicated by accusations against her during testimony before Deputy Governor Danforth. Most of them recalled only a month ago, Mary had claimed to be afflicted by various acts of witchcraft until John Proctor threatened to beat her for saying it.

And now, after the accusations against Mary, one of the afflicted children told Parris Mary was telling a different story altogether. Mary claimed she had come to her senses, as if out of a dream. She'd seen only false images. There were no witches.

When Parris immediately reported this to Mr. Hathorne, the magistrate signed papers for Mary Warren's arrest. To Parris, she had always seemed a good girl, but they needed to stop any backsliding. They needed truth.

Soon after the arrest warrant went out, Thomas Putnam informed Hathorne and Parris he had secured

Mary at his farm for questioning. At once, Parris called on Hathorne and they set off together for Putnam's.

Goodman Putnam led them into his barn, saying, "She was at the Proctor farm when we got her. She claimed she was tending the Proctors' unsupervised children."

He held the door for them to enter. "I thought it be best not to leave her at the Proctors' to do more mischief."

Parris was in front of the magistrate as they entered. He followed Putnam's finger pointing at a support pole in the barn where he had bound Mary. She croaked incoherently at the sight of the men.

Parris looked to Hathorne. If the magistrate was shocked at seeing the twenty-year-old tied to the pole, he allowed no one to see it on his face. But it stunned Parris. "Thomas, what evil has befallen this girl?"

"Ask her."

Mary croaked again.

Putnam interjected. "Several times she told my Ann and your Abigail the magistrates might as well examine Keysar's daughter, the one distracted in the head, than take notice of anything she and others have claimed."

Hathorne untied Mary's bonds. "Can you speak for yourself, child?"

She backed away from them, tripping on a misplaced farm tool, a hoe. She rolled to one side and covered her face.

Mr. Hathorne gave her a sip of water and she begged for more. Finally, she accepted his assurances that no harm would come to her if she spoke.

The young woman sobbed, "When I was afflicted, I thought I saw the apparitions of a hundred persons, but they brought on a distemper in my head and I could not tell what I was saying." She gulped down more of the water, her eyes darting from face to face. "When I became well, I could not say if I ever saw *any* of those apparitions."

Putnam cut in. "But upon bringing my daughter Ann and Abigail to this maid for a clearer discussion, those poor ones broke down as under torture! They said Mary had fooled them before, that she tricked them into believing she too suffered, but she was a liar all along."

"Enough of this," Hathorne said. "We shall send her to Mr. Herrick's custody and continue in a proper hearing."

* * *

Two days later, they led Mary Warren in front of the magistrates. Though ten children and women had claimed they were afflicted, only four were present.

The people in attendance had been chatting softly until Mary hobbled into the room and all went silent. As soon as she approached the magistrates, the audience witnessed what many of them had heard about but never seen. The afflicted ones became wracked with agony in front of everyone's eyes. Three of them were pointing to bloody marks on their arms where they were being bitten or pinched.

Tituba watched while keeping herself invisible. She had been drifting amid the lethargy that dogged her, especially after these kinds of sufferings occurred without her provocation. But… Mary Warren said she'd seen *false* images and who knew if she'd be more believable than the girls accusing her.

Hathorne began the examination. "Mary Warren—"

"I am innocent," she exclaimed.

Elizabeth Hubbard was among the distressed girls, and she lashed out at Mary. "You were, a little while ago, an afflicted person; now you are an afflicter. How can this be true?"

Mary stared at her childhood friend, her jaw muscles flexing and releasing. "I look up to God and take it to be a great mercy of God that I am no longer tortured by the Devil or any other being."

Mr. Corwin reacted as though startled at this reversal. "What? Do you take it to be a great mercy to afflict others, then?"

The girls writhed as if on command and shrieks about yellow birds and red cats came from them. As Mary seemed to silently implore them to give her a chance, looking from one pained small face to another, their cries of agony became louder. To anyone familiar with the scene of affliction by Satan's familiars could see, Mary was doomed.

Mary mouthed a few words no one could hear, and then swooned before dropping to her knees, and then onto all fours like a dog, head down and gagging.

Goody Putnam had been sitting close to the afflicted children. She stood abruptly and threw both of her arms upward, exclaiming, "I feel she is going to confess!"

Hathorne whipped his head from Mary Warren to Goody Putnam and back to Mary again. She was still on her knees, a long line of spittle sliding from her mouth to the floor.

Ann Jr. screeched as yellow bile came out of Mary's mouth. She pointed past Mary. "Oh, look! Look, Mother. Goody Corey, and John Procter and his wife—they have come *in their apparitions*! And they forbid Mary to confess!"

If this outburst confused the onlookers, Tituba smelled danger. When Mr. Hathorne called for a recess, Tituba watched Mary arise and stumble through the doorway. She followed her outside. No one looked at Mary, as though fearful she might hurt them if she returned even a furtive glance.

Tituba held her breath to marshal her strength as she approached Mary in the guise of a non-descript female figure draped in a hooded cloak. She was visible only to the shaken girl. She was unsure what she should say one way or the other. The maid was responsible for caring after the Proctors' children, and perhaps it would unburden the suffering Proctors if she were set free by the magistrates. Yes, perhaps an attack by another specter, actually drawing blood would set Mary straight. And besides, that might lighten Tituba's mood, and allow her to find renewed vigor.

When Tituba touched Mary's shoulder to draw her attention, the girl caught sight of her and staggered. Tituba reached for her again, still uncertain what tack to take. She whispered, "Listen to me child—"

Mary tore herself away before Tituba could finish. Those standing nearby heard Mary Warren collide blindly into the meetinghouse wall. The rough siding scraped her face and bounced her backward onto the muddy brown grass, conscious but unblinking, as if in a waking trance. No one touched her until the marshal gathered Mary up and carried her inside. He cleared a space on the first-row bench and laid her there. When the magistrates returned to bring them back into session, she was still lying in a daze.

It was obvious Mary Warren was not ready to resume defending herself, and Mr. Hathorne ordered the marshal to bring in the next accused prisoner. Tituba still debated whether to influence Mary further and waited to see how the proceedings played out next.

Bridget Bishop entered the room filled now with unsteady chatter that drowned the harsh scraping of her leg chains. She was rumored to have killed with witchcraft long ago, and she looked the part of a witch, hosting four dark moles protruding on each side of her pointed yellow chin.

"What know you of your first husband's death?" Hathorne demanded.

"If it pleases your worship, I know nothing of it. Nor do I even know any person in this room."

Hathorne interrogated her for an hour without gaining an admission. She gave as well as she got. But her flat unbelief in the whole matter did not move Hathorne. "Are you not troubled to see the afflicted persons so tormented?"

"I cannot tell what to think of them and do not concern myself about them—"

"I shall speak!" Mary Warren's ragged voice interrupted, the rasp of it almost inhuman in its tone.

She arose from the bench like a marionette yanked by strings. She advanced toward the magistrates, coming so close that both leaned away.

But then, returning to her girlish voice Mary cried, "Oh, I am sorry, I am so sorry. Oh Lord help me, for I will tell." She closed her eyes and raised her chin as she spoke. "They did, they did, they—they brought me to it." She keeled backward and collapsed to the floor.

Mary had returned to the afflicted girls' fold.

"Stand her up!" Hathorne demanded. "Make her face me." They turned Mary in his direction but her eyes were closed tight. "Who brought you to what?"

Mary's eyes stayed shut. "The black man said I should not speak a word, but I will speak, though he will kill me."

Mary bit her lip and blood trickled down her chin. She smeared it with the back of her hand. Not one of the afflicted girls uttered a sound as they watched. When her eyes shot wide open, she canvassed the entire room before stopping and pointing at the magistrates. "Avoid Satan, in the name of God, avoid!"

Her confession that followed was worthy of any story Tituba could have fed her. Seeming to believe every word of her own falseness to be true, Mary had broken from the Devil's clutches, glory to God; she was no longer hiding Satan's diabolical plan. And she spoke effusively how the Evil One worked on her body and soul until she briefly became a witch. But no more. Although she had lost her way until now, she would help the honorable magistrates by naming all demon helpers she knew of.

After Mary's revelations and promises, Hathorne looked speechlessly at his fellow magistrate. They put their heads together and concluded it best to release this prize from custody. The jail was filled, and since she had confessed and was ready to help root out others, it was best to keep her away from the witches in custody and out and about to identify others in compact with the Devil.

Tituba did not stay for the resumption of Bridget Bishop's interrogation. She was too weary to maintain her surveillance. Her persistent loss of stamina confused her, and she had to regain it. But how?

By the end of the day Bridget Bishop joined Giles Corey and Abigail Hobbs in jail to await final justice.

As the next weeks rolled by, Tituba mostly lingered in her jail cell, taking only occasional weary notice as groups of suspects, William and Deliverance Hobbs, husband and wife; Nehemiah Abbot Jr., weaver; Mary Esty, the wife of Isaac Esty; and Sarah Wilds, the wife of John Wilds were charged, arrested and hauled in front of magistrates for hearings whose results were foregone.

Groups of threes and sixes went into their hearings before being delivered back to jail to await their fate. At the same time, warrants were issued against more prominent members of the civil society. John Alden, a colonial hero, and Philip English, a wealthy merchant in Salem Town, were among them.

The examination hearings became public forums to find new witches, too. And some people showed their faces less often at them, afraid they might invite an accusation after a careless remark. At the same time, they all spread the latest accusations, which during discussions became exaggerated with each retelling. And everyone kept an eye out for anyone looking at them crossly. Puritan order was only a memory.

Tituba always kept watch on her original tormentor, Samuel Parris. She often listened to him meeting with men like Thomas Putnam or Jonathan Walcott. One day she overheard them agree, Parris would draft a letter for them to sign, a letter to the magistrates to stay on their toes to root out all undetected evildoers. From her prison cell Tituba smiled. The smile grew into chuckling that ended in tears, alarming her cell mates.

Chapter Twenty-three

Magistrate Hathorne was holding court in Salem Village's meetinghouse on a weekly basis to stay abreast of the flood of complaints, warrants and hearings arising from the surging spectral sightings.

Other magistrates in neighboring townships replicated the Salem Village hearings. Constables served fresh warrants on miscreants almost before the ink dried on them.

John Steele, one of Tituba's Boston jailors, had struck up a friendship of sorts, if any relationship between jailor and inmate could be a friendship. He kept her up to date on all the arrests and new hangings. He and a black freewoman from Jamaica were married. Now and then he also brought Tituba a sweet yam pudding whose taste recalled her childhood. A bite was usually all she could eat, but today she nibbled at it to keep Steele talking.

"All the magistrates are admitting tittle-tattle going back twenty years as proof of familiarity with the Devil. Everybody that breaks a leg or sprains their back thinks a witch is out to get them. Everyone pushes for the cases to move faster and faster.

"Travelers on the roadways from the farms are passing stories about new suspects going to jail. There's Martha Carrier of Andover, and Elizabeth Fosdick in

Malden. We've taken custody of Wilmot Read, Sarah Rice and Elizabeth How from Marblehead, Reading and Topsfield. And tomorrow a Captain John Flood of Rumney Marsh and Mary Toothaker and her daughter from Billerica are comin' here."

Their battle against Satan expanded as the radius of complaints grew: Mary Bradbury of Salisbury, Lydia and Sarah Dustin of Reading, and Job Tookey of Beverly joined Abigail Somes of Gloucester, Elizabeth Carey and Elizabeth Paine of Charlestown, and Mary Ireson of Lynn. There seemed no way to corral the flying satanic witches except to arrest them.

Over one hundred and forty were awaiting preliminary hearings or in line for criminal trial. Over fifty had confessed their guilt.

Tituba gave in to deep weariness as he talked. The terror she started was itself a living specter roaming the countryside, seeking victims. She should have been beyond joy, but she wasn't.

"Thank your wife for the food," she said, though she had hardly tasted it.

"Nothing at all." He knelt next to Tituba. "And here's the big news. They caught Reverend Burroughs up near Wells."

"The pastor in Salem Village from before?"

"Aye, and the warrant against him says he has been in league with Satan for years. They call him 'the little black-haired minister.' And they say Mr. Cotton Mather himself brought in William Stoughton from Dorchester to interrogate the man."

The jailor stood to his full height. "Me and mine are Baptists, but our minister said Mr. Mather thinks their Mr. Burroughs is unsound in doctrine and a heretic, which means they will treat him with special severity."

Tituba forced a smile of appreciation for the news until the jailor left the cell. Despite her misgivings about several of the falsely accused victims, she told herself this news pleased her. Someone was going after big game and had steered weak minds to capture a minister! A man of god in league with their devil. If this man fell.... She shook her head in wonder at the results of the powers she had used.

Mr. Hathorne confined George Burroughs in the Boston jail, and Tituba knew he was across the hallway from her cell. His upcoming private interrogation would be too important for her to miss. On the morning of it they left his cell door open, and she could hear everything if she remained still.

The preconceived statements and questions were true to form. She nodded at their simplistic form when she heard Mr. Hathorne say, "We know you showed tricks of superhuman strength to impress your parishioners instead of showing the humbleness of a true messenger of God."

Burroughs scoffed in reply.

Tituba reminded herself he was also true to form, the usual arrogant minister, as if answering was beneath his dignity. Then she recognized Parris' voice. "Consider your dire position, both physical and spiritual."

Mr. Hathorne continued. "You missed Sabbath communion several times in Boston, and Charlestown. And you, a mediator for Christ."

After a silence, Hathorne said, "Lt. Governor Stoughton, as a government official and a magistrate here in Boston, do you wish to question him?"

Tituba did not know who Stoughton was, but if he was with Hathorne and Parris, she expected he too presumed the man was guilty of the charges against him.

"Thank you, Mr. Hathorne," Stoughton replied. "And now, Mr. Burroughs, tell us why is it none of your children except your eldest have been baptized?" No answer again.

A new voice arose. "I should like to question this sorry fellow."

"By all means, Reverend Mather," Hathorne said.

Burroughs snorted, "Cotton Mather. You have changed little since we were classmates at Harvard, except to become fatter."

Mather ignored Burroughs' taunt. "Today I read a sworn deposition of Susanna Sheldon, who says your first two wives appeared to her wrapped in their winding sheets. They told her you killed them."

Burroughs laughed at Mather. "Still a willing believer in the absurd, Cotton?"

Tituba concentrated her attention. This interrogator must be the mighty Boston minister Parris seemed to fawn over. And here he was openly in the game of catching devils and not knowing there were none.

Parris took another turn. "You remember Ann Putnam from the village parish, do you not? She told us you came to her in your apparition and urged her to write in your book, and upon her refusal, you told her she must ignore any spirits claiming to be your wives and disbelieve anything they say."

"Bah!" The prisoner clinked his chains in his contempt. The others seemed to wait for an answer, for the cell was quiet until Burroughs shouted, "Did she say her husband, Thomas, withheld my pay because he falsely claimed I did not acknowledge money I borrowed for my wife's funeral? The one I am now said to have killed with wizardry?"

"Look at me, Burroughs."

"I'll look at whom I please *Mr.* Stoughton."

"So be it, but you shall listen. Mary Warren's sworn statement says, 'Mr. Burroughs had a trumpet which he blew to summon the witches to their feasts and other meetings near Mr. Parris' house.'" He must have been waiting for Burroughs to answer, for the room was quiet once more until Stoughton continued. "And here, Elizabeth Hobbs herself being charged as a witch confessed her sin and in doing so corroborated your leadership of witch meetings."

The little black-haired minister was doomed. The English were eating their own.

* * *

On May 13 word arrived in Boston that a ship carrying the new governor, Sir William Phips was merely a day out of port. Cotton Mather dispatched a rider to bring Parris to town as soon as possible.

Parris arrived the next day. "Your man said your father and the new governor are arriving, but what do you want of me?"

"We must gather Mr. Hathorne and Mr. Stoughton to meet the ship before any others reach Sir William."

Parris had learned by this time to avoid commitments, observe and listen carefully. Although he still felt some obligation to stand by his mentor, his faith in Mather was largely dissipated under the pressures of the seeming never ending disclosures.

Mather said the new charter arriving with the ship would empower the governor to create a special law court to hear the jury trials of the criminal witches.

Parris had expected as much, and could not understand the reason for the summons. The outbreak at home needed his attention. The Porter family and their friends now controlled the village committees, and at least one, maybe more, had whispered that the pastor was not attending to the spiritual needs of his parish.

Mather was still speaking. "… my father wanted Phips as governor and we have him. I now want Stoughton to take charge of the high court Phips must create to handle the trials and sentencing in the witch cases. Stoughton has always listened to my counsel, and we must convince the governor to appoint Stoughton as chief judge. Once he takes the bench, I shall intervene with my plan to save and rehabilitate our disturbed brothers and sisters."

Cotton Mather, William Stoughton, and a distracted Parris greeted the ship from London as soon as it docked. Sailors and longshoremen unloaded cargo while the visitors met with Increase Mather and Governor Phips in the captain's cabin.

After firsthand renditions by Cotton Mather and his colleagues detailing the precarious state of the province, and the most urgent need to punish the evildoers,

Governor Phips said he was willing to follow any reasonable advice.

"I have no heart for managing such spiritual disruptions. I much prefer to protect our people from invasion by the French while men like you are better suited to protect them from this abomination of the Devil."

Phips duly appointed William Stoughton to be the chief judge of a new court of Oyer and Terminer. It was a special court empowered to condemn the convicted to the hangman's noose.

Cotton Mather invited everyone to dine at his house after they finished their business, and all but his father and the new governor accepted his invitation. Mr. Stoughton sought an invitation for John Richards, whom he wanted as one of several additional judges on the new court.

Parris rode with Mather in his carriage after the meeting concluded. "Samuel, after dinner I shall broach my ideas with Stoughton that we of the church become involved with the cure of those afflicted and, just as important, the reclamation of those guilty of the sin of witchcraft."

Parris lost what little appetite he had for food, wishing, blasphemous as it was, he could fly back to the parsonage and away from his overbearing mentor.

Later, on the hour, everyone arrived for dinner. Mrs. Mather had transformed the parlor into a suitable dining area, and the men ate heartily while talking of England, the newly chartered Province of Massachusetts and the continuing rigors of claiming the new world for God's chosen people.

The discussion moved to their yearning for a rapid return to communal stability and then to the proper use of spectral evidence at the upcoming trials.

Parris listened as Mr. Richards, whom he did not know, said the unrestricted use of the spectral evidence concerned him. "Might slander arise from untrue perceptions? Or accusations be motivated by the malice of the accuser?"

"Perhaps," Hathorne said, "but that has not been argued in our proceedings below."

"But, William..." Mr. Richards directed his questions to the chief judge. "Our colleague and friend Mr. Saltonstall and I have discussed this, and he too has reservations. If the accused claim their spectral images are used without their consent, can we condemn a flesh and blood person even if someone proves the image?"

Stoughton glared at his fellow jurist. "I have complete confidence that the legal history cited by our host, Mr. Mather here, gives ample justification to use the specters as evidence of guilt."

Mather jumped in. "Your task is to extinguish this plague with swift justice."

Stoughton drank from his wine glass and explained his train of thought further. "I will never believe our great God would allow any innocent person to suffer from the Devil taking his image without consent from that person." He looked around to see if anyone would challenge him. Hearing none, he said, "If the proof is there, they must hang." He pointed to Parris. "What think you?"

"Me?"

"Yes, your family was attacked."

Parris inhaled deeply, stalling for time. He smelled swampy ground beneath the discussion and feared stepping carelessly. And, as a guest he knew Mather was about to disclose his idea to intervene in the prosecutions to save condemned witches who confessed their sins and repented.

He played it safe, remembering what someone recently had said about the evidence. "Witnesses have already testified to the images. Who are we to prove our witnesses are mistaken? Without them, you can render no verdict at all."

When Mather nodded to concur, Parris busied himself with the rest of his tasteless meal. He turned a deaf ear to what else they said. He thought of Betty and how he had sent her to live in Salem Town. Parris had not mentioned it to Mather during the rush to meet the ship, but he had visited Betty at the Sewell house in Salem Town before coming to Boston.

She was doing well there. Mrs. Sewell had nursed the child back to health, though she did not understand exactly what impact she made. She explained to the exhausted child she could shoo away the devil if he came to her. "Tell him to leave you be and he will."

Betty's bewitchment lingered for a while after she came to live with the Sewells, but in warm seclusion she regained her old self.

Mrs. Sewell was cautiously optimistic. "Neither of us can be certain if our tactic will continue to give the child peace of mind."

They had agreed to keep Betty's change of condition private until they were certain she was free of affliction.

Why should they risk the Devil discovering her whereabouts and harming her again, along with those protecting her?

At the end of the meal, the men prayed that God might guide them in their tasks. They departed one at a time until only Parris and Stoughton remained. Mather took Stoughton's arm. "There is another matter I must ask you to consider. Please stay and talk with Mr. Parris and me."

Parris stood off to the side as Mather launched into his unorthodox plan.

"We would never sit as judges, William," Mather said. "Certainly not, but as a… a resource of the court, for the good of the provincial and church community."

The divine moved to the hearth nonchalantly and stoked the fire, seeming to give Mr. Stoughton time to digest his proposition. But he turned and added, "Could not the Oyer and Terminer court delay or slow down the trials, and if neither of those, at least wait for an extended period before imposing sentence?"

Parris stared at the flames to calm himself, nervous Mather might call on him for support in front of Stoughton, who was slow to respond.

Again, Mather added. "I would lead certain ministers selected for the purpose, and Samuel here is one, in secure privacy, to counsel the afflicted. We would bring the convicted ones back to God's benevolence by securing full confessions and further cooperation."

Stoughton's face had gone slack at the proposal, but Mather continued as though he did not notice. "It is worthwhile at least to give the convicted ones a chance to save their condemned souls."

Stoughton must have been gathering his wits, for he did not directly respond until long moments passed. "Does your father support this concept?" And when told he did not know of it, Stoughton narrowed his eyes. "Do you not realize if this idea was approved, it would effectively dissolve the purpose of the new court before it began?" He was full red in the face as he continued. "This is entirely inappropriate under any jurisprudence in England or this provincial government. Our purpose, our court, is to punish the wicked we convict."

Mather glanced at Parris, and it was clear he wanted some help, but Parris had none to give.

"Let me add a warning to you, Cotton," Stoughton said. "You are asking for me to make you alone the central manager of fearsome power to condemn those not cooperating with your scheme. With this authority you could intercede after trial to grant clemency from a death sentence, or conversely hold the prospect of hanging over the head of some unfortunate soul. It is too much for one man to control."

Parris wondered if Stoughton's adamance was driven by worry he might lose too much of his power as chief justice. And with it, direct authority over the men sitting with him as judges. But that mattered very little as he listened to Stoughton. In him, Parris saw the Lord showing all the proof he needed; he had chosen a righteous path: trials, sentencing and execution in the promptest fashion. Then, at the end of it he and everyone could get back to their lives as they had been before this Divine test of faith.

"I shall not mention this idea to others, for your sake," Stoughton said. "It shall remain a matter for the new court, my court, to dispense justice."

Parris was already mulling his return to the hearings in Salem Town.

Chapter Twenty-four

Sleepiness pulled at Tituba once again, like a tide inviting her out to sea. She had languished in her jail cell while waiting for someone to announce her trial date. As the months passed, she found herself no longer able to fly and appear in various locations with only the thought to be anywhere.

Tituba was unsure what made her so low. She concluded it must have been the waiting that sapped her, since resting failed to renew her vitality.

More than physical weakness burdened Tituba. Sadness pervaded her when triumph should have. John Steele kept up the flow of information, but while the news had once given her pleasure, the continuing spread of accusations left her in unremitting melancholic moods.

As the arrests and hearings exploded in numbers, magistrates suspected parents of prompting their children to testify against them, sacrificing themselves to divert attention from their young ones. Several magistrates, upon realizing this, believed doing so was itself diabolical. They set none free on account of it.

When constables arrested Martha Carrier, they took four of her children into custody.

The magistrate examining her daughter Sarah asked how long she was a witch. She said, "Ever since I was six years old." The child explained her mother made her set her hand to a book out in Foster's pasture.

As Steele told Tituba about Martha Carrier's daughter, she had to tamp down an inexplicable urge to cry. "Then the girl says, to the magistrate, her brother Andrew been a witch too, near a month now for both of them."

In the quiet days in her cell, the awareness of her role confronted her increasingly. With each new story, Tituba's thirst for stirring unrest slackened another measure. What she had begun was ensnaring children, depriving them of the comfort of mother or father.

At last, the government announced the first trial date of June 2 in Salem Town, before Judge Stoughton's court of Oyer and Terminer.

The prisoner named stunned Tituba. It was Bridget Bishop.

"She's the easiest," John Steele said, "and the prosecutor picked her because almost everyone out Salem way knows she's been accused of hurting people for a long time."

Tituba had expected they would choose her before any others. She had been the first to confess. Could they have held off her trial because she might name more names? That must be the reason.

Only Tituba knew she had lost the taste for doing it.

On Bridget Bishop's trial day, Tituba wanted to roll over inside her Boston jail cell and sleep. But she sensed the tension from the courtroom. It vibrated inside her head more insistently until she could no longer lie on the dirty straw mat of the cell with her eyes closed.

Tituba held her breath to brace herself while sitting up. Even that small effort had become a chore. Up to that very morning, Tituba had harbored a faint doubt they would truly murder someone on the spectral evidence she had initiated.

She needed to witness how far they would go to win a battle in the spirit war raised by their devil.

Clearing her head of uncertain thoughts, slowing her breath, then her pulse, she opened her mind, willing herself to revisit Salem Town. At first, she could only muster a cloudy view inside the meetinghouse. It was like peering into a light fog, but the air was crackling. Someone would die upon the evidence being given today, and she felt power infuse her, strengthening her enough to go to the scene.

The people arriving chattered as they entered. They had come that sunny June morning to take part in their communal retribution and begin their deliverance from Satan's bondage.

Many from Salem Village were among the assembled people. They would have traversed the Ipswich road to Peabody before reaching Salem Town, all the while praying for justice. Thomas Putnam and his family must have picked up Parris, his wife and their niece Abigail since they entered together.

Being a solemn occasion, the hall was filled with muted whispering until someone pointed out the defendant. A shout, "That's her in the chains," set off a wave of gossipy talk. "Have you heard?" one woman said. "Even as they brought her, she exercised her devilment before arriving. When the prison cart passed First Church, she looked toward it and at that instant, a demon ripped a board loose from the roof to clatter to the floor!"

"What daring arrogance of her?"

"Yes, but for not much longer, I pray."

"Just look at her eyeing the room. The woman has survived two husbands and married yet again."

Finally, the crowd quieted again when Tituba saw Mr. Stoughton arrive with his five judges. The excitement in the room should have been inconsequential to her, but a wave of lightheadedness struck Tituba and broke her contact with the courtroom.

When she stirred again, realizing she had lost consciousness, Tituba could not immediately regain her sense of place. She was still in the jail, but how long had she been out?

Tituba shuddered, realizing she had faltered, unable to maintain her visitation of the trial.

She returned to the courtroom as the noises of shuffling feet and coughing yielded to Judge Stoughton's hammering on the table. "Very well, now Mr. Hathorne, please read from that portion of the record below relating to the appearance of her specter."

Hathorne stood at his place off the center of the bench, cleared his throat, and read from testimony during the hearing he had conducted months ago.

When he reached one place in the record, saying, "And someone declared that Bridget Bishop was present in her shape or apparition," a person deep in the crowd exclaimed, "There, up there she is!"

Mr. Stoughton seemed coolly in control as he growled at Bishop. "What do you know of such matters?"

"I have nobody to look to but God." Bishop was searching the rafters herself.

She came back to Stoughton. "I am innocent." To Hathorne and Mr. Richards, she added, "I know not what a witch is."

Deliverance Hobbs and Mary Warren had confessed to their own debauchery. And they gave testimony without question: Bridget Bishop was a witch.

Bishop snarled at them. "I know not whether there be *any* witches."

Stoughton pounced. "The denial of witches is a heresy, and on that ground alone we may find you guilty."

Evidence from various other witnesses Tituba had never heard of came next. Goodman Shattuck said a condition took his child. "He fell into terrible fits, his mouth and eyes drawn aside and gasping as if he was at the point of death. I believe it was Bridget Bishop caused it." He looked around the meetinghouse. "The doctors *agreed* my lad was under the evil hand of witchcraft."

A yeoman named Cook testified. "I was in bed. I saw Goodwife Bishop stand in my chamber by the window. She grinned and struck the side of my head, which very much hurt me. I saw her go out through a little crevice under that window. The opening as small as my hand."

Rebecca Bly and her husband had bought a hog from Bishop. "But afterward she quarreled with us about payment for it. That hog went into fits right then, jumping and knocking her head against the fence. It did not eat or let the piglets suck. Bridget Bishop bewitched that sow."

Goodman Lauder said, “One night, I was in bed and a great weight came upon my breast. I saw Bridget Bishop, or her likeness, sitting upon my stomach. She gripped my throat and almost choked me, and I had no strength or power to resist.”

They called Reverend Hale to come forward. “Years ago, I gave witness in favor of our sister Bridget in defense of a charge of murder.”

The possibility Bishop had a defense witness among the clergy aroused Tituba until Reverend Hale proved he was not that person.

“But now—I wonder how the victim back then could have committed suicide as the jury ruled. The death, upon reflection now, seems so unnatural.”

After the last witness testified, Chief Judge Stoughton gathered the judges in chambers to address some matter before sending the jury to deliberate.

Tituba drifted among them and was startled when Judge Saltonstall said he was aghast at the effect of the spectral evidence which dominated the trial. “It is the most damning evidence, subject to abuse. How can we permit it against this woman, where it makes a difference between facing shame upon being acquitted or being hanged?”

Judge Stoughton rejected the argument. And among the judges, only Mr. Richards seemed to acknowledge the point, but he did not vote with Saltonstall.

Back in the courtroom, Judge Stoughton gave the jury instructions on the allowable use of spectral evidence and cleared the way for that testimony against Bishop.

It did not take long before the jury sent word it had reached a decision. “Guilty.”

The verdict set off a scattering of applause, along with some calls of thanks, while others recited the Lord's prayer aloud. Judge Stoughton gaveled for silence before he signed the death warrant.

Mr. Saltonstall scribbled a note and passed it toward Stoughton before stalking out of the courtroom. He had resigned as a judge, effective immediately.

One day after Judge Saltonstall's resignation, news arrived that captured Tituba's attention. Judge Richards had asked Mr. Stoughton for permission to get one more opinion from the collective Boston ministers on the use of spectral evidence. And Stoughton agreed without argument. Was he willing to reconsider the Bishop verdict? Was there a possibility they might postpone Bishop's hanging? And what about the others waiting for trial?

When she learned the ministers permitted Cotton Mather to write the reply to the question, she understood why Stoughton had not objected.

The final report allowed the chief judge free rein.

John Steele recounted the rumored triumphant claim by Stoughton after the ministers' written report. "Mr. Stoughton said we are the law, and since he was the chief judge, he will be the final arbiter on points of law." The spectral evidence would remain admissible for all the next trials.

A raucous crowd gathered to watch Bridget Oliver Bishop's hanging on the 10th day of June, eight days after her trial.

Tituba told herself she needn't watch it, she'd seen enough of hangings in premonitory dreams, and nothing could be worse than them. But she could not avoid attending Bishop's execution. It was no less horrible as the woman swung out from the ladder after a push, easily at first, until she thrashed fruitlessly for five minutes before going still.

When Rebecca Nurse's trial was announced to begin on June 29, Tituba wished she could take her own life somehow rather than endure the continuing visions sure to come of more people climbing up the ladder to meet the hangman's rope.

Her stomach never unclenched as she huddled in the jail. Still they overlooked her turn in front of the judges and jury. And the prospect of endless days of second-guessing her time had flattened her. If only she could stop her mind!

Late in the day of the 29th, after they admitted all the evidence in the trial, Stoughton sent the jury out to deliberate Goody Nurse's fate. Their return stunned everyone. They had found Rebecca Nurse not guilty.

Stoughton harbored no doubt of her guilt, though, and he sent the jury out again with instructions to reconsider all the evidence.

The jurors followed his orders, but after a while they returned, wanting to ask Rebecca one more question for clarification.

But she surprised them all by refusing to answer for herself. Her failure to speak convinced any holdouts in the jury that Judge Stoughton was right. Guilty and insolent.

And so, they voted a second time and Stoughton signed the death warrant.

Nurse's family later claimed the elderly woman could not hear the question posed by the jury. Didn't they know? Deafness was the reason Rebecca Nurse did not answer. But their offers of proof were not enough. The judges declined to reopen the case.

Tituba's nerves frayed like the worn ends of a rope. She tried to block the repeating thoughts of what happened to the old woman and what was in store for her. She bashed herself with ugly flashes of her manipulations of Goody Putnam that day months ago. She had added fuel to Goody Putnam's fanciful memories, knowing even then what Ann said would help condemn Rebecca Nurse.

She remembered Putnam's words so clearly as she gave in to Tituba's encouragement: "My strength being as I thought, almost gone, the apparition of Rebecca Nurse set upon me in a dreadful manner upon first light. She wore only her shift, and brought a little red book, urging me to write in it."

Thinking about it now, Tituba could not ignore the irony; she had manipulated Goody Putnam's natural urge to protect her daughter against affliction, and used her willingness to say and do anything for her child. Like Tituba wished she'd done for Akanni.

How long ago, it seemed, she had reveled in the pain she administered, hurting both afflicted ones as well as those accused of doing evil. Their suffering dulled her own as she spurred on the pandemonium. That admonition from Mama had been drowned out as she listened only to her need for revenge. "Never use your powers to hurt others." And now she could not stop her ears from it.

Even if she knew how to stop the witch hunt, Tituba felt sapped of energy. Yes, she deserved her own turn on the gallows. But welcome as it might be, it would be the lesser punishment for defying the ancient occult laws. After her mortal death, her soul would dissolve into nothingness, forever banned from traveling to the stars, never to see Mama again.

A little over a month after Bishop's hanging, they executed Rebecca Nurse, Sarah Wildes, Elizabeth Howe and Susannah Martin on the 19th of July.

Tituba watched each execution from her spectral perch, then replayed them in her imagination afterward, punishing herself by making the hangings more gruesome. Twisted necks, lolling tongues, purple faces, vein-streaked arms and hands, gurgling, gagging, kicking feet before silent swinging in slow passes back and forth.

She also remembered the faces of those come to watch the executions. Some with hands to mouths hiding gasps, or grins, or thin grim lips, seeing justice done and Satan rebuffed. Among the viewers were always children, leaning into their mothers, heads pushed deep into the folds of the voluminous skirts and aprons. Some adults held them up so they might see the hangings and know the result of rejecting the laws of their god.

In early August the biggest fish came to trial. George Burroughs, the failed heretic minister, stood no chance of acquittal. Neither did Martha Carrier the next day after testimony by her own children. The jury convicted George Jacobs, John Proctor, Elizabeth Proctor and John Willard after less than a day of trial for each of them.

The government announced more trials and still it did not call Tituba's case. Was this punishment from the supernatural plane? To remain in thrall to an uncertain fate as she watched others die?

Sometimes she fought back during arguments with herself, but no matter how many ways she twisted the justifications for her revenge, there was no satisfaction for Tituba. She leaned against the cold stone wall of her cell and closed her eyes. Even if she had wiped out every English man, woman and child in the province, her Akanni remained dead and she would remain in jail, alone.

Waiting for death at the hands of the English was intolerable, and dealing with her conscience, unbearable. Tituba chose another course to hasten her oblivion. She neither ate nor drank and wrapped herself into a cocoon of self-loathing. Except for her slow breathing, Tituba became responsive to no one.

Chapter Twenty-five

Governor William Phips returned to Boston on September 22, mere hours after they executed the next batch of condemned men and women on Witch Hill in Salem Town. He had been on the Maine frontier conducting military exercises and out of touch for two months.

Phips came home early because Salem's and Boston's elite had sent alarming reports about the witchcraft prosecutions. The trials and hangings paralyzed the economy and spread fear rather than ending it. Phips sent for Judge Stoughton, Increase Mather and Cotton Mather. They needed to convene within forty-eight hours and he wanted answers.

Parris was in his study when a messenger arrived. The sinking sense he was losing his congregation had been layered on his other troubles, and God had not given him guidance. Less than half of the covenanted members were attending communion on the monthly Sabbath Day. He had to find the cause of this falling off, return to the basics of his ministry and bring them to Christ.

And blocking him from attending to his congregation was the seeming endless invasion of Satan's horde of familiars. It was clear the accusations and hearings and hangings were not bringing them closer to final victory. The more suspects they bound over for trial and convicted, the more witches the Devil sent. But he could not shirk his holy duty to press the battle.

Elizabeth interrupted his wallowing. A messenger from Cotton Mather was downstairs, and he needed Samuel's help in Boston.

"Again?"

Parris wanted to refuse. He didn't need another lecture about saving convicted witches. But the messenger said he couldn't take no for an answer. He waited, looking determined.

Parris had not told Mather he abandoned any interest in saving the souls of the accused witches, and didn't want to face him.

He hemmed.

The group who had supported Rebecca Nurse were avoiding his lectures and worship services and making their reasons plain to other congregants. Perhaps Mather might have some insight in ways to regain his flock. He was still an experienced churchman.

"Very well, I shall ride to Boston."

"Ah, Brother Parris," Cotton Mather greeted him, looking distracted. "We must prepare to meet with the governor. He wants to know how the province has gotten what he calls, 'out of control.'"

"I am at your service. And perhaps you might also help me. It seems we in my parish also have several control issues."

Mather appeared not to have heard him, but he had, hadn't he? Parris' stomach lurched. This was not a promising start for any attempt at *quid pro quo*.

Mather was flipping through papers as he talked. "Did you know the accusations have reached the mother-in-law of Jonathan Corwin, and even the wife of Reverend John Hale is disputing allegations against her." He stopped searching the papers. "They have accused my father's cousin!"

Parris almost replied by asking if Mather heard of the faction against him in Salem Village, but he decided it was better not to say what was on his mind.

Mather continued flipping pages. "Yesterday I heard a rumor someone might call out Lady Phips."

Parris wanted to still Mather's hands and say, I need support more than Lady Phips. She has the governor at her back. But he held his tongue.

"Will you and I alone meet with the governor?"

"Mr. Stoughton, my father and me." Mather looked to the side as if checking whether someone might overhear them. "A gentleman in the government informs me the governor is looking for a scapegoat. London has noted the disruption in our trade with the mother country. Ships are not being loaded since our tumult paralyzes every part of the province."

That word "scapegoat" struck him. Parris reached for Mather's arm and swallowed to steady his voice. "I am uncertain how I might help here. You see my congregation is rather discontented with me and—"

"Just follow my lead. Then we shall see if I, or perhaps my father, can give you some help with the control problem in your congregation."

He fought an urge to leave Mather and head home. Had the man ever been helpful?

By the time Cotton Mather finished assembling the papers and herding Parris to the carriage, the meeting at the governor's palace was already under way.

When they arrived, Phips, Stoughton and Mather the elder were in deep conversation and the two late arrivals heard Phips' raised voice. "Twenty are dead, and still you want more blood!"

None responded to Cotton Mather's soft apology for their tardiness.

Phips was red-faced as he spoke to Stoughton. "You have from the beginning hurried forward on these matters with great precipitancy, and by your warrant caused the sheriff to seize and dispose of the estates, goods and chattels of the executed without my knowledge."

Stoughton looked at Cotton Mather for support, but Mather was studying his shoes.

The elder Mather caught Stoughton's attention, and Parris thought he trembled as he spoke.

"Your doctrine that juries must reject the accused ones' claims that they denied the Devil access to their specters is beyond my contempt."

Cotton half-raised his eyes to his father as Increase Mather spoke to him. "I cannot help but wonder that any man, much less a man of such abilities, learning, and experience as you and you, Mr. Stoughton, should take up the persuasion that the Devil can assume the likeness of an innocent."

The senior Mather glared from the one man to the other. "It is a persuasion destitute of any solid reason to render it probable. And now *we* must clean up this mess."

Colonial good order had always depended on a foundation of faith and law. But the abuses of the last seven months had cracked it, perhaps beyond repair.

Governor Phips said he would issue a decree prohibiting convictions based only on spectral evidence as a first step to regain order.

When Increase Mather motioned that his son could excuse himself from the discussion, Parris followed him.

During the ride back to Cotton Mather's home, Parris felt the carriage walls closing in on him. Considering the discussion at the governor's chambers, he realized the chances of getting Mather's help to preserve his job were near zero. These men concerned themselves with larger matters than a country preacher's uncertain hold on his congregants.

As they parted, Mather said, "Perhaps I shall discuss your concerns with my father at a more propitious time. But that time is not at hand."

"Perhaps."

Parris said little else before parting. He was alone in this struggle and he wondered if God was still on his side. That woman, Tituba. His emotions flared. She—she….

When Parris arrived home, Elizabeth had news. "A committee of four came here to present grievances. The men will return tomorrow morning. Francis Nurse is among them."

Parris' stomach flipped as she spoke. They were moving against him. He should not have gone to Boston. But he at least now had a few hours to prepare, having missed their unannounced visit.

"I shall take my meal in the study. I need to pray and think."

The next day, the four-man committee wasted no time getting down to business as they all sat in the main room of the parsonage. "The people are not content with your ministry," Joseph Porter said.

Parris fought to keep his face neutral as he considered the bluntness of Porter's remark. "Brothers in Christ, I know there has been talk about our leadership during the recent crisis of faith. If this meeting is over my rate of pay, I will abide by a delay in payment."

"We are considering more than your salary, Mr. Parris."

Porter stood. "You must have noticed, some of us have stopped attending meeting since the persons under diabolical power and various delusions were permitted free expression during services."

Parris caught Porter's glance to Rebecca Nurse's widowed husband Francis as he spoke further. "Your preaching on our molestation from the invisible world has been conventional, but you could have taught more charity toward some of our people."

"It is not for you to judge me."

"But we do. And you lent your authority as pastor to tales which destroyed many of our brothers and sisters. Our shame will linger on long past this time. Perhaps forever."

Parris had the grim image of himself at the reins of a wagon loaded with his family's possessions, driving away from the parsonage. He could not endure that fate once again. If he needed to beg them, he would. "I know bitter animosities have come between too many of us. And your words are a humbling experience for me after the recent horrid calamity which has hurt me deeply."

They were unaffected at the reminder of his own suffering. It was Barbados all over again, not to mention the mercantile failures in Boston. No compassion from anyone.

He pressed on. "I do own that God is now righteously spitting in my face for the errors I may have committed." None of the stony grimaces softened. "But I sympathize with all who have suffered through Satan's wiles and sophistry."

When the other committee members stood up, Parris knew at that instant he lost his pulpit. What Porter said next was verbiage going in one ear and out the other. These ungrateful people did not deserve a faithful pastor. They had driven out the last three men before him. And now they discharge me, he thought. God, why have you turned from me?

"… and so, we are sorry it has come to this, Mr. Parris. But we must have your resignation and the deed to the parsonage. You have a fortnight to announce your resignation or we shall begin an action at law."

Chapter Twenty-six

With the change in weather as a warmer season came, Tituba felt something, a thrumming inside her. It persisted until she could not ignore the sensation intruding on her dark lair of perpetual sleep. She squeezed her eyes tighter by reflex, but got no relief.

Soon she was thrashing like a disoriented swimmer carried by a ground swell toward the shoreline of consciousness. At last, exhausted by the mental exertion, Tituba gave up the struggle and opened her eyes, reluctantly back among the living. Goody Steele, the jailor's wife, had been bathing Tituba's face and upon seeing her charge's open eyes squealed delightedly.

"And so, you have returned!"

Why am I disinterred from my peaceful slumber?

She tried to ask. "Wh…chk-k…." but her tongue was a fillet of salted cod.

"I cannot understand you, but there is no rush." She dabbed her own eyes with the wet wash cloth. "For six months have I spoken to you every day with no reply. You will speak soon enough." Goody Steele cradled Tituba's head and tipped a cup of water to her mouth for a sip.

Tituba wanted no water.

How many more did I kill?

"Well, the first thing you must know is that they have paroled everyone."

Tituba blinked her incomprehension as Goody Steele continued in a rush. "Governor stopped Mr. Stoughton from using ghostly specter evidence as proof in the trials. Stoughton, he was furious, and he kept trying to catch witches. But nobody else got convicted or hanged."

The fate I deserved instead of them.

Goody Steele blotted Tituba's welling tears. "Wasn't long after, the government said all the prisoners could go home."

Tituba tried to spy the cell for others, but her neck was too stiff to move.

"You are the only one remaining in jail."

As it should be.

Tituba envisioned innocent prisoners leaving in silence, as confused at their release as they were upon their being charged and arrested. She alone knew why everything had begun.

Goody Steele explained the government had condemned the use of spectral evidence and the trials soon came to a stop. With the news, Tituba's spirits rose. But just as quickly, she felt that crushing sensation return and grip her chest.

There will come no accounting for my crimes, which deserve the gallows.

When John Steele entered the cell, his wife pointed at Tituba. He broke into laughter. "At last!"

Tituba managed a lethargic nod. *What did she care for his pleasure?*

"I told her what happened," Goody Steele said.

He kneeled to Tituba and spoke just above a hush. "After the trials ended, the afflictions themselves evaporated into thin air like the coming and goings of the fanciful specters." He shook his head. "But now, none among us dares speak of the blood lust last summer. Nineteen in total hanged and Giles Corey pressed to death under the weight of stones." Steele stood.

All because of me.

"Satan drove us all mad."

You think me, too, but not me.

Steele helped his wife raise Tituba to sit up against the wall. "And so, you may leave, too, if your master pays the prison bills."

Tituba's mind could not break from her role in the horror so recently ended until she thought of Skitôp. A surge of bile gagged her. Had he survived the hysteria? Her hand moved a fraction with the urge to touch her Skitôp once more. Where was he?

She fainted.

John Steele's wife kept tending Tituba day after day, keeping her warm and demanding she take incessant sips of broth until she could swallow bread and butter. During the intervals between Goody's nursing, Tituba's mind bounced between her culpability for murder and wild fears for Skitôp's wellbeing.

At her request, Steele searched out meager news of John Indian. "The village dismissed Samuel Parris from the pulpit. He's fighting in court for his back pay and word is, he's selling his Indian man to raise money. Mrs. Parris has died, and he ain't paid for her funeral yet."

Tituba inhaled slowly. Parris' misfortune made her feel neither joy nor sorrow. Contempt? Yes. He had killed her son, hadn't he? But that Parris might sell Skitôp to hard labor on her account cut deep and her weak spirit gave way to a fit of coughing. Steele hunched his shoulders. "Maybe you and your man will find each other someday."

"Thank you for learning what you have," she wheezed. How long had it been since she'd acknowledged decency from any Englishman?

"Warden says Mr. Parris won't pay your jail bills either. If he doesn't, the law will make him sell you at auction and use the money to pay the warden."

An urge to cough gripped Tituba again and though her lungs needed to rest, she forced herself to speak. "How much are these bills you speak of?"

"All the fees of your confinement? Don't know how much, but you've been in jail for more than a year so it's a tidy sum for food, shelter, the cost of the chains and so forth. If Mr. Parris doesn't pay, you stay in jail until someone buys your debt at a discount. Nobody wins that one, eh? Not the warden nor Parris, nor you."

Tituba wondered why anyone would want to buy her? A self-proclaimed witch.

She tried to comfort herself that Governor Phips had quashed the campaign of finding and killing witches. If she got any relief, it lasted mere seconds.

During the nights when she jolted awake wanting the final relief of death the prospect of another lifetime of slavery tortured her.

Death was better than living in debasement, though it meant the immediate reckoning with her spiritual punishment for hurting others with her powers, forever denied entry to the astral plane. But she deserved every punishment.

Death, though, was merely an aspiration beyond Tituba's reach, chained as she was to the prison wall, dependent on outside forces for her fate.

During her solitary days, Tituba revisited her past and dwelled in it. Doing so was easier than contemplating her future. She knew it was a compulsion promising nothing except greater sadness and shame, but Tituba couldn't help herself.

Why hadn't she stopped the witch hunts before her psychic powers dissipated? Until it was too late. And she could only watch the chaos?

While chewing over those mad times, Tituba realized her first bouts of conscience had coincided with her growing fatigue. The greater the burden of guilt, the weaker her abilities became. And at the end, she barely summoned the last reserves to cocoon herself into oblivion. What irony: her power allowed her to create a trap with no release.

Condemned to be among the living again, Tituba could not escape her self-judgment: *I am a murderer and I deserve to die.*

Tituba had shed many tears over earlier misfortunes, crying until she was a dried husk; Mama beaten to death by the evildoers, the master's abuse in ways beyond counting, and the abandonment by Mama when she needed comfort and guidance. And until this hateful existence in jail, she'd thought the worst was when Akanni died, and she gazed upon his frozen body.

As Tituba mourned not only for herself, but for the people she'd wronged, her tears seemed endless. She cried for the old ones like Rebecca Nurse, but also husbands and wives, and parents and children who lost their dearest ones. Would they recover from their losses? Even if they could, Tituba convinced herself she never would.

One afternoon, Goody Steele visited with fresh fruit and a pint of cider. And while Tituba nibbled, Goody remarked how the colonists were loath to acknowledge their wild accusations and the wrongness of the hangings. Their collective failure to speak out against the absurdity of the claimed afflictions permitted the spreading accusations. "None of us is free of that guilt," Goody said.

None of us.

"So many falsely admitted to witchcraft and named accomplices, or cowered in fear of it… some say for self-protection… though it is scant justification." She pinched a split seam of Tituba's blouse in an absent-minded way. "And after their own doings, from the villagers pointing fingers to the city folk flocking to the hearings, from the government to the churches, none dares to call out what madness happened." She stood to depart. "We're all the same, hiding from responsibility, aren't we?"

Tituba mulled what the jailor's wife said after she left. Of course, she included Tituba's well-known role of confessing and accusing, but Goody Steele would never believe the whole story if Tituba explained it to her. No one would have.

But. What was unsaid by Goody Steele struck Tituba. She was not alone in shame. No. Not a single other accuser or judge or minister had admitted to their credulity.

Her first reaction to this was anger. They kept the witch hunting alive even after she stopped manipulating them. But then Tituba reminded herself she was the worst of them all.

The jailor's wife unknowingly offered Tituba a fragile line. The English were co-conspirators with her and together none could forget the unforgettable. Nevertheless, Tituba could not see the line nor grasp it, nor begin a climb out of the morass of her conscience.

The next morning, a faint commotion in the jail's hallway distracted Tituba. Voices. Several men. When they stopped outside her cell's iron-studded oak door, she drew up her legs and hugged them, tilting her head to listen.

The high pitch of the warden was snappish. "Here is the key. Open it." He banged his staff on the stone floor.

Tituba's mind froze.

One key jangled after another until the warden shouted, "Use the large one, there in your hand, dolt." His tapping his staff sounded more insistent. "We must get rid of this witch before the buyer has second thoughts. I shall not spend another ha'penny to keep her."

A *buyer*? She yanked on her chains, but there was no use in that. And where could she go if she broke them? Hide in a filthy corner? Tituba's heart pounded, flushing her neck. Another enslavement loomed.

The key twisted back and forth in the lock, but it did not turn.

Oh, for the means to end her misery with a thought.

The stale air in the cell was always heavy to breathe on account of the stink from waste buckets, clothes and rags reeking of body odors, and the mildew on the damp stone walls. And now, it seemed like liquid, each aching gasp worse than the last.

Another owner. Who? She was hot, then chilled, and sweat itched her face. A swipe smeared salty grime into her eyes, stinging them.

Through the tears, Tituba surveyed the wet stones and mortar of the opposite wall. She had once passed through those walls to terrorize, but not today. She turned inward, searching for the dark place where she'd hidden for so many months. Tituba exhorted herself for one last power. Concentrate!

But she found what she'd expected. Impotence.

Bereft of energy, Tituba weakly surveyed the floor, the ceiling, and the walls, perversely wishing to remain within the comfort of the prison…

When the mildewed stone wall seemed to move a fraction, she tore at her teary eyes, despite the burning. Even at the height of her powers she could not move stone with a look. Yet the wall was morphing into a translucent purple curtain.

Why could she not catch her breath?

The purple shade of color lessened. And there…, was that a figure there?

A sky blue and yellow gele scarf like one her mama treasured covered the figure's head, and Tituba strained to better see it. The pain in her chest gave way to rapid shallow breaths. Sweat kept hazing her vision! Who was this image come to her?

"Mama?" Tituba asked timidly, then again and a third time, but the figure ignored her. Tituba's view cleared somewhat, and she saw the apparition moving away. "If you are Mama, stop and have mercy! Grant me an end to this misery!"

It receded further in silence.

"Pity me."

There was no response.

Tituba lashed out with the accusation that had lingered inside her since Mama's death. "You betrayed me!"

The image stopped moving.

"You *made* me the appeaser. And you made me fail my son."

The object stubbornly refused to acknowledge her until Tituba shrieked. "And just as I am unforgiven for my evil deeds, so too I shall never forgive you."

At last it turned toward her and Tituba gaped. The face. It was Mama's brutalized face. But when its lips parted to speak, the voice Tituba heard was her own. "You blame your mother for her sins against you, yet you seek absolution for your own profane actions. You beg for aid to escape from the consequences. How is this, Tituba?"

Tituba sputtered, unable to reconcile the face with the voice.

"You could have made your own choices. Is this not so?"

"I ..."

Tituba searched for a sign of compassion, even a small smile, but the visitor was turning away from her.

"Yes!" Tituba shouted to stop it. "I could have chosen my own path!" She said the words even as she remained unconvinced they were true.

The figure faced her again. "What is past is over, but you will not escape its consequences."

The translucent haze began building again. "To survive, forgive yourself..."

Tituba squinted to see through brightening purple, afraid she might miss the next words from it.

"Then, come what may—"

The oak door of the cell groaned and exploded open like a gun shot. And even as the sound distracted her, Tituba knew whatever she'd experienced a moment ago had ended.

Any parting spectral words remained unsaid, but Tituba needed to hear nothing more. An existence without constant guilt might be possible. If she forgave… beginning with herself.

Tituba greeted the first man through the doorway with the final phrase from the image still in her mind. *Come what may.*

The second man through hefted a blacksmith's hammer to break off her cup lock shackles. When he bent to crack the leg irons, he exclaimed, "What is this?" Each iron cuff was wide open. He looked at Tituba as if wondering what other powers of witchcraft she possessed.

The warden saw them, too. "John Steele will feel my discipline for leaving off the cuffs. The witch might have flown off and I'd've lost my payment for keeping her."

The warden prodded the two men. "Stand her up. Move. If we are a trice late for the release at noon, I shall have to feed her again."

They brought Tituba out of the front doors of the jail seconds before a church bell rang the hour. The sunlight blinded Tituba, and but for the blacksmith's hold, she nearly tripped over the steps leading down to the street. She raised her hand against the brightness, shading her eyes to get a clear look at herself.

Tituba's once well-kept clothes had changed colors from blue and white into tattered shades of gray. The skin on her arms, once smooth and glowing, was cracked and ashy. She bent to scratch an itching spot on her leg and felt the wide callus rings on her ankles where the shackles had rubbed. Still sun-blinded and leaning from one foot to the other, Tituba stumbled when the warden pushed her forward. He shouted to someone. "Here's your property—if you pay for her,"

Tituba caught sight of a man at the bottom of the steps. He wore black outer clothes with a clean white shirt. She could tell he was not a Puritan because of his flowing beard.

The man squared his shoulders and barked back to the warden. "Hand me the bill of costs to review before vee settle up."

"And I shall see the Assignment of Rights to this one. I'll not have legal trouble after we turn her over to you." They exchanged documents, barely perusing them as if they knew the contents well beforehand.

Then the warden read the Bill of Sale aloud to the otherwise empty street: "We hereby give public notice of this transaction. Whereas the sale of the Negro woman, Tituba, for good and valuable consideration between the parties…"

Tituba stopped listening as he rattled on. What difference did the words mean to her?

After the warden finished reciting, the man taking Tituba pulled out a bag of coins and they counted the money there on the jail steps. Once finished, they shook hands, saying done and done.

After the blacksmith escorted Tituba to the street, she dared look the waiting man in the eye."M-master, where are we bound?" Beginning today, she would never again cower before any man.

"We go to my home in New London in Connecticut until you fulfill your debt." He gave her his hand, and she mounted his single horse cart.

My debt? She had trouble understanding because he spoke with a thick accent. If he meant money, that was an absurdity. Did this bearded stranger not know African slaves in Massachusetts had no right to lend or borrow?

He joined Tituba on the bench seat of the cart and slapped the reins. The horse pulled them away from Prison Lane at a slow walk. "You vill tend to my four motherless children and keep house for us. The oldest of *meine kinder* is five and the youngest, a girl, is less than one year."

He steered the horse. "My wife died as she brought the baby to this life. I have neglected the needs of the children because my work demands too much of time and we must eat."

Still stunned by the spectral visitation in her cell, and the seeming epiphany for survival, not clear she could even reach the goal, Tituba forced herself to listen to her new master. It seemed a debt was ridiculous, but the idea intrigued her. To what end might a slave repay any debt?

"My children need mothering, while I search for a woman of my race to marry. After ten years of service, your debt in the sum the warden demanded will be satisfied. And you will be a free woman." He wiped his nose and looked at her. "Do you understand?"

Tituba nodded; uncertain she'd heard that one word. Free.

"I do not think it proper to keep a slave for life, but do not think me an easy master on account of my opinion. You will work very hard to earn your freedom."

Freedom! And the stunning prospect made her want it so much, she feared this might be an illusion. But he *had* said it. In ten years....

He seemed disinclined to speak further, and Tituba was content to dwell on what he said, repeating his words silently as if to cement them into an unbreakable promise.

They continued to ride without speaking until Tituba spotted ship masts protruding above the rooftops. They were nearing Boston harbor, and the swaying masts at anchor conjured slave ships, driving a cold spike through Tituba, forcing out a gasp as if she'd been punched. She gripped the edge of the seat for purchase, flashing a thought of Akanni's attempted escape, but the new master seized her arm before she could leap.

"I must meet a Mr. Green at a tavern ahead for business and dinner. Then we leave Boston, for Connecticut."

She readied to pull free of him, unconvinced, but his ironlike grip on her arm relaxed, surprising her. "Do not fear this place." Whether he understood her terror or believed the strange waterfront was frightening Tituba was impossible to tell, but she decided his reassuring words and touch were true. One way or the other, she would handle the consequences. *Patience.*

"My name is Gerechtigeit."

She squinted at him. So many syllables. "What does your name mean in English?"

"I shall tell you what my name means on another day, but now Gerrick will do. They all call me Gerrick."

He hurried the horse as they passed through a busy intersection. "And," he slapped the reins again, "you have no reason to fear the future. I do not believe in English witches."

Upon realizing she was holding her breath, Tituba let out a long slow exhale. Patience.

They rode on for a while longer and she distracted herself by considering the other distance she'd traveled recently. Oblivion, the renewed desire for death, self-abuse, and always thoughts of Akanni. She was still unsettled by what exactly happened in the purple haze of the jail cell before they took her away, but the message was clear. Forgive. And yes, patience. Those would be her strength forevermore.

Tituba drew an easier breath. The prospect of ten years of servitude was not insignificant. But it was not overwhelming either. And the duty to care for Gerrick's children promised, perhaps, badly needed time to salve her still unsettled mind.

Yet doubt crept back. Somehow this new path seemed too clear-cut, and soon she was kneading trembling fingers. In ten years, a future free of bondage. And then what?

Gerrick's slow pace as they approached the waterfront of the harbor gave Tituba time to consider her unanswerable question. There was one thing she had seen during her servitude under the Parris family; they bargained for everything they wanted.

How might this Gerrick help her prepare for life after her indenture ended? Dismissing her old tendency to appease, Tituba came up with a plan. She cleared her throat. "Master, if you teach me to read and to write words, I shall serve you longer—until your newborn child reaches sixteen years."

Gerrick laughed but there was no harshness to it. "Such a generous offer." He pulled the cart to a stop and a long moment passed before he spoke again. "Ya, it is a good bargain for me and since I am a printer, I shall teach you reading and writing." Then he smiled. "And perhaps a trade."

They rode another half mile, bouncing over the rough cobbled street, but Tituba hardly felt the uncomfortable jolts.

When Gerrick called his horse to stop alongside a brick building on a wharf, Tituba broke from her reverie.

"This is the tavern of my friend. He has good food like from home. You may come in to wait until I finish my business matter. Then we shall eat and be back on our way."

Gerrick was tying the beast to an iron post when a cargo wagon creaked next to them.

Tituba peeked at its cargo through the slatted board sides. Men…Africans. The smell of their fear wrenched Tituba back toward days gone by, but she resisted the temptation to dwell on the past. Her destiny—was freedom!

A white man driving the slave wagon jumped from the front seat and gave orders. His prisoners, six in number, came off the back end where two other white men checked their chains. They led the prisoners into a small adjacent meadow out of Tituba's sight. She heard the driver charge his men. "Watch the cargo until I finish eating. Then you may take your meal inside."

Gerrick started toward the building entrance and motioned Tituba to follow, but she inhaled the cool evening air as if it could fortify her against any lurking memories brought on by the chained men in the meadow. "Please, master, permit me to savor the cool breeze a little longer. I have been confined so long."

"If you ran, I would catch you, and we would have to dissolve our agreement." His kindly smile was more gentle chiding than a threat, and she returned his smile.

The sky in the west was pink and gold. Tituba searched for tranquility and watched the sun paint the clouds, listening to the easy creaking of the mooring hawsers of the docked ships.

The shadows were growing.

A ragged cough seemed to come from somewhere near the empty cargo wagon. It evoked thoughts of her distant Skitôp. She hoped he was bound far from Parris.

With darkness settling, another cough sounded and this time Tituba peered at the wagon. She hopped down from the cart to get a closer look, intending to then join Gerrick inside the tavern.

At the rear of the wagon, Tituba tossed a glance at a sack of grain that leaned against the front of the dim cargo bed. But a chill raised her flesh before she turned to walk away. "Skitôp?" She breathed it more than speaking her lost lover's name, a vague premonition perhaps, a worry he was not well. And she sighed for him aloud. "Oh, my lost Skitôp."

When Tituba spoke her man's name, the rounded shape of a head lifted in the far end of the wagon bed. She scrambled toward it, heedless of the rank-smelling straw strewn inside.

It *was* him.

She touched his chest with her palm, but he did not respond. "You are sick?"

She wanted to search for signs of blood on his clothes, but it was too dark to see. Even if there was light, the tears glazing her eyes blurred everything.

As he moved slightly, his chains spoke first. Then came his voice, hoarse, a whisper. "I was hired out to a farmer near Andover. When I told him Samuel Parris owned me, the man cursed him. He cursed you too and said the judges should have hanged you."

Skitôp lowered his head. "I stabbed him in the leg."

Tituba caressed him and he flinched in pain. "They laid me open with fifteen lashes, and I spent three days in the pillory for harming an Englishman." His short laugh stopped under a grimace. "And now they say I am bound for the West Indies and the cane fields."

Tituba wanted to console him; he was still alive at least, but no words seemed right. After long moments passed, she said, "We should have run long ago as you wanted, my beloved." A knot swelled in her throat, cutting off further talk until Skitôp sniffed. "One other captive says they will load us onboard a ship tomorrow to sail on the morning tide, but they will not take me."

Tituba knew it was impossible for him to break the thick irons.

She wept softly, knowing the remaining moments would be their last time together. In loving silence, Tituba waited with her man until Gerrick appeared in the tavern's doorway, loudly calling farewell to his friend. She had a brief notion to hunker down in the wagon with Skitôp, but when she put voice to it, he refused. "Go on. That would not help you or me."

Tituba kissed Skitôp one last time, inhaling his scent before scrambling back to Gerrick's cart. She waited for Gerrick to unfasten the horse tie and mount the cart, avoiding his eye so as not to betray her emotions.

The night sky was cloudless and filled by uncountable stars as they slowly drove away on the long straight city street. Tituba imagined her Skitôp back among his Pequot people. An image to keep of him, a free man. But when Gerrick pulled the reins to turn a corner, she twisted for a last look in Skitôp's direction. She located the wagon just in time to spot a silhouette of a man jumping from it and dissolving into the darkness.

Tituba caught her breath, afraid to believe her eyes, and gazing upward, caught sight of a bright star that seemed to wink at her.

The first surge of joy since… farther back than she could remember arose in her. And she let go a laugh in spite of herself.

The End

NEW WORK FROM DAVE

Coming in Spring 2022

You can now enjoy the story of Tituba in audiobook form.

Dave has narrated the unabridged book and brought the characters to life in the way he originally envisioned them.

Check for it wherever you buy books.

DEAR READER

I hope you enjoyed this story. Book reviews, star ratings, and word of mouth spread the word for authors like me. If you enjoyed *Tituba* please leave a review wherever you bought it. Thanks. Dave

ABOUT THE AUTHOR

Dave Tamanini

I practiced law for over thirty years. Before that, I was a civil rights investigator of race and gender discrimination. Now, I cherish family, work at keeping and making friends, and write fiction in Harrisburg, PA.

Please sign up to follow my author journey and news events at www.DaveTamaniniAuthor.com

ACKNOWLEDGEMENTS

It's hard to count up all the people supporting this book and my work on it over the years. Some of them are: John Paine my excellent editor, Robin Vuchnich my cover designer, Liz Simcox at the Dauphin County Bar Association, who planted a seed for this story, The Authors Guild, The Alliance of Independent Authors, the leaders and talented members of The Fourth Wednesday and the Midtown Scholar critique groups, my friends and my family. Thank you, one and all.

Made in the USA
Middletown, DE
22 June 2024

55835097R10191